SEWARD'S FALL

Stories

By

Darren Gordon Smith

Largo & Sons, Publishers

This is a work of fiction. All the characters, organizations, and events portrayed in these stories are either products of the author's imagination or are used fictitiously. Any resemblance to actual persons, living or dead, is entirely coincidental.

SEWARD'S FALL. Copyright 2015 by Darren Gordon Smith.
ISBN-13:978-0692571385 (Largo & Sons)
ISBN-10:0692571388

Printed by CreateSpace
Also available on Kindle

Cover photograph copyright 2015 by Darren Gordon Smith

Special thanks to my beautiful and editorial wife, Nancy Long, as well as Staci Layne Wilson, and Mia Bruno.

SEWARD'S FALL

'TWA: A MÉNAGE OF FOOLS

I.

"Aaron?" The woman had a cheerful but insistent tone. He waited for her to continue, to get on to whatever merchandise or God she was selling. Despite his "Solicitors and Jehovah's Witnesses Do Not Ring" sign, salespeople were always at the door.

"Aaron Jenkins, right?"

"Yep. Do I know you?" He brought his *Teachers Do It with Class* mug to lips and gulped scalding hot coffee, wincing as it went down. He hoped the caffeine would kick in soon. It wasn't that early in the morning, but it was Saturday, his day to sleep in and relax, and he wasn't fully awake yet. He didn't want to be rude, but Aaron was in no mood for a sales pitch.

"You probably don't remember me – I'm Tanya. But back in New York I went by Alys? That's Alys with a Y."

Aaron vaguely remembered, somewhere in the recesses of his memory, that someone had once used that "Alys with a Y" line, but he couldn't remember who.

"I'm sorry," Aaron said, "I don't recall–"

"You remember Denise McIntyre, don't you? From N.Y.U.?" Of course he did. In his last semester of college he had dated her. They had little in common but Denise was hot and sexually uninhibited. And could that gal drink! He recalled wistfully how she'd always be hammered when he, well, hammered her. Actually, they'd both be wasted. After he graduated and moved back to Hamlin, they'd lost contact. He hadn't thought about her in years.

A hot breeze blew past them. Tanya aka Alys re-adjusted the bangs on her bob cut. Her hair was jet back and shiny. She donned a 1920's do that was in style in the East Village when Aaron was going to school. He must've seen that look come and go at least a half dozen times.

"You probably don't recognize me," she laughed. "I had wavy red hair back then." Aaron took another boiling swig from his mug, coughed and sputtered, and then thought for a moment. Maybe she *did* look familiar. She was tall, about his age – in her mid-thirties, and she was pretty, albeit in a hardened way. Her flapper hairdo seemed incongruous with her miniskirt and tight tank top, though he couldn't blame her for wearing something cool for an already sweltering summer morning. Nor could he blame her for showing off her sexy figure.

"Do you remember that night?" she asked. "You and Denise were at The Kettle of Fish, and I came by and we were all doing shots and, you know, we went back to your place and had a three-way?"

Yes he remembered. Well, kind of. Though he'd been drunker than at probably any time in his life, he did recall certain bits and pieces of that night. Unlike most of his guy friends, having sex with two women hadn't been high on his Bucket List. But, after more than a few shots of Stoli's, followed by a dozen pints of Newcastle, he wasn't about to turn a threesome down when it was offered. And it was. But once he got into bed with the two ladies, he started to get the spins. And during his sloppy intercourse with each of them, all he could focus on was how his bladder was about to burst from all the beer, and how he felt like throwing up from every last ounce of vodka. Then, he had a hard time climaxing before finally passing out. So the whole experience wasn't all that great. On the other hand, despite his complete stupidity in having sloppy unprotected sex, he considered himself lucky that he hadn't picked up an S.T.D. or two from Denise and whoever the other woman was.

"Yeah, I sort of remember that night," said Aaron.

"I sorta do too," she laughed. "So what's up?"

"What's up? Well, life's good," Aaron said. He hoped his summation was enough to avoid recounting the details of all those years since college. Anyway, aside from the recent challenges with Lauren trying pregnant, for Aaron it was largely true: life *was* good.

Tanya's face grew serious. "Listen, I need your help. It's about Denise. Can I come in?"

He was just about to tell her that he hadn't seen or heard from Denise since senior year, when, out of nowhere came two kids: a boy and girl. Aaron stepped out on his stoop and looked around – where did they come from? The kids must've been standing by the neighbor's garage or something, but it was freaky how they just appeared. They looked like twins and had to be about the same age as his wife's middle school students.

"Oh, hey guys!" Tanya put her arm around the two. "I'm sorry, Aaron, but my son really needs to use your bathroom and my daughter could use a drink of water."

Aaron was one of those teachers, the ones we hear about in election years, who actually liked kids, so he felt sympathetic. But, he knew that if the boy really needed to pee he would've done it in the neighbor's Bougainville's, so he must need to do Number Two, and Aaron wasn't crazy about some strange kid taking a dump in his bathroom.

"Um, sure, come on in," said Aaron, "But we only have a few minutes. My wife Lauren will be home very soon, and she'll, well, she'll need to get to sleep." In truth, Lauren rarely napped, even when she was exhausted from teaching her adult E.S.L. class on Saturday mornings, but it was the best excuse he could come up with to get them out of there. Aaron hurried the woman and the kids inside the house, while looking around to see if the neighbors had been watching. It's not as if what Aaron had done with the two women years ago was a crime or anything (unless you consider getting too wasted to enjoy a three-way a crime), but he *was* a high school teacher, and these days you had to avoid even a hint of any kind of impropriety. The fact that Tanya aka Alys with a Y was already discussing their sex life on the front porch made him suspect that this woman had a big mouth.

He showed the boy to the bathroom. Then he escorted the girl to the kitchen, where he invited her to choose between any number of beverages, except for the beer and Lauren's fertility booster drinks.

Aaron looked around for Tanya and found her in the den, reclining in his LaZee-Boy. He took a seat on a chair next to the sofa. Tanya seemed to be hypnotized by one of his Op Art Mobius Strip drink coasters.

The girl came in from the kitchen, bearing her choice of beverage – tap water - which she thoughtfully brought in with four glasses. Then came the sound of the toilet flushing and soon the boy joined the girl on the couch. The tween-aged twins quickly took out their respective smartphones and zoned out. Aaron hoped the woman would state her business about Denise and leave before his wife came home.

Lauren, Aaron's high school sweetheart, had known that he had dated other women in college (they'd both dated, by mutual agreement), but he had never told her about that drunken ménage a trois. Not that he would ever hide anything from Lauren; it's just that he'd never really been in the mood to go into the details of that sexual experience, especially when it was so, well, disappointing.   Nor was this, in modern organizational jargon, a good time to "circle back and loop" his wife on it now.

Aaron leaned forward. "Well, Alys –"

"It's Tanya now."

"OK. Tanya, it's good to see you, but –"

"I see you've done really well for yourself," she said, her eyes scanning the four corners of the room. "You have a *lovely* house."

Aaron smiled and thanked her, though he couldn't tell whether she was being snarky or not. Maybe she just had a tone of voice that always sounded sarcastic.

"Yes, it really is lovely," Tanya added. "Very, ah, suburban."

Aaron again thanked her, whatever the hell she meant by it. Then he asked, in a louder voice that he hoped didn't come across as rude, "So, Tanya, why are you here?"

"Well, it's nothing bad, don't worry." Tanya pointed to her children, "By the way, this is Tristan and this is Isolde."

"We're t-w-e-e-i-i-ns," said Isolde, in a high and affected vaguely English accent.

"No shit, Izzy," said Tristan, since not only did they look so much alike, they were even dressed identically. They wore the same green Izod shirt and chinos that looked like they'd just been bought off the rack. Their pants still had sales tags on them. "And I go by T.B."

"'It stands for Tristan Banes," Isolde said, with a nervous giggle.

"Nice to meet you," said Aaron. The kids smiled politely and went back to their phones.

Tanya got up and sat herself on the arm of the sofa next to Aaron and touched his knee. "We've come here to ask you to help us find Denise."

"Denise? Oh, look, I'm sorry," he said, "But I haven't seen or heard from her since college, and we only dated for a few months. So I really can't help you."

He had just taken the woman's hand off his leg when suddenly Lauren came in, laden with textbooks. Before Aaron had a chance to say anything, Tanya leaped to her feet, and with a wide smile, rushed to Lauren with an extended hand.

"Hi," she said, "You must be Lauren. I'm Tanya. I had a thing with Aaron and another woman way back in college."

"Oh..kay...?" Lauren stammered. She dropped her books and glanced toward her husband. Aaron opened his mouth to say something but no words came out.

"Jesus," said Tristan, rolling his eyes, "Do you have to tell everyone?"

"Sex is nothing to be ashamed of dear," answered Tanya, and, turning back to Lauren, added, "I don't do group sex that much anymore, anyway. Unless the vibe is right -"

"Honey!" Aaron suddenly blurted, like a cork just popped out of his mouth. "Remember that…'out there' girl that I dated towards the end of my senior year? Well, this ISN'T her, this is Tanya, who used to be Alys with a Y, and anyway she and Isolde and Tristan just got here and …."

He ran out of breath; that was fortuitous since he didn't even know where he was going with all of this. After a brief pause, he calmly said, "So why don't we all sit down and listen to what Tanya has to say?"

"Yes," said Lauren. She eyed the room, looking for an available chair. "Why don't we?"

Lauren left the room and came back with a tall kitchen stool. She sat, looming over the already crowded den. Lauren smiled at the guests and somehow seemed unfazed by the situation. But Aaron knew his wife well enough to sense her irritation by the tightness of her smile. Even when she wasn't irritated she had a controlled, almost prim demeanor. Her WASPY, pretty girl-next-door looks only reinforced that image. Only those who knew her well would see her outgoing nature, and sometimes even her silly side. Aaron was especially concerned about not upsetting his wife right now. She'd already been through a lot these past few days: first, she was dressed down in front of her class by her new principal, and then Dr. Mengyao told them that the latest round of fertility treatments they'd gone through had borne no fruit. For five long years they had tried to conceive.

But even during the best of times, Aaron's college days were a sore subject with Lauren. She had dated other guys when she'd gone off to college, but that didn't keep her from not wanting to hear about Aaron's collegiate exploits. He was a decent looking guy back then, and being one of the few heteros in Greenwich Village in those days helped his chances with women considerably. Now, years later he still kept himself in shape. And, unlike his friends who spent their weekends playing golf, he still had a full head of hair.

Tanya broke the strained silence. "I was just about to tell your husband that the reason I'm here is I was hoping he would help me find Denise."

"Denise?" asked Lauren, eyeing her husband.

"That's the 'experienced' gal I dated. But I was just telling Tanya that I don't have any idea where Denise could be, since, as you know, I haven't seen or heard from her since college."

"Actually," said Tanya "We did finally locate her, but we need your help. Look, here's what happened – to make a long story short, or a short story long, whatever the case may be - after Aaron, Denise and I had that 'twa, she and I hooked up again and we started dating. We had already fallen in love by the time I found out that I was pregnant."

"With tweeeeiiiiins," said Isolde, with a giggle. Aaron smiled politely and took a sip of water.

"YOUR twins," added T.B., making brief eye contact with Aaron, before going back to his smartphone.

"WHAT?!" said Aaron, spitting out his water. Aaron looked to his wife to see how she'd react, but she was staring at Tanya.

"Yes, it's true, Aaron," said Tanya, "They *are* your kids, BUT before you get all upset, I'm not asking for anything from you. Denise and I had a civil union, she adopted the kids, and we were going live happily ever after. And we did, for several years. Until…" Tanya started to tear up. "She broke our hearts into a million pieces and left us. She said she no longer wanted to have anything to do with me or her own children. She was the parent they loved and called Mommy Number Two. We couldn't find her for years, and now that deadbeat Denise owes thousands of dollars in back child support and is hiding from the law." Her voice started to quiver. "Let me tell you it hasn't been easy being a single mom trying to get by…" she began to sob.

Lauren reached in her purse for a tissue and gave it to Tanya, who wiped her tears and loudly blew her nose with it.

"Look," Aaron said in a shaky voice. "I'm sorry, but, well, I know it must've been very tough on you having to get by without Denise - T.B. and Isolde seem like good kids and all - but to come here after so many years and claim that I'm their father –"
"You ARE the father," said Tanya. "I didn't do guys back then. You were the first and only guy I'd ever been with at that point in my life."

Oh God, thought Aaron. A virgin. Kind of.

"Anyway," Tanya continued, "The DNA confirms it; that's how come I found you - from a genetic database. I was told that they took a swab of your DNA when you were arrested."

Aaron turned to his wife, who looked more confused than angry. "Honey, it was some stupid college prank, getting drunk, and trying to steal the big cube sculpture at Astor Place. Something I almost forgot about. I only spent a night in jail, no fine, no nothing. But I don't remember them taking my DNA."

"Well they did!" said Tanya. "Maybe you were too wasted to remember it, but they got your sample, put it into some international registry, and that's how come I found you. And just yesterday I got a lead on where Denise is hiding. It turns out she's near you, in Seward! So we'd like you to give us a ride."

"That's got to be, what, two hours away?" said Aaron, "150 miles from here? That's a long way. I'm sorry, Tanya, but we can't help you."

"Actually, it's only 97.8 miles from here. Look, here's the printout of the directions." Tanya took a folded piece of paper out of one of her boots. Aaron saw that Tanya didn't have a purse and her tank top and miniskirt clearly had no pockets. Tanya turned first to Aaron and then to Lauren, giving them a pained and desperate look. "We don't have a car! Denise left us with nothing!" She began to cry again.

Aaron was about to ask how they had gotten to his house without a vehicle (one certainly couldn't rely on the piss-poor public transportation in Hamlin) when Lauren addressed him. "Sweetheart, I'm sure we can at least give them a lift. We'll just drop them off in Seward and drive back."

"That's all we're asking," said Tanya, through muffled sobs. "And then you two can just drive back. Please! We have nowhere to turn, no one else to ask." She doubled up her tissue and cried some more.

Aaron was about to give in when Tanya looked up from her snot rag to add another stipulation. "Oh, and Lauren, could you please let Aaron come with me to the door when we find Denise?"

Without waiting for his wife's response, Aaron cried, "Absolutely not!" He didn't want to get in the middle of Tanya's tiff with Denise. He was also incensed that Tanya was asking his wife for permission, as if he wasn't allowed to decide for himself.

Before Lauren could respond, Tanya added, "Please, Lauren, make your husband come with me and the kids to see Denise. These are *his* children, after all."

"Pending a paternity test," said Aaron.

"OK," said Tanya, "Pending a test, have it your way." She daubed her eyes and then gave him a serious look. "But - and I'm not trying to be mean or anything - you know that if we can't get Denise to pay up, ultimately, you, their father, will be responsible. You'll have to pay all back child support plus interest, and help support them for the next five years, at least until they're 18. We're talking hundreds of thousands of dollars. I'm just saying."

Tanya's not-so-veiled threat made Aaron furious, but he didn't want to make a big scene in front of the kids, especially in the unlikely event that they really *were* his. Aaron knew that if the twins were really thirteen years old (they looked younger to him; maybe they were just small for their age?) it was at least possible that he *could* be their dad. Aaron calculated that the end of his last year at N.Y.U. was almost fourteen years ago, and, adding another nine months from the date of that unpleasant orgy for conception and birth, there was at least a remote chance that the kids were conceived by him and Tanya.

"Honey, why don't we get ready and take them to Seward?" Lauren said, in the form of a question that really wasn't. "It'll only take an hour and half to get there."

"And an hour and half back!" cried Aaron, to no avail. If it had been up to him he wouldn't have gone at all, but Lauren, he could see, was already on edge and the last thing he wanted was to upset her further. Plus, his wife had good instincts, an intuition which he often relied on, so maybe she was on to something here. Maybe Lauren knew that dropping these three off in Seward would be the only way to get rid of them.

And so, Aaron reluctantly agreed to make the trip.

In record time, Lauren packed snacks for T.B. and Isolde, while Aaron grabbed an industrial strength bottle Diet Mountain Dew to properly caffeinate him for the drive. They all jumped in Lauren's car and headed for Seward.

II.

Aaron's gut rubbed against the steering wheel as he backed Lauren's tiny coupe out of the garage. It made him aware that he still had another five pounds or so to go on his diet and a few thousand more sit-ups before he regained his former abs of steel. Sadly, his SUV was in the shop, and Lauren's car was a tight squeeze for all of them. But she always insisted that he drive, no matter which car, which was fine with him. He loved long stretches of road, and he knew that he did his best thinking behind the wheel. He figured that the drive to Seward would at least give him time to wrap his head around this whole situation with Tanya, her kids (his kids?), and Denise. And to let him figure out how to smooth things over with Lauren once he dropped them off in Seward.

Since Tanya was a nearly a half a head taller than his wife, Lauren offered to let "their guest" (her words) sit up front. Lauren got in back, in the middle, with Isolde on her left, and T.B. on her right.

Fortunately, Lauren taught history and social studies to eighth graders and was adept at quickly developing rapport with kids that age. She was even better than Aaron, and that was saying a lot. So it wasn't long before T.B. had become more personable and Isolde dropped her freaky twin act, and they both were laughing and cracking jokes with Lauren. The kids were bright, and surprisingly knowledgeable about history too: Lauren had them play her "History Jeopardy!" game, and no matter how obscure her questions became, she couldn't stump them. And, perhaps unsurprisingly, given the fact that they were named after two Wagner protagonists, they had an appreciation for opera. For kids their age, they had a passion for, or at had least knowledge of, a surprisingly eclectic mix of disciplines - 19th century literature, medieval weaponry, even Asian geo-political history.

Lauren and the kids seemed to be having fun, but for Aaron, the drive upfront with Tanya was long, tedious, and annoying. Tanya talked nonstop: about people he didn't know, sexual acts he'd never tried, and of her innumerable grievances against Denise. He tried to tune her out, at times listening in the history game with the kids in the back (how on earth did they know the date of Zimbabwe's independence?), at times thinking about his own memories of Denise.

Why hadn't she told him about Tanya's kids - who were supposedly his too? *Denise could've found*

*me anywhere, online or in the alumni directory for
chrissakes, just to let me know. Still, that's supposing
that those kids really ARE mine.* He glanced in the rear
view mirror. *They DO look a little like me, the thick
eyebrows, the green eyes, their wavy black hair. But
maybe it's just my imagination. After all, they look a
little like Lauren too. Hell, all kids kind of look the
same, anyway – small, mostly bipedal hominids, with
opposable thumbs.*

Aaron took a sidelong glance at Tanya, who
was looking straight ahead at the road before them –
and babbling. She prattled on about how tough her life
was growing up with a controlling mother, how Denise
had started acting like Tanya's mother, and how Tanya
had come "this close" to an abortion, but couldn't
afford one. Sneaking another peek, he concluded that
his death-seat passenger had a fine set of breasts, which
made him reassess her face. Sure it was hardened,
almost beaten down, but, with her almond shaped and
olive colored eyes, and her thick, sensuous lips, she was
still a fine looking woman. When he mentally replaced
her shiny black hair with her former red curls, the
fragmented memory of Alys/Tanya, Denise, and that
night started to come back.

Back then, Aaron had been a month away from
finals, so by this time he would have been "dating" (his
euphemism for fucking) Denise for about three
months. Following their drinking binge at the Kettle of
Fish, he remembered the three of them stumbling down

Bleecker Street and somehow making it back to his dorm room. Luckily his roommate was out of town. Wasted as Aaron was though, he probably wouldn't have noticed if his roomie had been there and filmed the whole thing. He remembered going to his little dorm-sized fridge - to get a Coke to mix with the rum the girls had brought. When he turned around, the two ladies were in his bed and stark naked. He recalled Denise lifting her head from Alys' crotch and turning to smile at him; the light from the lamp on his bed stand reflecting her moist and glistening face. Then the girls pulled him down on the sheets, undressed him, and he was really getting into it - until he entered Alys and immediately knew that this was all a mistake. With each thrust, his bladder hit against her thin body, against her pubic bone, causing him to think of nothing more than how much he needed to pee. When Denise took over from Alys, climbing on him and mounting him, her athletic and violent undulations made him cry out in pain.

At some point he had to throw the woman off him, run to the john, wait for his erection to subside, and then piss like a racehorse. His head was spinning and he could feel vomit rising in his throat. While he splashed cold water on his face, he could still hear the girls in the bedroom; they were either moaning or laughing at him, or both.

By the time Aaron stumbled back to bed, Alys was already on her hands and knees, impatiently waiting for another fucking; Denise fondled his semi-erect penis and pulled his member into Alys. But banging this girl doggy style was even worse. His brain started bouncing against his skull. Suddenly the whole dorm room spun like a Tilt-a-Whirl, his bladder started filling up again, and the girls' sexy talk and moans felt so loud that his ears pulsated. His whole body felt spasms of pain. He couldn't wait to get the whole thing over with and was relieved when he finally ejaculated. He couldn't really call it an orgasm, since describing it that would imply a level of pleasure that definitely wasn't there. Once he climaxed, he immediately pulled out of Alys, crawled to the bathroom and puked his guts out.

He crawled back, but didn't quite make it to the bed. When he awoke the next day, he was still on the floor and the ladies were gone.

As if reading his mind, Tanya took her eyes off the road and asked, "So, did you enjoy our little 'twa?"

"Our what?" asked Aaron.

"Our 'twa, ménage a trois, you know, the night with you, me and –"

"OK, Tanya, I get it." As uncomfortable as he felt talking about it within hearing range of Lauren, he felt even weirder about the kids hearing it too. Aaron was far from a prude, but he and Lauren had decided a long time that ago that, if they ever had children, they wouldn't even curse in the kids' presence - let alone talk about the "mature themes" they warn you about in PG-13 films. Of course, he knew from observing their friends who have kids, that being absolute in one's parenting rules (like no TV, ever) rarely works for long. Still, he reasoned, you had to set the bar somewhere.

He whispered to Tanya, "Aren't you afraid about the kids hearing you, you know with all the sex talk?"

"Shit, no! They've known about the night they were conceived since day one. And they're 13 years old, for fuck's sake. I certainly had my share of poon by then."

Tanya pulled out a pack of cigarettes - unfiltered Camels. Before Lauren could say anything, Aaron told her to please not smoke in his wife's car. Lauren was acutely sensitive to the fumes. Tanya rolled her eyes, but put her cigs away. He looked around at the sights on the road, wondering about the billboard that advertised "Logistics"(whatever that was), and wondered why the company would name itself "P.U.S. Supply." He tried to ignore Tanya but he could feel her eyes on him.

"Well," she asked, "Aren't you gonna answer me? Did you enjoy our three-way that night?"

Lauren's voice came booming from behind him. "Yes, Aaron. Did you *enjoy* your little three-way?"

Aaron blushed.   He hated being put on the spot, knowing that whatever words he chose would be the wrong ones. "Well, yeah," he fumfered, "It was … OK. I mean, I guess, it was cool."

"Just 'cool'?" Lauren asked. He knew she hated weasel words like that. "And precisely what does that mean?"

"Honey, please. Let's just drop it, OK?" Aaron clenched his teeth and checked the a/c temperature for the umpteenth time. He just wanted quiet but something was nagging at him. He turned to Tanya and asked, "Did Denise know that T.B. and Isolde are allegedly my offspring -"

"Don't use that word 'allegedly'," said Tanya. "You're going to give the kids a complex."

"Yeah, Aaron," said Lauren, piling it on in an annoyingly self-righteous voice. "Don't talk like that in front of the children."

He tightened his grip on the steering wheel. He couldn't tell if Lauren, who was prone to taking the side of students over teachers, was truly worried about the twins, or whether she was just talking that way because she was pissed at him. If only he could have had a few minutes alone with her before they'd taken this trip. At least that way he could've sussed her out about Tanya, the threesome, the twins, and his prior arrest.

Lauren might not have liked how he spoke in front of the twins. But Aaron was starting to get pissed too: she has to know that it's TANYA who was really messing up those kids, not him. If he weren't their father, then Tanya had given them false expectations. But if the kids were really his, then Tanya barging into his home unannounced with the kids in tow, was a horrible way for them to be introduced to their real dad. Just what had Tanya told the twins about him, anyway? And how did these kids feel about Denise, their so-called Mommy #2? He had a lot of questions for Tanya, but decided it was best to say nothing for the time being to avoid any further drama.

Breaking a long silence, Tanya said, "To answer your question from before, Aaron, yes, of course,

Denise knew that you were their father. But by the time they were born, we were already living together and she was gung ho about us building a life together and raising the twins as a couple. By the way, it was Denise's idea, not mine, actually it was her INSISTENCE that I NOT try to find you. She was adamant that she did not want you in the picture."

"Oh, really, and why not?!" Aaron demanded.

"Well, I don't want to upset you or anything, but she – not me, but Denise – felt that you wouldn't be a good parent. I guess it was on account of you screwing her while you had a high school sweetheart, or something. That, and your willingness to take two girls to bed. That last point, Denise strongly felt, made you an especially unfit parent."

"Oh yeah? And what about HER?!" Aaron banged his fist on the steering wheel, accidently honking the horn. The bus in front of them immediately changed lanes. He floored the engine, passing the bus driver who flipped him the bird as they went by. Aaron leaned toward Tanya and said, in what sounded like a growl, "Well, fuck her, then. "

"You did," said Tanya. "And you fucked me too!" She giggled.

Aaron said under his breath, "Then I *really* fucked up."

"Language!" cried Lauren. "Aaron, we really mustn't use that kind of talk in front of young ears," He looked in the rearview mirror to see her frowning at him. Tanya giggled again.

Aaron ignored his wife. "Look, Tanya - Denise was wrong about just about everything, although it's true that I had a high school sweetheart. Still do. Right honey?" He cocked his ear to hear Lauren's response. She made none.

"Anyway, Lauren and I were together since high school. But then we went to separate colleges, a long way apart. Lauren dated other people and so did I. My point is that it's ridiculous, hypocritical even, for Denise to say that *I* did anything wrong."

Again, Lauren was mute.

Aaron was becoming increasingly irritated at his wife's silence. He really could have used some support right then. But now was *not* the time to get into that. If it turned out that T.B. and Isolde were his kids after all – crazy as that might be - he did not want to make a bad first impression. Anyway, he knew better than to project his anger onto his wife, when in fact Tanya, this bitch who just sprung all this stuff on them, was his real target. Upon further reflection, he couldn't blame Tanya for being so desperate that she felt she had to track him down, though a head's up would've helped. It wasn't as if Tanya was asking *him* for child support. But he knew if he didn't play his cards right, that's exactly what she'd do. The more he stewed about all this, the more his rage focused on that evil, lying, temptress and abuser - the one who started this whole mess!

Tanya, again as if reading Aaron's mind, said, "You know, Denise used to hit me when she thought I was out of line. Look at this." She held up her forearm so that both he and Lauren could see her scar. "This is where Denise burned me with a skillet for not having food on the table when she got home."

"How disgusting!" cried Lauren. "Aaron, how could you have dated such a bad person, someone so vile, so lacking in human compassion?"

"Honey, c'mon, I didn't know she was like that. It's not like we spent a lot of time discussing philosophy or corporal punishment. Or cooking, for that matter."

"Yeah, I know," said his wife, "You just fucked her. Pardon my French, kids."

"'Fuck' is not French," observed Isolde.

"No shit, Izzy," said T.B. Then the boy turned to Lauren and said with a grin, "Excuse my NON-French." Lauren, who usually took a dim view of potty mouthed kids, let out a chortle.

"So, Aaron," asked Lauren, "Any *other* reason you hung around with Denise?"

Aaron knew there was no point in responding. Obviously, there had been no other reason to hang around that despicable, barely human piece of swill - except to jump her bones.

Lauren leaned forward. "So, Tanya, why'd you stay with Denise for so long? Is it the usual 'she keeps saying she'll change and I believe her' thing or what?"

"Well, yeah…" Tanya answered in a trembling voice. "That, and her torture porn. I liked her snuff role playing video games too." She pulled out her wadded-up tissue out of her boot and wiped her eyes. "What you need to understand, is that Denise and I had a love/hate thing, but it was *thing* nonetheless. Me and the kids withstood her violent temper and she kept saying she loved me. But then one day Denise comes up to me and says, 'this place is a fish mart and I'm looking for a sausage fest.' And I was like, 'what is that, a line from something?' and she says 'no, but it should be.' And then she just ups and leaves. That's just like her: flippant and cruel. And it was bad enough for me, but you can imagine what it did to our children."

"She's heinous!" said Lauren.

"I couldn't agree more," said Aaron, "But, Tanya, this woman physically hurt you. So who knows what she could do to you now. OR to any of us. That's why we should just drop you guys off downtown and head back. I am NOT about to put my wife in harm's way."

"Then why don't you drop Lauren off downtown ?" Tanya asked. "Maybe she can grab lunch or something , while the rest of us go to Denise's?"

"No!" said Lauren, "I'm not afraid to confront this woman." Then she added, in what to Aaron sounded like a sanctimonious tone, "We all need to handle this together, for the sake of the children!"

Aaron finally agreed that they all would go to Denise's, but only if Lauren stayed in the car with the twins. Also, Aaron and Lauren would leave at the first sign of any trouble. Under no circumstances, he said, would he take Tanya and the kids anywhere after that. Tanya would either have to make up with Denise or be solely responsible for getting her and the kids out of there.

III.

They made record time to Seward. Aaron was always a fast driver (he claimed to be a stickler for time-efficiency), but being cramped in Lauren's tiny coupe with the five of them made him really drive like a bat out of hell. Luckily, Lauren was too distracted by her history game to notice that he'd been averaging ninety miles an hour most of the way.

As they slowed to reach downtown, they saw an old woman twirling a sign for a fast food chain. First T.B., then Isolde asked when they were going to stop to eat.

"LATER," said Tanya, "So just shut the fuck up!"

Aaron winced and looked at the kids in the rear view mirror. He didn't even have to look back at Lauren to know that she would be shocked to hear a parent like that to her children. But the twins didn't even object to Tanya's rude cursing. Either the children were well-mannered, unlikely as that might be, having been raised by a crass loudmouth like Tanya, or they were quiet for fear of getting the shit kicked out of them. Either way, Aaron felt sorry for them.

Tanya glanced at her directions and had Aaron make a couple right turns into a neighborhood with

1950s tract homes and cars parked on the lawns. The town looked like it had seen better days. A few streets even looked downright sketchy. But Seward did have a certain charm, with its wide, wooded boulevards and rolling hills.

Suddenly some guy on rollerblades careened down a hill, went through a stop sign, and almost hit their car. Aaron and everyone else in the car nearly had a heart attack. Luckily, Lauren didn't reprimand him. Tanya said nothing. She just quietly, and almost in a meditative fashion, gave the rollerblade guy the finger. Then she yelled something unspeakable. They drove up the hill and as they did, ticky –tacky houses gave way to '90s Mc Mansions, and finally to even larger custom homes on quarter acre lots.

"Hey, nice neighborhood," said Aaron. "For this dump of a town, at least."

"I don't think Seward's dumpy at all," said Lauren. "My uncle Kurt, you know, the lawyer, lives here. I've thought of us moving here and teaching at the high school my cousin Rachel used to go to."

"Living up *here,* yeah, well *that* would be nice," he said. "But I'm sure you'd need a lot of money to live up in these parts."

"Denise is rich," said T.B. "She's an A.P.C."

"No, she's a C.P.A.," said Isolde. "Right, Tanya?"

Tanya nodded. She downed some pills that she'd fished out of the bottom of her boot. Then she started to take slow, deep breaths.

"Oh, yeah, that's right," said Aaron, "I remember Denise was an accounting major. She must be pretty good with numbers, right?"

"Numbers? You mean, like orgies?" asked Tanya. She didn't look like she was kidding.

"No, I mean figures," said Aaron.

"Whose figure? Mine?"

"That's not what I mean. I mean, wasn't she good at math?"

Tanya didn't answer. She resumed her deep breathing. From her seated position she also went into a routine of stretches and butt clenches.

T.B. said, "Izzy and I don't really remember much about Denise."

"We don't even remember what she looks like," said Isolde. "We were just babies, I think."

Aaron looked at Tanya. She, in turn, scowled at the kids and again told them to zip it. Aaron hoped that his wife noticed, as he did, that the kids' stories didn't quite jibe with Tanya's. How come they call her by her first name, anyway, instead of calling her Mom? And just how long *had* Tanya and Denise been together?

Before he could ask Tanya, they arrived at their destination. Denise's place was the crummiest house on the block – a run-down, shotgun-style bungalow.

"If Denise sees me," Tanya told Aaron, "She won't open the door. You and Lauren better go up and knock."

He hesitated. Finally, he said, "Alright, *I'll* go. But Lauren, honey, you just stay here with –"

"Hell no!" cried Lauren as she threw open the rear passenger door. "Let's roll."

Lauren took his arm as the couple walked up to the front steps. There was a bike and a motorcycle in the driveway, so maybe someone was home. Aaron knocked on the door and, sure enough, a woman answered. Denise no longer had her black hair in a bob cut from when Aaron knew her (like Tanya's current hairstyle). This lady had short, spiky blonde hair which reminded him of a cross between Annie Lennox and the "Stop the Insanity!" TV woman. But Aaron knew it was Denise alright. She was wearing tight shorts, a sports bra, and a headband, and she was drenched in sweat. She had obviously just come from some kind of intense workout like aerobics or sex.

A look of recognition came over Denise's face. "John?"

"No," said Aaron.

"Oh, sorry." She thought for a moment. "It's Cameron, right?"

"No. My name is-"

"J.P.?"

"No, it's - "

"Wait, don't tell me. P.J.? Gordon? Clyde? Jacob? Dewey? Herb? Mohammed?"
Aaron kept shaking his head.
Denise was stumped. "I know we used to fuck, but I'm sorry, I forgot your name."

"It's Aaron, from N.Y.U. Oh, and this is my wife, Lauren."

"Eric! Why, of course, I remember you."

"Aaron," Lauren corrected her.

"OK, whatever," said Denise, eyeing Lauren from head to toe, "Eric, you've certainly done well for yourself. You always did like the older ones, didn't you?" She extended her hand towards Lauren. "I'm Dee, but my lovers call me Denise. So, why don't you call me Denise?" She winked at Lauren. Lauren blushed.

Just then, Tanya jumped out of the car and marched up the driveway. Denise looked terrified as Tanya ran up to the porch. Denise tried to slam her front door shut, but Tanya was already there to stop it with her foot.

"You heartless, thieving, conniving, embezzling, cunt!" Yelled Tanya. She would've hurled herself into the door had Aaron not held her back and muffled more of her foul epithets with both hands over her mouth.

Lauren bravely put her face up to the crack in the door as Denise kept trying to shut it on Tanya's foot. "Denise, please! Tanya just wants to have a few moments to talk – "

"Tanya?!" cried Denise, still pushing back on the door. "Oh, is that what you're calling yourself these days? What happened to 'Joanne', 'Natalie', 'Patricia',

"Skye", "Marie-Therese", "Paula"? Oh, and remember, 'Alys with a Y'?" Her nostrils flared in anger. "Get this whack job away from my house right now or I'm calling the cops!"

"But," said Aaron, still holding on to Tanya and covering her mouth, "She brought the children. Don't you at least want to see *them*?"

"Oh, great," said Denise, "She's getting her kids involved again?! Hold on; don't let her take another step in. I want to show you something, OK? Just a sec." She closed and locked the door.

Aaron kept a firm grip on Tanya while they heard shuffling around inside. A few moments later, Denise slowly opened the door a crack and pushed some papers in Lauren's direction. Lauren grabbed the pile and leafed through the documents. Most of them appeared to be legal pleadings. Lauren had worked as a paralegal before getting her teaching certificate, so she had some familiarity with legal mumbo-jumbo.

"These are restraining orders," Lauren told her husband. "Like here, it says 'the respondent, Alys Majestyk, aka Natalie Prince, aka Tanya Sinque, upon completion of her incarceration and drug treatment program, is permanently enjoined from harassing the petitioner or otherwise coming within 100 yards of her for a period of 99 years.' And these are police reports…assault, harassment at work, death threats directed against the victim, Denise aka Dee McIntyre." With a frown, Lauren flipped through the rest of the stack.

Through the door, Denise said. "Now, do you see what I've had to go through? Twelve years of hell trying to get away from that prick hole. "

"OK, Denise," said Lauren. "I get what you're saying about Tanya. But what about your children?" They looked back to see T.B. and Isolde standing by the car. Lauren had told them to stay inside but she couldn't blame them – it was too hot to stay in there, even with the windows rolled down.

"MY children?" Denise laughed bitterly. "They're not mine. Look, I'm sure they're good kids – I mean I haven't seen since they were babies – but they're definitely not mine. Me and this Muff Job from Hell only dated for a few goddam months, and that was a dozen fucking years ago." Denise paused to wipe a dribble of sweat that trickled through her cleavage. "I hope Alys or whatever name she uses now, didn't give you that cock and bull about how we were somehow domestic partners and how I supposedly adopted her children. Did she?"

"As a matter of fact, she did," said Aaron. He tightened his restraint on Tanya, who was shaking with rage.

Tanya bit his hand and suddenly broke free. "Denise, they're YOUR kids, too, you crotch rot!"

"No, they're YOUR kids, you piece of shit for a mother! You know, the ones you made *your* mom raise while you were in an out of rehab, remember?"

"Don't you dare bring my dear mother into this!!" Tanya's eyes grew savage.

"Look, I don't know who to believe," said Aaron, "But Tanya, you've got to keep your voice down –"

"Why don't *you* keep your voice down, limp dick!" Tanya turned to Lauren. "Your husband has to be the worst fuck on the planet."

"He is not! How dare you?!" Lauren shot back. Aaron had to keep her from slapping Tanya's face. Lauren added, "He may not be the greatest lover in the world –"

"What? Geez, Lauren," said Aaron under his breath.

"But he's my husband! I'll not have you talking about him like that, especially in front of the children."

"Yeah, and anyway, you guys, cut me some slack," Aaron added lamely. "I was drunk off my ass that night."

"Well, that bitch is lying again," said Denise, "I hope *you* don't believe Alys about our 'twa."

"What do you mean?" asked Aaron.

"I'm saying, Eric –"

"Aaron," Lauren corrected her again.

"If you're the guy the guy I'm thinking of, then you were pretty damn good with me AND psycho twat here. "

"Psycho?!" cried Tanya. Aaron tightened his grip around Tanya's waist. "If you've been talking to my parole officer, well *she* can eat my pussy straight up. And you can ask anyone, my friends, my lawyers, all my therapists, and they'll tell you, I'm saner than anyone you've ever met. Everyone knows that – Denise, YOU fucking know that! YOU are the crazy one. Goddam, you stink hole, I could kill you right now!"

Tanya struggled, breaking free of Aaron. In a split second she pulled something out of her boot and jumped on Aaron's back. She pulled a long knife on him, resting its sharp edge right on his Adam 's apple. Lauren, seeing her husband in peril, seized up.

"Denise," said Tanya, in a slow and menacing voice. "I'm going to tell you for the last time. I want my money. And if I don't get it, this loser's dead meat."

"I don't owe you shit," said Denise. "I ought to be charging YOU for all the legal bills and lost billable hours it's cost me just to get you out of my life."

"I'm serious, Dee, this fool's gonna get it!" said Tanya. Aaron didn't dare move his head, but he shifted his eyes to look at Lauren, who met his gaze with a helpless expression. Then he glanced imploringly at Denise.

"Are you off your meds again?" asked Denise. "You can slice this fool, dice him and make him into soup, for all I care."

"Oh, you used to say that I 'made soup in your panties', Denise, just like the Spanish say. Remember our trip to Seville?"

"That was years ago," said Denise. "Now, soup time's over. So go ahead and kill him. And kill yourself, while you're at it, you putrid snatch." Denise eyed Lauren from head to foot. "And you can kill his mother over there –"

"His 'mother'?!" cried Lauren, "How dare you!" Lauren reached her arms through the crack in the door to throttle Denise. Denise slammed the door on her hands. In the confusion, Aaron managed to break free of Tanya. He tried to grab his wife and pull her away from the door. The last thing they saw was Tanya charging toward Denise, knife first.

Aaron and Lauren were just about to call 911 when they heard a siren blaring in the distance. A police car drove up, but the cops were too late: before they put down their burritos, got out of the squad car and adjusted their belts, Tanya had already plunged her knife into Denise's sternum. She stood over Denise's body, trying to extricate her knife out of Denise's ribs. The officers, fearing that the assailant would take off on foot and they wouldn't be able to catch her (each of them weighed over 300 pounds) shot Tanya in the back multiple times. Within minutes, both Tanya and Denise were dead.

IV.

The officers questioned Lauren briefly and then turned to Aaron. Their investigation focused on his ménage a trois, and involved such prurient questions as,

"Did Suspect #1 ride you cowgirl style or was it reverse cowgirl?"

The officers were unable to get anything out of the despondent children, other than the fact that they were the ones who had called 911. Lauren insisted that the children were their foster kids; neither T.B. nor Isolde contradicted her. The officers then told them that they had finished their investigation. The cops high-fived each other and let them all go.

Lauren returned to the back seat with Isolde and T.B., while Aaron got behind the wheel. He offered to give the kids a ride anywhere they wanted to go. But, through pained sobs Isolde told him that their grandmother, the only caregiver that they'd ever known, had died last week. Now they had no one to take care of them and nowhere to go.

"I guess it's just you and me from now on," said T.B. to his sister, bravely trying to hold back his tears.

"We're orphans," said Isolde, wiping her eyes.

Lauren drew them into her arms. "No, don't say that. You are not orphans."

Aaron started the car and drove them back down the windy streets toward the Interstate. In a few minutes the freeway opened up and Aaron floored it. In a blur, tract homes gave way to industrial parks, billboards advertising personal injury lawyers, and finally long stretches of countryside and mini-marts. Hot winds rustled against the speeding sedan. Aaron could feel the road whizzing by underneath them. But inside the cabin there was only silence. He looked in his mirror to see the children asleep, resting their heads on Lauren's shoulder. He caught his wife's eye. She smiled at him and tenderly reached out and touched his shoulder. A few minutes later he heard Lauren snoring peacefully.

In little over an hour they would all be home.

IN(TER)VENTION

I

Invention #1

He was late and he knew it. He was also drunk, and knew that, too. How else could he have been expected to get through an excruciating evening with Mom and Song without first stopping for three fingers of rye? And how was he to know – for he had never been to The Palsied Pup before – that he would get there just as Happy Hour was starting? And that he could afford two g & t's for the price of one? Though he was as frugal as ever, it seemed unwise not to take advantage of an offer like that. It's not like they paid him nearly enough at that cheap digital rag to even nurse a $4 Bud during the insufferable concerts and talent shows they'd make him review. Luckily, he carried a flask, just in case he had to watch yet another derivative band preening around as if they'd invented the three chords that inevitably would make up their set.

Now, after a dozen or so drinks, he was fortified and ready to do his duty: to see his folks. He'd taken a train and a bus all the way out to the hinterlands of Seward in the pouring rain. And now, after leaving the bar, he still had a two mile walk just to get to their place.

To pass the time, he hummed Blind Melon's No Rain, Bob Marley's Misty Morning, and Johnny Cash's

Five Feet High and Rising. He rattled his brain to remember some of his other favorite songs about rain. He cursed himself for losing his iPad at The Hoary Chestnuts set last night. Oh well, he'd just have to conjure his favorite tunes in his head, just like Lester Bangs and Leonard Feather, and all the great music journalists of yore.

Ian was soaking wet and exhausted by the time he got to Mom and Song's mansion. OK, he'd often admit to his drinking buddies, it's not really a mansion. But it was a big house. And its ostentation, like the circular driveway he was walking up, never set well with him. Especially now that he was broke again. Mud, silt, and pebbles found their way into his holey sneakers. If Mom and Song weren't so stingy with their money, he thought, trudging the stone path to the porch, he could finally get a good pair of boots.

He stood at the imposing set of 10-foot high doors and rapped on a brass knocker. He expected his mother, or Song, or maybe their housekeeper Natty, to open the door. Instead it was Dean, Larry's husband, who greeted him. What was he doing here? This was supposed to be a quiet dinner with his mom and step-dad. Then, after dessert, Ian planned to ask them for another loan.

But before he even entered the parlor (his mother's name for the spacious living room) he sensed that something was up. Dean was normally a high testosterone, Army and law enforcement type of gay guy. But now he was somber and subdued. Dean paused before opening the door. He scratched his flat-top and said, in an irritatingly soothing voice, "Ian, Mom and Dad and your brother have invited a few us here to talk to you."

With a flourish, Dean opened the door to reveal a group of people sitting in a semicircle. Mom and Song were there, of course, both offering sad smiles. And there was Ian's brother, Larry. Two of Ian's cousins were there, as was his Step-Uncle Chen. Also present were two classmates Ian hadn't seen since kindergarten, almost twenty years ago. Finally, there were three strangers – an abnormally skinny teenage girl, a bloated middle aged man, and a tiny, shriveled nonagenarian of indeterminate gender.

The middle-aged stranger held out his hand and said, "We wish you well, Aidan," and gave him a kiss on the mouth.

"His name is Ian," Missy corrected the man. As Ian extricated himself from the stranger, Missy whispered to her intoxicated son, "Take a seat over there," pointing to the center of the semi-circle. Ian looked around for a chair but found none; was he supposed to sit on the floor at their feet?

Step-Uncle Chen brought in a folding chair from the garage, put it at the center of the semi-circle, and motioned for Ian to sit. He did.

Missy continued. "You need to listen to what we have to say. Larry, tell him."

"We have certain concerns about you, and Dean, as you may know, has been studying for the past year and is about to get his license as an Interventionist."

Dean cleared his throat. "InterveNOR."

Ian raised an eyebrow. "So, you're going to lead an intervention before even getting certified?"

"Correct-a-mundo," said Dean.

"And is this your first one?"

"That's none of your business," said Dean.

"Ian," said Larry, "There's no need for you to get defensive."

"I'm not getting defensive. If anyone is getting defensive, it's –"

"Clearly, you're being defensive," Larry pointed a finger at Ian, "And passive-aggressive too, so just drop it." Ian hated his brother's pop-psych power plays but decided to let it go. In Ian's more rational moments like this, he knew there was no arguing with his sanctimonious and none-too-bright sibling.

Dean straddled a metal folding chair, cleared his throat and declared, "Let's roll!" This may have been Dean's first intervention, but the burly former police officer and Army drill sergeant quickly took charge of things.

Ian counted a dozen people surrounding him. He felt like Jesus, except none of those present were his disciples. And, unlike the Son of God, Ian knew that not one, but ALL of these people would betray him. Most already had.

"OK, folks, let's get busy!" said Dean. The Intervenor leaned on the back of his chair and pounded his fist with peremptory authority. "OK, we have a quorum. Now, unless anyone, EXCEPT the Intervenee – and that means you, Ian – has any objection to the commencement of these proceedings, let the Intervention begin!" He rang a tinkly bell.

Ian, sensing Dean's extreme earnestness, took another look at the motley crew that had been assembled. He let out a chuckle. Then he made a serious face of his own and turned to his mother. "Is this intervention about my lateness problem?"

"No, dear," said Missy, "It's –"

"Or my earliness problem? You know, premature ejaculation?"

"Heavens, no. We didn't even –"

"Oh, I know! Is it because of my chronic fingernail biting?"

"No, son –"

"My vintage Arabian porn collection?"

"No, we don't care about –"

"I'm just kidding, I don't have one; my smut's all new. Plus, I'm not that into horses." He pretended to wrack his brain. "Oh, I get it now. I didn't even think you guys knew. This intervention is because I'm becoming left-handed, right? I was already thinking of seeing a shrink about that my ambidexterity."

"Sweetheart, no –"

"Is it my poison pen review of Taylor Swift's 1989?" The visitors looked confused, but Ian gave them bitter laugh. "Sorry, I was just joking. Of course you would never read anything I write." He furrowed his brow into a frown. "But seriously, folks. Is it because

I'm short?" He stood five-foot-seven though, no shorter than his brother or Chen. Missy shook her head.

"Is it because of the way I dress?" He was wearing a fedora hat, a London Fog trench coat, and a t-shirt underneath which advertised the Cameron Crowe film Almost Famous. Every article of clothing he had on was soaked.

"No," said Larry. "But it's pretty corny, especially for someone who fancies himself a writer."

Ian ignored his brother. "Is it my auto-repetitive mastication syndrome?"

"Your WHAT?" Mom asked.

Ian loudly chomped his teeth.

"Don't get smart with your mother!" barked Song. Normally, he was a quiet, almost mute older gentleman. But when provoked, Song reverted to the tough-as-nails Marine Corps captain he'd been before his retirement two decades ago.

Larry said, "Ian, we're all here because we need to talk to you about your drinking and how it is affecting you and those who love you."

Ian wondered who those loving individuals might be, but chose to bite his tongue.

"That's right, we heard your drinking sucks!" said a tinny voice coming from a laptop computer that lay open on the coffee table.

Ian leaned forward to look at the monitor. There were dozens of people each on their own webcam, displayed in a moving slide show in three rows of three. It looked like the Brady Bunch on the Hollywood Squares playing Chat Roulette. Ian couldn't tell which one of the talking heads had just spoken. In fact, he didn't recognize any of the faces who appeared on the screen. The whole online set up struck Ian as ludicrous. He let out a snort.

Dean smiled, oblivious to Ian's derision. "Pretty cool, huh? There's this site on the Internet that conducts virtual interventions."

Ian was trying, really he was, to be civil. He just wanted to get the whole thing over with so he could make it back in time to meet up with friends for drinks at The Second Opinion, a neighborhood bar, catty-corner from Seward Memorial Hospital. But he couldn't suppress another laugh. To Ian, the term "virtual" went out with Electronic Bulletin Boards, Megabyte Mondays, AOL and LOL.

"Cyber-virtual interventions, huh?" Ian said to Dean. "What will they think of next? Chat rooms?"

Dean's already tight smile turned to a grimace. He wasn't one of those friendly, big smile guys by nature. But Dean looked like he was trying his best to be personable and caring, skills this Intervenor gig apparently required.

"OK!" Dean peered around the room to see if there were any African Americans in the room. There were none. "Let's call a spade a spade. Buddy, your drinking stinks and you're a goddam alkie –"

Missy cut in. "I think, well, what Dean is trying to say –"

"Please, Mom," her son-in-law interjected. "Address me as The Intervenor."

"As you wish. Anyway, what The InterveNOR is saying is that we are all concerned, Ian. We're worried about what you are doing to yourself, what with all the wine, vodka, and who knows what else."

"How about the gin and tonics whenever I crank up Oasis? Do they count too?" Ian asked helpfully.

All eyes turned to Dean. "Without resorting to the Interventionor's Manual, then I'm just shooting from the hip, but I'd say they probably count."

"Of course they count!" said Missy. "But I love you. WE love you. And we're just worried sick about you."

"Because," said Larry, who had a knack for stating the obvious, "We don't like what your drinking is doing to you."

Ian paused. "I think I'm starting to get the picture. So, is there a consensus here that my responsible enjoyment of alcoholic beverages has a deleterious effect on me and everyone around me?"

"Yes!" was the chorus from everyone in the room. Some tinny voice on the Brady Bunch monitor yelled, "Praise Jesus!" Another tinny voice asked what "deleterious" meant.

Ian sunk toward the floor, feigning ignorance and embarrassment. "I understand completely now. I guess I just never knew that drinking to excess was bad."

He thought about telling these fools that, for every Bon Scott, John Bonham, and F. Scott Fitzgerald, there were millions of other heavy drinkers who are exceedingly happy. But Ian was cornered and he knew it. These pinheads, led by the grand wizards of pinheads – Larry and Dean – wouldn't be satisfied until Ian quit doing the one thing he enjoyed. The only thing that helped him deal with spending even a single hour with his revolting family.

"Ian, you say you understand?" asked Dean.

"Yes. And I think we should look into rehab," said Ian.

The members of the group smiled and everyone high fived each other, except for Step-Uncle Chen, who spoke no English and really had no idea what was going on.

"Oh, and thank you all for caring." Ian started to fidget.

Dean was obviously pleased with himself. "How's that for one-stop therapy, huh?" he asked the group. Dean answered his own question by adding, "Pretty darn good if I do say so myself."

Suddenly Ian doubled over in pain. "I'm sorry," he said, through clenched teeth, "But my bladder is bursting. It's been one heck of a long trip. Excuse me for a moment." He stood up, though not quite erect, held his bladder, and waddled out to the bathroom.

Actually he did need to pee, but not that bad. Ian had a more important reason to leave the group than urination. And that reason had nothing to do with popping a squat, either. Ian lifted the toilet seat and did his business. But he didn't flush. Keeping the light and the overhead fan on, he crept out of the bathroom, silently closing the door.

Then he snuck into Song's study. The light was off but Ian knew his way around Song's sacred little room in the dark well enough to get to the closet. That's where the old man kept his guns. Ian found the steel box that held the firearms, but the damned thing had a padlock and chain around it. Then he found a wooden chest with its top left open. Ian took out his cellphone to illuminate its contents: an assortment of knives, daggers, swords, scythes, and machetes. He almost sliced his thumb trying to dig into the box to look for more.

Finally, Ian found something that would do the trick: a rusty, old dagger with a razor sharp edge.

He got back on his feet. But he stood up too soon and felt woozy. Though he was dizzy and disoriented, he was determined to end it all right then and there.

He tried to direct the blade into the side of his neck. But his vertigo got the best of him. He slipped, dropped the knife, and fell to the ground. He found himself flat on his back, with the knife planted firmly between his shoulder blades. He tried to move so he could bend his arm back and release the knife, but the weapon only dug in even further, piercing skin and muscle. When the knife hit a nerve ending, Ian let out a piercing, anguished cry.

Hearing this, the group of interventionists ran to the bathroom, to the bedrooms, and finally to Song's study.

Dean turned the lights on to reveal the bloody scene before them. Fortunately, the middle-aged stranger, Ken, was a paramedic. (He was a new neighbor who'd been invited over by Missy after he mentioned that he'd been to a couple interventions in the past and enjoyed the food.) Ken immediately examined Ian's injuries. The poor young man was still clinging to life. Ken staunched the blood and called an ambulance. Then he gave Ian mouth-to-mouth resuscitation, notwithstanding the fact that Ian was breathing normally. Since Ken said he had some pull with the city's ambulance services, they came within 90 seconds, instead of the 45-minute wait that was typical for their area.

The first responders turned Ian on his side and put him on a stretcher, leaving the knife in his shoulder for fear of causing further blood loss if they removed it. Ken sat in the back of the ambulance and continued to give Ian mouth-to-mouth, until one of the EMTs told him to knock it off.

The reason the knife landed where it did, instead of Ian's neck – in other words, the reason he lived, instead of hitting his jugular vein or an artery and dying immediately – was simple, at least to Ian: he had survived BECAUSE of his drinking. Had Ian not been feeling the effects of Happy Hour he wouldn't have been dizzy and slipped, and therefore the knife did not reach its intended target.

II

Invention #2

Yes, Ian's alcoholism saved him. Sort of.

Once he was rushed to the hospital, he lay in critical condition, fighting for life in the ICU. Missy, Song, Larry, and Dean sped to the hospital, where the four of them nervously sat in the waiting room. The rest of the interventionists stayed at the house, where, in their grief, they decided not to let a Costco vat of red velvet cake ice cream go to waste.

The waiting room was mostly empty except for a couple of families sitting at the other end. The two couples – Song and Missy, Dean and Larry, sat face-to-face in the dim light. The fluorescent lighting was subdued, either to make the room feel tranquil, or perhaps as the hospital's cheap-ass cost cutting measure.

Song held his wife as she sobbed, shook, and caterwauled. "My son! Oh, my son!" She repeated this over and over, to the disapproving glares of the other people in the waiting room. Missy daubed her eyes with a tissue that was already soaked with tears. She leaned forward toward Larry and Dean and asked, "Oh, God, what have we done?" She let out a wail.

"There, there," said her husband, unable to find anything else to say.

"It'll be OK, Mom," said Dean. "It's not uncommon to have unresolved feelings come up during an intervention."

"Unresolved feelings?!" cried Song. "Ian – her son… OUR son – is clinging to life right now and this is NOT the time for your intervention psychobabble!"

Larry pressed a finger into Song's chest. "Don't you dare talk to my husband in that tone! It's very disrespectful."

"And it's not very constructive!" said Dean, a little too loudly.

"Both of you, please!" said Missy. "I can't bear this. Oh, why did we do this horrible thing, this stupid intervention? Why couldn't you leave my poor Ian alone?"

"Because, Mother," said Larry, "Ian was killing himself and we couldn't stand by and just watch him make one bad decision after another. Like, him quitting dental school to become a music journalist! Jeez, in a day when journalists can't make a living and newspapers are closing left and right, it's like Ian dove right in after the Titanic and yelled, 'Wait for me!'" Larry's stupidly jovial face suddenly turned serious. "And most important, Ian was killing himself with alcohol."

"So YOU say, dear. But we went on your word and on Dean's word that Ian had a problem."

"Let's be clear, Missy," said Dean. "I was present solely in my capacity as the Intervenor. I am not, nor can I be, a percipient witness to Ian's drinking. I was called here because Larry asked me to, and I wanted to help..." Dean put his head in his hands and whined to no one in particular, "Jeez-Louise, there are so many liability issues with these things. I knew I should've drawn a contract. Or at least a CYA letter."

"Shut up, Dean," said Larry. "You can't Cover Your Ass this time, so don't try to pin this all on ME. We both know you've seen Ian get tanked before."

"I don't know, maybe once."

"It was definitely more than once," said Larry. "So cut the shit."

"Language!" said Song. "You know better than to talk like that in front of your mother."

"How's this for language?" Larry asked his step-father. "Fuck. You."

"Oh, yeah? Well fuck you, too!" Song stiffened, as if he were expecting a salute in return. "Don't forget, I can still bend you over my knee and spank you, young man."

"Step-Daddy, I'm not a child anymore," said Larry, "Haven't you noticed?"

"I wouldn't know, by the way you're acting," said Song.

"Larry, please," said Missy, "Just stop it! You ARE being childish. You're a grown man for Pete's sake, you're 33 years old."

"I'm 34. You ought to know your own son's age!"

"Oh, Larry. I'm ashamed of you, making this big fuss while your poor brother is back there clinging to life…" She blew her nose again. "Oh, poor, pathetic little Ian."

"Mother, that's poppycock! My 'poor brother' wouldn't be clinging to life if it weren't for your husband's collection of weapons!"

Song's face shot a fiery red. The vein running up and down his forehead pulsated. He held his breath and searched for the right words to express his anger at his insolent step-son.

Dean beat him to the punch. "Now wait a minute, Larry, dear. This is a Live Free or Die issue so I don't really think you should be criticizing your father –"

"STEP-father."

"Whatever." Dean scratched his head. "But there's absolutely nothing wrong with knives. Or guns. Everyone knows that knives don't kill people –"

"Save it," said Larry. "We've heard this all before: 'Guns don't kill people. Only people kill people.' And only people kill people – with guns, knives, and bombs."

Both Dean and Song looked confused.

"Well, anyway," said Dean, "I'm just saying that you can't fault Dad –"

"Stop calling him 'Dad'!" said Larry. "He's not YOUR Dad! And he's not MINE either. He's not anyone's dad. He's a non-dad with children. Kind of like a reverse bastard, I guess you could say."

"Larry!" cried Missy. "You will not be naughty like that. Song has been your daddy since you were 12 years old."

Larry looked sheepish.

"As I was saying," said Dean, "There's nothing wrong with Dad – or Song, if you will – having a knife collection OR a gun collection." Dean stopped to scratch behind his ear. "That said, and I'm not being critical, but it is a legitimate question as to whether it was negligent or not to maintain a collection of lethally sharp blades in your home without safely locking them up."

"What did I just hear?!" bellowed Song. "When you're treading on my Second Amendment rights conferred by the Almighty, you're treading on thin ice, pals'y."

Missy wiped her nose with another soaked tissue. "Honey, please don't get angry, but Dean's got a point. You can't just leave your guns and knives lying around like that."

"I didn't leave my firearms lying around!" Song banged his fist on the end table next to him. A 10-year-old Reader's Digest and one of the doctor's yachting magazines fell to the floor. "Those blessed guns WERE locked up! And the knives – I wasn't expecting to have this intervention in my house –"

"OUR house," said Missy, "It's not just yours."

Song took a deep breath. "I know, dear. I misspoke, OK?"

"Boy, I'll say," said Larry.

Song ignored him. "Missy, sweetheart. It's just that I didn't want to do this thing at our house."

"And you think I did? I wouldn't have had it at our place, either, or anywhere, if Larry and Dean hadn't MADE me do it!"

"Mom," said Dean, "Nobody made you do anything. It's not like we came over and put a knife to your throat –" Missy winced at the imagery of that cliché. Dean seemed unaware. "Nor did we put a gun to your head –"

Missy let out a sharp cry. "Stop!!!!! Just stop it! Oh, poor Ian! My poor, poor son!"

"I'm sorry, Mom," said Dean, "I didn't mean it to come out like that."

"Yes, you did. You and Larry are always trying to hurt me."

"No we're not." said Larry. He paused. He wanted to be truthful to his mother. "At least not most of the time."

Song pointed his finger at Larry and Dean. "And you don't think that your stupid intervention – and what it did to Ian – didn't hurt your mother?"

"Hey, that's a cheap shot," said Dean. "Nobody expected this to happen."

"YOU didn't expect it," said Song, "Because you'd never conducted an intervention before. Oh, for the love of God, you don't even have your license yet!

Dean, you clearly didn't know WHAT you were doing. And, without even being a licensed Interventionist –"

"I'm an Intervenor!"

"– you used our Ian as a guinea pig."

"A GUINEA? YOU'RE CALLING ME A GUINEA?!" yelled Dean, who'd lost part of his hearing when he was an Army sharpshooter. "I may have Italian blood in me but I'm 100% American, I'll have you know!"

"I didn't call you a guinea. I used the term, guinea pig –"

"See?!" yelled Dean, in a voice that everyone in the waiting room could hear. "He's using that word again!"

"I heard it, too!" said Larry, though his hearing was normal. "And he's calling you, a decorated police officer, a pig!"

"That's enough, Larry," Song said, "You're just begging to be disciplined."

"Yeah, and I'll press charges if you do! Anyway, where do you get off saying my husband doesn't know what he's doing? Dean is smarter than you and Mom put together."

"If Dean's so smart," asked Song, "How come he's hiding behind a mask of stupidity?"

"I will not sit here and have you making homophobic comments about my sweet, smart, and brave husband!"

"I'm not saying anything homophobic, you asshole." Song felt the sudden urge to spit on his step-son.

"Language, please!" said Missy.

"Language?!" yelled Song. "Oh, I got to be like, 'I no speaky Engrish,' is that it? Like I'm your little Asian rickshaw driver? Well, I got news for you, Missy: this Korean slash Chinese American is every bit as American as you are!"

Missy fished another Kleenex out of her purse and wiped her eyes.

"You can't talk to Mom that way!" cried Dean.

"She's not your mother," said Song.

"And she's not yours, either!" Dean knew he wasn't making sense but was too angry to care. "And no one was making fun of your ethnicity or questioning your patriotism. You know you're just talking bull –, well, out of respect for Mom, you're talking gobbledygook."

"Gook?" Song yelled. "Did I just hear you call me a gook?" Song jumped up, and got in Dean's face. "How dare, you, sir! I will not stand for any racism, nor will I allow this insolence – from you or from anyone. Not when I was out defending this country, defending YOUR freedoms in 'Nam."

Dean stood up and pounded his chest. "Yeah, well, I was in the Army, too!"

"The Army, ha! A bunch of pansies. I'm Semper Fi."

"So I'm not just a faggot to you, I'm a pansy now?!" Dean was so angry all you could see were the whites of his eyes. "You wanna step outside and see who the real pansy is?!"

"Alright, both of you," said Larry, "Let's just cool it. And Song – "

"I've told you a million times to call him 'Dad'," said Missy.

"Alright, Mom. Dad! Enough with the homophobic slurs!"

"How dare you talk to me like that, you disgrace of a step-son." Song reached into his jacket to grab his pistol. "Your brother NEVER would've spoken to me like that." He paused to load his gun. Then he yelled out, "Now, here's a bullet for the next scoundrel who calls me a homophobe!"

Three people at the other end of the room noticed the short man holding a firearm above his head and ran for their lives.

"Two can play that game," said Dean, reaching into his holster to grab his Lugar.

"That's it!" said Larry. He stood up and buttoned his jacket. "I've had it with both of you. I'm going outside for a goddam smoke."

"Not without cleaning your mouth with soap and water first!" said Missy.

Larry ignored her and left the room.

With Larry out of the way, Song pointed his gun directly at Dean, who pointed his at Song. The older man asked, in a voice loud enough for even the hospital staff to hear, "WHO DO I HAVE TO KILL AROUND HERE TO PROVE FOR THE LAST TIME THAT I AM NOT A HOMOPHOBE?!"

Missy sunk in her chair. Within minutes a security guard came and ordered Song and Dean to put their weapons away. Missy looked to the ground, silently whimpering. She hated the irascible side effects of her husband's heart medicine.

The security guard, a small, round, older lady, walked Song and his step-son-in-law to the hospital parking lot. There they saw Larry, who was pacing and nervously toking on an e-cigarette. The guard told Song and Dean that, as per hospital protocol, she was required to inspect their weapons and to log their serial numbers. Sensing their apprehension, she assured them that state law forbade her, or any official, from confiscating firearms at a hospital, school, senior center, or church.

Song and Dean still refused to let her inspect their weapons, saying that the whole thing sounded like socialism.

The altercation with the guard escalated, and in the confusion, the two men discharged their weapons. Larry, apparently forgetting that his brother was in the ICU, cried out, "Help me, Ian!" Then all was still. Song, Dean, Larry, and the guard lay in a bloody pool next to a row of doctors' Porsches.

III

The Writer

    In a dark and dingy room, a silhouetted figure of a man with a fedora sits at a desk. Next to him is an ancient Burroughs typewriter, a 100-year-old machine made by the ancestors of Naked Lunch author William S. Burroughs. Next to the return tab a burning cigarette rests in between tokes.

    The blue glare from his computer monitor gives the writer a ghoulish mien as he furiously types. His features are young; his eyebrows, cynical. If his tweed jacket and winged-tip shoes weren't so dingy he'd resemble his New Journalism heroes Gay Talese and Tom Wolfe.

    With a dramatic click of the keyboard, the writer signals to the heavens that he has just finished his requisite two chapters and he's now finished for the night.

    He takes a drag off his cancer stick, slides his beat-up Bo Diddley guitar off the bed, and finally downs the last of his gin.

IV

The Reckoning

    Ian awoke to the incessant buzzing of his cellphone. He looked at the clock. It was already past noon. He was supposed to be at his brother's for brunch at 10 o'clock. He could have called Larry to cancel, but Ian was broke and, as usual, he was up for some free food. Luckily, having slept in his clothes, he was already dressed, so he splashed some water on his face, put on his fedora and cabbed it over to Larry's.

As soon as Ian arrived, Larry came out to greet him and to pay the cabbie. Then Larry led Ian inside. Mom and Song were sitting on the couch with stern expressions. Ian was just about to apologize for his tardiness, when Dean came out from the kitchen with a tray of coffee, tea, and pomegranate juice.

"In case you're wondering, Ian," said Dean, "This is an intervention and I'll be your Intervenor for today."

WHAT?! Ian's heart pounded. His mouth went dry. An intervention! And before he even had breakfast and a couple mimosas? This can't really be happening!

Ian looked around the room. "Where is everybody?"

"What do you mean? Who else would be here?" asked Mom.

"Who else cares about you but us?" asked Song.

No one, Ian guessed. His life was sad enough already, and now this?

Ian immediately excused himself and ran into the bathroom. He furiously searched for some method of suicide: pills, razor blades, something to electrocute himself with. But he found nothing. Not even a roll of dental floss to hang himself with. They must've hidden everything before he'd gotten there. The bastards! He tried to sneak out to check the couple's bedroom, when Dean spotted him and escorted him back to the living room.

So now Ian would have to sit through the whole thing: the speeches, the hugs, the torture, all that mealy-mouth stuff. He felt envy for the prisoners at Gitmo – if only they'd just water-board him. Or, better yet, vodka-board him. The whole scene was even worse than he could have ever imagined. And, unlike what he had written the night before, Ian's annoying family stood united as each member prattled on and on about their love and concern for him.

Unable to off himself right then and there, Ian resigned himself to his fate that day. He'd have to just sit there and listen to this shit, just like Bangs being forced to review James Taylor. Or like Dave Marsh, being forced by Rolling Stone to slog through a Journey concert. But rather than just sit there and be miserable, Ian decided to use this whole intervention thing as a learning experience.

And what Ian learned that day is that you can't just commit suicide any time you feel like it; things like that take planning. And, most importantly, if you choose to consume large quantities of alcohol on a daily basis, you have to make sure that you completely alienate everyone around you. That way, no one will ever care enough to hold one of these stupid interventions.

O! SALESMAN!

The cubicle was shaking and the lurching, sweating Frankenstein of a salesman was on a roll. His massive limbs made the already cramped prefab desk look like it was swiped from a 2nd grade classroom. Tapping an insistent rhythm on his size sixteen wingtips, Jeff was on the phone with his umpteenth prospect today.

"Can you *see* the potential here? Doesn't this deal make sense to you? Can you *feel* yourself being the envy of all those creeps who laughed at you before you took action on this deal and got STINKIN' RICH?"

"Um…My Mommy says she'll be – uh, what did you say Mommy?" there was a long pause, followed by the distant voice of someone yelling. "She'll be with you in a -"

"Wait! Are we ready to seal the deal on this, or what?"

Jeff could never resist working his sales chops on anyone, and no one in Seward or anywhere in the state was immune. This morning it was the deaf man who lived in the apartment above him. His newest victim was a toddler.

"Give Mommy the phone. Hello, this is Ms. Charles," the woman said in an impatient tone. "What are you calling about?"

"Are YOU ready to close this baby, Missus Prospect, er, Missus Charles?"

"Close what? What are you calling - ?"

"Missus Charles! You're a smart woman, you make good choices don't you?"

"Who IS this – "

"Opportunity is knocking right now, Missus Charles! What are *you* waiting for?"

"Look –"

"Can you see the Big Picture here?"

"I don't know who you are or what you want, but don't ever call here –"

"Missus Charles, are you afraid of success?"

"Am I what? How dare you call at this hour! And how dare you give your shitass sales pitch to a four year old, and, wait – Lucina, stop! Stay away from my glass! Mommy told you not to touch her glaaaaaass!! God damn you! You're a bad, bad girl…."

Jeff was just getting started with his spiel when he heard a CRASH on the other end of the line. Next, he heard the sound of a hard SLAP! And then a little girl sobbing through a muffled receiver.

Jeff wiped the sweat dripping from his forehead with his damp hanky. By now his whole body was drenched and his white shirt looked like it was plastered on. He cranked up his headset so he could hear his own voice over his pencil drumming. That's because he had that RUSH song stuck in his head, the one where Geddy Lee does this falsetto yell "Salesman! O! Salesman!" Whenever Jeff thought about that song he'd start air drumming, which would get him jazzed to make some cold calls. Jeff's fidgety legs were now getting spastic as he bounced his knees up and down to the beat. The other sales reps in his cubicle tried to ignore the shaking; they pressed their headsets closer to their ears. Chad, his pain-in-the-ass desk mate, even got up in a huff and stormed out. *Poor Chad*, Jeff thought, *he won't make it in this boiler room with that kind of loser attitude.*

"I know you're skeptical!" he continued, over the sound of more slaps and children's cries. "Who wouldn't be? You don't know me from Adam. Heck, sometimes I don't even know MYSELF from Adam, ha! But I do know this: I know how to make moms *just like you* into entrepreneurs!"

With the child slumped on the floor in tears, Ms. Charles caught her breath and glared at the broken shards on the floor. Then she saw the receiver. The salesman's spiel was still audible and she grabbed it, ready (to mix her own metaphor) to rip this douche bag a new asshole.

"Didn't I tell you, whoever the hell you are," she yelled into the receiver, "To never EVER call -"

"Yes, I'm with you one thousand percent! That's right, and no Charles, especially this Missus Charles, would ever walk away from the opportunity of a lifetime! Even your daughter, Lucinda gets it! Just think! A little girl named Lucinda Katelyn Charles, age four and a half, residing at home with her mother at 54 East Fourth Street, in Old Town Seward gets it!"

"HOW THE FUCK DO YOU KNOW MY DAUGHTER'S NAME?! What kind of creep are you? Lucinda! You stay on the floor and think about what you did!"

"Ma'am, Lucinda's on the floor looking to you to see whether YOU are going to awaken that giant within! Wake up, Missus Charles, and smell the coffee!

Lucinda thinks outside the box and you should too! I know you'll want to get with the program, even if-"

"Lu, what the hell did Mommy just tell you-"

"YES, EVEN IF YOU ABUSE YOUR DAUGHTER LUCINDA, MISSUS CHARLES!"

"What?!!"

"Yessiree, you need help, you know it and I know it, why this is my fourth call to you today, and you're my best prospect. I've heard all the slaps, the hits, and all your threats. And I've heard sweet little Lulu screaming."

"You better mind your goddam -"

"And naturally all the little toddler's tears have been recorded for 'quality control' purposes. But we don't have to bring the little sweet one's cries for help to the attention of my supervisor, do we? She'll just have to call child services, and you'll pay a pretty penny to get Lulu back. Or worse, you'll have my girlfriend, District Attorney Van der Kloos, on your ass, sorry, I mean, your buttocks. I can tell you (from experience!) you won't like that. BUT you're in luck: where others see problems, I see opportunities! We can make a deal, can't we? Of course we can. That's why we accept all major credit cards, no problemo! We're here to provide one stop solutions, right here, right now. As we say in the biz, "operators are standing by" so WHAMMO! LET'S ROLL UP OUR SLEEVES AND DIG IN! What'll it be, Missus Charles, Visa, MasterCard, or Amex?"

He heard rustling on the other end of the line. As much as Jeff loved to hear himself in action, he knew that when you're ready to reel the sucker in you'd better close your mouth. Inside his throbbing skull, Jeff silently counted: one-alligator, two-alligator, three-alligator.

"God damn you," said the woman. Yep, he had a live one there!

"First, I'll need your name *exactly* as it appears on the credit card."

"Alright, alright, how much is this thing, whatever it is, gonna cost me?"

"Missus Charles, think about what it'll cost you if you *don't* take advantage of this once in a lifetime opportunity."

"Oh, alright, here's my credit card. The name on the card is Danielle Kristi Charles. That's spelled D-A-N-I-E-L-L-E…K-R-I-S-T-I…"

Yep, another call, another sale. Jeff got the card number, expiration, and secret code on the back, and said to himself, *I freakin' love this job.*

THE STICKY NEST

I

When daybreak came, Martin crashed, slumped back and buck naked in his indoor Jacuzzi. The jet stream had ceased bubbling a long time ago. The water was yellow and smelled of beer and urine. A few cigarette butts floated on top. At some point his fellow revelers must have had said their goodbyes. All, except for Peri, one of Martin's three lovers, and her friend Khang, the best sword swallower in Martin's circle of partiers. They had both nodded off under a mound of clothes, popcorn, and cotton candy at the foot of Martin's huge, circular bed.

Suddenly, a blast of "Big Girls Don't Cry" bellowed from upstairs. Muriel had always been a morning person; always chipper, and usually whistling in her tuneless and shrill warble as she'd make her morning tea. Then she'd head out to one of her many volunteering gigs like the local hospital Candy Stripers, The Lady Lutherans, or the Chaperones of the Lutheranettes. Lately, though, Martin's mom was waking up at an even more ungodly hour than usual. And she had taken to cranking up Frankie Valli and the Four Seasons at deafening doo wop decibels while vacuuming the entire house.

Peri and Khang woke up with a start. Martin, who was comfortably numb in his tub of beer and piss, was dreaming in falsetto; all the bad guys in his dream had high, nasally voices and spoke in Low Brooklynese – like Joe Pesci before his Snickers bar. Eventually, though Martin aroused from his slumber by Muriel's industrial-sized vacuum.

He looked at the clock. Christ, it's not even seven in the morning. In a whisper -Martin had a massive headache and couldn't handle any more noise, not even his own - he asked his sword swallowing buddy what day it was. Khang, was rushing around, frantically sorting through refuse to find his clothes. He said that today was Sunday. *Good,* Martin thought, *Mom will be leaving for church soon.*

Khang found his pants, someone else's shirt, and a couple of mismatched socks. He roused Peri, reminding her that they both had to book out of there to get to Traffic School. Peri, though puffy eyed and pale, got into her street clothes (Thomas Pink, Juicy), put on some lipstick, and dashed out the door.

But not before she gave Martin one last sloppy kiss. Khang respectfully waited outside. For a moment, Martin wondered what kind of relationship Khang had with Martin's stripper-lover Peri, if any. But then Martin realized that he didn't really care.

The insistent male falsetto coming from upstairs, the kind of singing his mother knew he hated.

And her jacking the thermostat higher and higher just to make him sweat, all of this made Martin curse her. But it would take more than 150 decibels of Frankie and every one of his Seasons *and* the hotter-than-Death-Valley-in-Hell heat to get Martin to move out. He inserted ear plugs, slid under the covers of his bed, and in zero to sixty, was fast asleep, snoring with abandon. Now his dreams were now peaceful and devoid of any wise guys and that dreadful doo-wop.

Martin didn't awake until 4:20 p.m. He knew the exact time because that's when the ice cream truck made the rounds for workers just starting the swing shift, while playing its chimey, demented tune. It took him a few minutes to lift his head, and then a few more to lift the rest of his partied-out carcass. He checked his little fridge for something to eat but found nothing but a can of Coors Lite. Apparently no one was hard up enough last night to keep their buzz going to touch that swill. Martin looked under the bed to find his early morning Pringles, his deliciously processed potato chip & particle board slabs. But hot damn! The box was empty.

He'd have to go upstairs to the kitchen to grab a bite. If he was lucky there might be some of Muriel's leftover goulash. Thankfully, the house was now quiet. His parents must still be at church. Normally, he would have just traipsed upstairs in his boxers; he could easily handle his mother's vitriol about his choice of clothes or lack thereof. But now it was freezing cold in the house. Despite the winter chill, Muriel must have put the a/c on when she left, undoubtedly to try to freeze him out. He slipped on a bathrobe and a ski cap and headed upstairs.

The kitchen was spotless, just as Muriel liked it, except for the dirty dishes, pots, and utensils that Martin and Peri and the rest of his revelers had used last night. Muriel had the unwashed dishes perfectly stacked up with a sign on top saying "MARTIN: CLEAN THESE AND USE SOAP AND SCALDING HOT WATER! WE DON'T WANT YOUR SINFUL FRIENDS GIVING US A DISEASE! The dishes could wait, his stomach could not. He looked in the pantry but found nothing good to eat. He could smell something wonderful had come out of the oven. But whatever Muriel had baked was gone. That meddling little shrew must've taken them this morning, probably to give to one undeserving Lutheran or another. Martin fired up a pot of coffee and made do with a bowl of Sven's Grape Nuts. The coffee helped his headache and the cereal gave him enough strength to face another day of partying – and dealing with his parents.

He was about to head down to his room when he heard the front door open, signaling that Muriel and Sven were back from church. While still chomping on the particular type of gravel they call Grape Nuts, Martin heard somebody else coming in with them, someone with a female voice. He shuddered. *Oh Jesus, not another girl they're trying to fix me up with.* He knew that these set ups were nothing more than a ruses to get him married off so he'd ship out. *As if. I'm never moving out and I'm never getting married,* he thought. *Unless they legalize polygamy – then it's game on.*

Martin heard his dad going downstairs to look for him. By then, Mom was already walking toward the kitchen. She stood in the doorway and yelled, "Yoo-hoo, Marty!"

Her son turned around with a glare. "You know I hate that name."

"I know, Marty," said Muriel, in an annoyingly cheerful voice. "But it's a charming nickname. Are you decent?"

"Sure, Mom, I've hidden my latex, chucked the handcuffs, and covered the piercings on my hairy wazoola. So yeah, I'm free to meet unwanted guests."

"We don't need that kind of language around here, young man," said Muriel. She escorted a pretty young woman into the kitchen. "I'd like you to meet a very nice girl from church. Courtney, this is Martin. Martin, this is the very talented and intelligent Courtney."

Courtney blushed. "Hello and how do you do? Your mother has told me so much about you."

"Well, I don't want to get in the way," said Muriel, without a trace of irony. "I'll let you two get better acquainted." She left the room. Martin grimaced. He knew that Mom would be listening in from the laundry room.

He offered Courtney a seat. She was kind of sexy, in a girl-next-door-meets "Girls Gone Wild" sort of way. But he could tell right away that she was too young – like she was fresh out of high school. While Courtney seemed genuinely sweet, Martin already had a full sex life, what with Peri and the two other young women he regularly hooked up with. And this Courtney girl looked like she'd be high maintenance. He was sure she'd require dinners, jewelry, nauseatingly cute emoticon emails, and the obligatory three dates before she'd put out. Besides, this was the umpteenth woman his mom had tried to set him up with, and naturally, he'd grown sick of her meddling. Fortunately, though, he'd been through this dick-dance many times, so he knew to tell Courtney just enough of his life story to get rid of her.

It worked. In a short time, Courtney gave him a warm hug before running out of the kitchen crying, "Oh, Martin, that's all...so sad..."

She found her way to the front door, and, still whimpering, managed to say, "Goodbye Mr. and Mrs. Kihlstrom, wherever you are. Thank you for having me over." She hesitated.

"And Martin." She stopped to wipe her face. "It was nice meeting you. My gosh, you've been through so much. You really should join us at church sometime." She timidly opened the front door and left.

Muriel emerged from the laundry room and ran into the kitchen. "What the dickens did you say to that girl? You didn't go into all that poppycock about the past?!"

Martin laughed bitterly. "Yeah, Ma, I went into the poppycock."

"You'll never find a wife with that kind of attitude," she told him "And, you need to fix yourself up. Oh, for corn's sake, is that vomit in your hair?"

He took off his ski cap, ran his fingers through his blond curls and brought them up to his nose. "Yeah, smells like puke alright," he said, looking wistful as he recalled the good times from the night before. Anyway, we've been through this a million times. My maximum is three lovers at a time, you know that. I can't do a fourth. And, even if I dated another woman, even if I *married* her, I'm still wouldn't move out."

"Sven!" she yelled down the hall. "Sweetheart, talk some sense into our boy!"

But Sven either couldn't hear her or was ignoring her. He was probably in the den, building another one of his ships in a bottle. Without her husband there to back her up, Muriel gave an exaggerated sigh and stormed out of the kitchen.

Martin finished his breakfast and headed down to his room. Or *rooms*, to be more accurate. His pad was a converted garage and basement, a two-story, four- roomed party animal's fantasy, complete with a hot tub, two stripper poles, a fireman's pole for sliding downstairs, a pool table, arcade games, four big screen TV's, and a killer sound system. Just about everything that a young man who parties every night and has no job could possibly want. He played a couple games of Parcheesi and folded some origami, his newest kick, making cranes and geese. Then he took a nap before the Sunday night party people came by.

At eight o'clock, they started arriving. Sunday's partiers consisted of a dozen old high school buddies, a couple of old lovers, a couple of new lovers, and a mixed set of strippers. Also present was some dude Martin had met near the bank selling Quaaludes, and a tall guy with a nitrous tank whose real name Martin could never remember. That bloke would always exclaim "Jesus H. Christ!" whenever he ran out of

nitrous, alcohol, or smokes, so that's the moniker
Martin gave him.

The revelers chowed down mushroom pizzas
with psilocybin, imbibed Everclear Jell-O shots, and
medicated themselves with cannabis delivered from an
octagonally-shaped plastic bubble contraption called
"The Volcano." A few sat around playing craps. Some
played pinball. Still others zoned out to video
projections of German *scheisse* flicks, old-time
Mexican silent films, and loops of Giada de Laurentis
licking her fingers off of an array of desserts. The party,
as usual, went on until the wee hours of the morning.

II

Martin awoke with a start when Muriel blared
Sweating to the Oldies. He had barely slept an hour.
The last of the partygoers left at 4 a.m., but his special
friend Lavonne had come by after that to give him one
of her incomparable massages. That kept him up for
another two hours. Now he was startled by the sound of
pounding upstairs and what sounded like Richard
Simmons bellowing, "It's my party and I'll cry if I
want to!" Though Martin was aware that his mom had
been trying (with little success) to lose her matronly fat,
he also knew that this noisy, early morning workout
was really for *his* benefit. Or, rather, his detriment. He
heard his father pleading, "Muriel, I can't dance
another step, I'm dying out here!" and his mom yelling

"Sven, that blasted Martin is 29 and needs to find his own place to live, so just keep dancing!"

Martin put in his earplugs, made a mental note to buy a pair of fancy noise cancelling headphones, and fell back to sleep.

When he finally woke up that day, it was late afternoon. Today was Monday, and Mondays were his days for fastidious metrosexual grooming. Chet, a retired barber who lived down the street, came over to give Martin a haircut and shave. As usual, he paid the barber with a shoebox full of joints and a $100 tip.

Martin's Monday transformations were remarkable: he'd wake up looking like The Dude from *The Big Lebowski*, and by the time he'd shit, showered, and shaved, he was transformed into a more handsome Jeff Bridges, like his heartthrob role in *The Last Picture Show*.

When Martin was drunk, stoned, and wearing shabby pajamas -as he usually was - it was easy to forget that he was basically a handsome young man. At six feet tall, he had wavy, strawberry blond hair, blue eyes, and an impish smile. Peri and Lavonne both thought that he looked like Ryan Gosling. But Ming, Martin's third lover, thought that Martin most resembled the would-be actor Channing Tatum, "without the Aspergery eyes."

Martin's Monday Makeovers were his one concession to the workweek rituals that people who have normal schedules keep. Nearly all of his friends held down 9-5 jobs, and sometimes he'd feel lonesome during the day when there was no one to hang with. His lifelong best friend, Blair – a former Lutheran altar boy like himself – was gone; he offed himself two years ago.

When the sun went down and his antique grandfather clock struck seven, Martin began his toilet ritual. He combed his hair, splashed on some aftershave, and put on his neatly pressed slacks and button-down shirt. Finally, he put on his Hugh Hefner-style smoking jacket and headed upstairs.

Just as he expected, his parents' Monday night bridge club was in full swing. Two card tables were placed in the middle of the floor in order to accommodate the four players on each side. Muriel and Sven sat at the couch on one end of the table.

The usual suspects were there: Harlan and Candice, Earl and Agnes, and Eugene and Betty. Sven didn't notice his son's arrival. Muriel did, but she just scowled and tried to ignore him.

"Hello, bridge people!" Martin announced with a big smile. Everyone, except for his parents, put their cards down and gave him a warm greeting. When

Muriel and Sven started the club last year, Martin had ingratiated himself with the group with the intention of making him look good and, of course, making his parents look bad. But since then, Martin had developed a strange affection for these older folks. They were friendly, funny, and some even silly. And they drank like fish. He wondered why on earth these cool old coots would ever hang with his parents.

Martin offered to make everyone beverages: tea, coffee, or some of his infamously strong drinks. They laughed at the last option, but all, except Muriel and Sven, took him up on it. He served Blair's parents, Harlan and Candace, their gin and tonics, then gave them both hearty hugs. Back when their son was alive, they probably would've stiffened to the touch – they weren't touchy-feely people by any means – but now they warmly embraced Martin. He knew they appreciated how much he had loved their son.

When Martin and Blair were growing up, Harlan and Candace were one of the richest folks in their largely middle class neighborhood. In fact, they had the biggest house of anyone he knew. But now their fortunes had changed. The town itself had gone downhill due to a loss of manufacturing jobs. Foreign investors, flush with incentives from the too-big-to-fail banks, bought up most of the homes in Seward and now acted as absentee landlords. The neighborhood where Harlan and Candace lived had become sketchy and even dangerous. The couple had both been aerospace engineers. They retired with good pensions. But five years ago, the company they'd spent their lives working for went belly up and, with it, their pension funds disappeared.

After years of struggling to find work, Candace finally found a job last year as a maid to a rich and arrogant young family. As scions of prominent families who owned two of the biggest businesses in town, the husband and wife were both members of the lucky sperm club. They were the kind of people of privilege who, according to Candace, were born on third base, thinking they'd hit a triple.

A few weeks after she started her job, Candace convinced the rich couple to hire Harlan as their butler. Candace told the bridge group that she hated that her bosses called her Candy, a nickname, she had told them repeatedly, she hated. And though the rich fucks were reasonably civil to Harlan in private, he told the bridge group that whenever guests came over, he was required to call his bosses "Sir" and "Ma'am." Their snotty children even called him "Boy", a moniker that, his employers curtly told him, came with the job.

The bridge group commiserated with the older couple. Martin added, looking directly at his mom, that some people are so incredibly rude.

Martin decided to change the subject to something more pleasant. He complimented Betty on her new hairdo (hair dyed bright red, heavily processed to hide her female pattern baldness). Then he congratulated Betty's husband, the handsome and silver haired Clark, on his new job as the ticket taker at the local Cineplex.

When Agnes, the oldest in the group, told everyone that she'd just finished her first week as a sign twirler for a fast food chain, Martin kissed her hand.

"I'll be back in a sec with more drinks," Martin told the group as he dashed into the kitchen.

Betty turned to Sven and Muriel, "Your son seems to be doing better. He's looking quite handsome, too, these days."

"He ought to be doing well," said Muriel. "He doesn't do anything all day except loaf around and have wild orgies and who knows what, with the lowlifes he brings home. And let me tell you, he makes sure he gets his beauty rest every night."

"Muriel, dear," said Sven, hoping to avoid any arguments, "*You* look like you get your beauty rest too."

Clark looked up from his cards. "Martin's a good kid, don't get me wrong, but if it were MY son,

I'd have given him a swift kick to his potty maker and sent him on his way years ago."

"Believe me," said Muriel, "We've been working on it. I mean, what 29 year old still lives with his parents? We've tried everything –"

"Now, now, dear, it's complicated," said Sven, "Let's not get into this."

"That's right, Muriel. Let's just play bridge," said Candace, clearly hoping to avoid Muriel's incessant carping.

Candace and Harlan had kicked Blair out of the house when he was nineteen. This added to the young man's serious depression. And, they now believe, it led to his subsequent drug overdose. Candace looked helplessly at her husband.

"I agree," said Harlan. "Let's just play another rubber of bridge." He shuffled the cards, but apparently couldn't help jumping back into the hornet's nest. "It takes years and a lot of patience and forgiveness to recover from that kind of abuse."

Muriel rolled her eyes. "*Alleged* abuse."

Sven gave Candace and Harlan a sympathetic look to avoid insulting their guests. Muriel was about to add something, but her husband kicked her under the table.

Meanwhile, Martin was in the kitchen making a couple of Long Island ice teas for Betty and Candace, and shaking an apple martini for Earl. With the kitchen door closed, he strained to hear the group's conversation. It helped that these golden girls and guys were mostly hard of hearing and had to talk loudly to be heard.

As Martin jigged the cocktail shaker he suddenly felt his eyes sting. Then they began to tear, as if he'd just been maced. (He knew that feeling because Muriel had pepper sprayed him last year after he ate one of the tarts she'd reserved for the church bake sale.) Martin sneezed three times, steadied himself, and then sneezed again. But the sneezing brought no relief. He still felt a tickle in his nose and his throat was scratchy and parched. He wondered for a second whether he was becoming allergic to martinis; the very thought made him shudder.

Then he heard a meow. He looked up to see a plump and furry Persian cat sitting on top of the fridge. Martin immediately guessed that his mother had adopted the beast because she knew he was highly allergic to cats. Martin sneezed seven more times.

OK, Mom, he muttered under his breath, *this means all-out war.*

He came out to the living room with a tray full of drinks. "Here you go everybody," Martin said cheerfully, but in a Rod Stewart-with-a-tracheotomy rasp. "Excuse my voice." He stopped to hack a dry cough. "Looks like Mom and Dad got a new cat. I love felines but I'm just seriously allergic to them, especially the long hair breeds."

Candace turned to Muriel. "If you knew your son was so allergic why in God's green planet did you get a cat?"

"Because it's OUR house, Candace, not Martin's," Muriel shot back.

Martin turned to his mom with a smile. "I'm sorry, Mother, but that's not quite correct. You see, I was glad to be able to help you two after Dad was laid off, giving you money to bring the mortgage current and putting a trust deed on our house to protect you against your creditors. I guess that's one good thing that came out of my abuse: the settlement, which gives me the ability to help the people I love."

His voice, hoarse as it was, sounded sincere to everyone. Everyone, except his mom, who squirmed on the couch. Sven put his head down, pretending to be engrossed in his hand of cards. Martin bent down to give his mom a kiss on the cheek but she pulled away.

"Of course," Martin went on, "Dad had no idea what was going on at All Saints Lutheran. As many of you know, he's never been much of a church goer. But Mom, ever the pious one, signed me up with the Young Lutherans, and, of course, we all know what that youth pastor did…" Martin paused for dramatic effect, though he wasn't acting; he was genuinely pained.

"That's enough!" Muriel snapped. "Nobody knew or suspected –"

"Actually," Martin corrected her, "I did tell you what was going on a number of times, but each time you said it was all in my head."

"Well, it was, and still is," said Muriel, "For you, anyway, Mr. I-Don't Have-To-Work-a-Day-In-My Life-Since- I –Won-A-Big Lawsuit!"

"Muriel, please!" said Sven.

"Yes, Muriel," said Harlan, putting his arm around his Candace, "With all due respect, let's not go there…." He looked down, his eyes growing moist, undoubtedly thinking about what had happened to Blair.

Martin saw Harlan's pained expression, and he too looked to the ground.

"Oh, Clark, honey," said Betty, putting on a happy face, "Tell everyone our news about that new local chapter of Eldertude we started."

"Eldertude? What is that?" asked Martin. He looked for an empty chair to sit down. There was none; Muriel had made sure of that. But he found a tiny spot on the sofa next to his mom and sat, nearly plopping down on her lap.

"It's like PETA for old folks," said Betty. "Except, instead of helping to save circus animals or taking service dogs away from blind people, we try to raise awareness for the plight of seniors – like *us*."

"If you ask me, it's a terrorist group," said Harlan.

"As if somebody asked you," said Candace with a little wink. Everybody laughed.

Martin leaned forward. "Now I'm *really* interested."

"Well," said Clark, "Eldertude is kind of what you young folks might call an in-your-face type of group. We're out there to do the things those pansies at AARP are afraid to do."

"Like, we go out and *really* stick up for senior citizens." added Betty. "Eldertude is founded by anonymous members who stage demonstrations and sit-ins - and, well, *other* activities - so that we seniors can fight to get all the social security and housing subsidies we're entitled to. And Eldertude makes sure that younger folks, especially middle agers - those blasted Gen X'ers! - understand that there are millions of us out there. We will not be ignored!"

"Oh, no one could ignore you, Betty," said Martin, with a warm smile. "Not with your beautiful red hair."

"Oh, Martin," Betty said, running her fingers through her processed perm.

Clark laughed. "I'm warning you, young man, to stay away from my lady."

"OK, Clark, you win, she's yours," said Martin, with a twinkle in his eye. "So where does this Eldertude group meet?"

"We don't have a spot for our local chapter yet," said Betty. "Every place is so darned expensive. We need a very private place. Nobody who's associated with Eldertude uses their real names because of our, uh, activism."

"And because of the damn cops," said Clark. "Sorry for my language, Muriel."

Before Muriel had a chance to respond, Martin said, "That's OK. Our delicate ears can take a mild oath now and again. So, how much does it cost to rent a *damn* place?"

Muriel elbowed him in the ribs.

"Well, with the meeting hall," said Betty, "And all the gear –"

"Guerilla-type gear," Clark interjected. "Night vision goggles, radar detectors, heat sensors, jet packs, the whole nine yards. Just to get started we need to raise five grand."

"That sounds like a worthy cause," said Martin. He took out his wallet and searched around for an old battered blank check he kept in case of emergencies. In between his crumpled receipts, ancient condoms, and the powdery remnants of a Valium tablet, he found the check. Someone lent him a pen and he wrote it out for $5,000 and endorsed it to Clark and Betty Stapleton.

"Here you go," said Martin, "But, please don't cash it until tomorrow when I get my next settlement payment."

"Oh Martin," said Betty, "You're such a wonderful young man."

"You can say that again," said Clark, "But Martin, I don't know - that's a lot of money. I'm not sure we can accept such a generous gift."

"Please do," said Martin, "I want something good to come out of my abuse." They took the check. Clark shook Martin's hand while Betty gave him a kiss, leaving bright pink lipstick marks on his cheek.

"Muriel and Sven," said Clark, raising a glass, "Here's to Martin, a jolly good fellow."

Muriel waved him away. "Oh c'mon!"

Candace snapped, "Muriel, for God's sake, at least *you* still have your boy!"

Muriel was uncharacteristically speechless. The guests all toasted Martin.

All of a sudden, the young man sneezed again. And again. The cat had caused his eyes to swell and he now had a throbbing headache. "Well, I better let you all get back to your game," said Martin. He bid everyone adieu and went back to his pad. Once there, he cured his pain with a few strategically administered bong hits.

III

Smoking a few bowls of Yellow Cur cannabis while lying in bed and watching re-runs of *1,000 Ways to Die* made Martin mellow and then sleepy. He called his friends and told them not to come over tonight. His buddies couldn't believe it – Martin hadn't missed the Monday party for three years. Everyone said they hoped he felt better and told him to get well soon. At least in time for Tanqueray Tuesday. He called Lavonne, who usually came over on Monday nights, for schnapps and sex and told her he'd have to take a rain check. He sat in bed and started to watch some old Western on TV. He quickly dozed off.

He was having a heavenly dream about doing peyote in a teepee while making out with a sexy tribal council of naked Native American women, when he was awoken by pounding on the door.

He looked out the window and saw flashing lights. The cops! Martin slid his pot stash, jug of moonshine, handcuffs, and nun-chucks under the bed.

He opened the door to find two officers, a tall woman and a short and stout woman.

"Are you Martin Kihlstrom?" the short cop asked.

"That's me, guilty as charged. Is there something wrong, officers?"

The taller cop spoke. "We've received an eyewitness report of marijuana smoke emanating from these premises."

"Who's the eyewitness?" asked Martin.

"We can't tell you that, sir." Both officers yawned. They looked genuinely sorry about having to come here in the middle of the night on such a minor infraction. "Unfortunately, we're required to investigate and write up a report."

"Officers," said Martin, "I understand and I'll be straight with you. The smoke is from my medicinal cannabis." He reached into his back pocket – Martin had taken to sleeping in his clothes - and pulled out his wallet. Next to his expired driver's license, a conspicuously placed Seward Police Benevolence Fund medallion, and a joke "Get out of Jail Free" card, was his doctor-issued pot certificate. "See, I'm licensed. It's because of the Lutherans. It's a long story, but I'll tell it to you if it will assist in your investigation."

The cops didn't want to hear the Lutheran story. Maybe they weren't interested or maybe they'd heard it all before. "Everything seems to check out," said the taller cop. "We'll be on our way. Sorry to have disturbed you, Mr. Kihlstrom, and have a good night."

Martin smiled at her. He hadn't noticed until now how pretty she was, or just how tall: Martin was six feet tall and she was about an inch taller.

"I will have a good night. And when I smoke a bowl I'll be thinking of you." He looked on his night table and saw that he'd forgotten to hide his bong.

"Well, thank you, sir," she said. "And, if I may make a suggestion – use a vaporizer – it makes less smoke.

"Plus, it uses less product and it's better for your lungs," added the short cop. "Or so I've been told."

The tall cop introduced herself as Officer Gonzalez and gave Martin her card. She told him to call her if he noticed anything suspicious in the area.

Martin thanked the officers for their vaping advice. He invited them to party with him on their night off, and then waved goodbye.

Fucking Mom, narcing on me! She'll pay for this.

He'd decide on her punishment later. He grabbed his stash from under the bed, took one final bong hit, pulled a sheet over his head, and crashed for the next ten hours.

IV

When he finally awoke he felt good. His throat wasn't scratchy and his head was clear. Clear enough to hatch a plan to get revenge against his nightmare of a mother. He guessed that, through his stoned haze of sleep, his subconscious must have been working on a solution to this great and pressing problem.

Martin remembered a novelty gift one of his former lovers had given him before she shipped off to Iraq. *Poor Lloyda,* he thought. *She never came back.* He never thought he'd have a use for it until now.

His immediate concern, though, was to satiate his hunger. He stuffed the novelty item into his bathrobe pocket and went up to the kitchen in search of a can of his potato -inspired slabs. There, he found Sven at the kitchen table, trying to pry out one of his ships from a rectangular bottle. When Martin said hello, his father looked at him with diffused eyes and gave him a weak smile. Martin sighed, noticing just how old his dad looked. Ever since Sven was forced to take an early retirement a few years back, and after what had happened to his daughter, the man had become listless. In the first year of his retirement, Sven had occupied his time by completing a series of model ships. But now, years later, he had dozens of only partially finished projects scattered all over the house.

"Dad," asked Martin, "Did you take my Pringles?"

"Your what?"

"You know, those delicious, highly processed coasters of salted cardboard; the ones that almost look like potato chips?"

"Oh those? Son, I'm sorry, I got hungry last night…"

"Dad, it's OK, have as many as you like. It's just that I'm just starving. Are there any left?"

Sven nodded and pointed to the pantry. Martin grabbed the can and chomped down the remaining slabs in a single bite.

"Where's Mom?'

"I don't remember what she told me," said Sven. "Maybe she's volunteering at the hospital today, or maybe the church. I hope your mother will be back soon to make my sandwich."

How sad, thought Martin, *he's so dependent on that repugnant woman that he just sits there feeling hungry, waiting for her to make him his lunch.*

Martin went to the living room to hide his little surprise. He found the perfect place too, right between the cushions in the sofa. He carefully placed the item there and covered it up with some ladies undergarments that had somehow found their way into his pockets.

Then he heard the front door open.

"Well look who's here!" said Muriel, She was wearing her hospital candy striper outfit. "Martin-I-Just-Wake-Up-Whenever-'Cause-I'm-An-Allegedly-Molested-Bum-Kihlstrom."

"Mom," said Martin, "It's a little early for your ineffectual sarcasm and misplaced venom."

"A little early?! Why, I just finished a full shift volunteering at the hospital and you just woke up! Anyway, aren't you supposed to be in jail?"

"Nice try, Mommy Dearest, but I've got a pot card."

"Oh, I forgot, you need your dope to handle the stress of not working or doing anything but having parties and having relations with your lady friends. And I use the term 'lady' quite loosely."

"As indeed you, of all people, should," said Martin.

"What the dickens is that supposed to mean?!" asked Muriel.

"You two, please," Sven called out from the kitchen. I can't live with this constant yelling and – *a-chooh!"*

"Gesundheit," said Martin.

Sven blew his nose. "It's that darn – no - that *damn* cat."

"Honey," said Muriel, "Watch your French."

Sven ignored her. "Muriel we have got to get rid of that thing."

"Yeah, Mom, get rid of that fucking cat," said Martin. "I know you got it to try to kick me out but now you're punishing Dad too."

"You're darn tooting I'm trying to kick you out," said Muriel. "Here!" She shoved a book in Martin's face. "This is something YOU need to read."

"I see you're sinfully reading something other than God's Little Big Book."

"Shut up, you. Look here, it's called *Straighten Up and Fly Right out of Here.* Once you read this you'll know exactly why you need to find yourself a place of your own."

She tried handing Martin the book but he shooed her away. "Martin, it's for your own good."

"MY OWN GOOD?" said Martin, surprising even himself about the intensity and loudness in his voice. "WHAT DO YOU KNOW ABOUT MY OWN GOOD AFTER WHAT YOU LET HAPPEN TO ME?!"

"You know darn well nothing happened."

"And you know *darn well* it did."

"If it did, that was your choice. How old were you, 17 or something?"

"I was 13!"

"That's old enough to have said no. And *that's* supposing the whole thing really happened . You know that nothing was ever proven."

Martin took a deep breath. He spoke to her in measured tones, as if he were speaking to child – a child he was planning to kill. "We've been through this a million times, for chrissakes. Or maybe *not* for Christ's sake, but the bastard killed himself before trial. And if you think this was all made up, why don't you ask Candace and Harlan why Blair, you know…"

He choked up. Bringing his old friend into this seemed almost like a sacrilege. But Martin was so angry, what with his scratchy throat, the sneezing, and after the late night visit with the cops. He'd had ten years of counseling after the alleged incident and, for the most part, he was ok. But whenever he'd get into it with his mother it was like a scab being reopened; it felt like he was back to square one.

"I don't have time to listen to this malarkey," said Muriel. "I've got the church ladies coming over tonight and we've got to clean up –"

"But first, Muriel," Sven pleaded from the kitchen, "Can you please make my lunch?"

"One second, dear." She pointed a finger at Martin. "I am warning you now to leave us alone tonight. Do not come upstairs. Do not, under any circumstances, interrupt the Lady Lutherans. And do not, for the sake of your soul, try to embarrass us -or yourself - while we're conducting prayer."

"Now, Mother, why would I do that?"

"Who knows why you do anything, my disappointment of a son. For corn's sake, why did you come up here last night and disturb our bridge game? These dear people are some of our closest friends. How dare you try and make fools of me and your father!"

"Actually, I was only making a fool of you."

Her nostrils flared. Then her face turned to crimson. "And, what in the Lord's name was that all about, giving money to Betty and Clark for that crazy group?"

"It's *my* money, and I'll do what I want with it," said Martin. "And that includes saving this house from foreclosure, as you'll recall. So let's cut out all of this malarkey and call it what it really is: bullshit."

"There's no reason to be vulgar, young man. Or, rather, our not-so-young man."

"I won't debate you on matters of age or vulgarity. I readily concede you win on both counts. Besides, I think Eldertude is a great idea."

"A great idea?! I don't think they know what they're getting mixed up in. Somebody at church told me about those people – these Eldertuders, or what have you. They're violent nuts. Terrorists. And you know full well that Clark, bless his little heart, isn't the sharpest tool in the shed. Oh, poor Betty! They're going to get themselves arrested, or blown up."

"Then, Mom, maybe YOU should join them."

Muriel reached for her broom and smacked him with it. Then she prodded him down the stairs. He had just reached the door to his place when all of sudden his cell rang. It was Ming, his third lover. Martin liked to keep his lovers in threes – one was too intimate for his tastes; two was ok, but a little dull; and more than three women at a time became unwieldy. The ladies he "dated" accepted that he would be shared. They felt sorry for what he'd been through, plus he was a cute guy. And Martin was financially generous with each of them – a major plus, since his lovers were usually in desperate need of money. Anyway, there weren't too many eligible young men with steady incomes and cool pads in Seward.

Ming told him that she'd just blown into town. Martin knew she had gone to Florida for her mom's tattoo school graduation but he couldn't remember when she said she'd be back. She asked if she could come over tonight. Of course, he told her; he hadn't seen Ming in a while and was starting to miss her. Plus, he could use her computer expertise for some fun he had planned for that evening.

V

At seven p.m. sharp, Muriel assembled the Lady Lutherans in the living room, while Sven went into the den to work on his U.S.S. Merrimack model. Before long, the group of a dozen worshippers stood in a circle around the coffee table and joined hands in prayer. Some prayed for the health of a stricken loved one, some prayed for their husbands to find work again, still others prayed for world peace. Muriel, of course, prayed for her son to move out.

Helga, the eldest of the group, said she was feeling faint from standing up and praying for so long on an empty stomach. All of a sudden, she collapsed on the couch. Helga caught her breath and realized that she was sitting on something - something hard, though, for her, not entirely uncomfortable. She reached behind her to find a big clump of ladies' undergarments jammed between the sofa and seat cushions.

Muriel saw the wadded up panties and blushed. She prided herself on keeping a clean house. "I'm sorry, Helga... sometimes I fold laundry here and, uh, I guess some of these must have slipped through the cracks."

A few of the younger ladies tittered, as if Muriel had just made a naughty joke.

Upon closer look at the errant laundry, Muriel saw that those weren't the granny pants she wore.

These were some tramp's panties – with holes in the crotch, no less! And sheer black stockings and a garter belt. Muriel practically yanked the clothes out of Helga's hands - and out popped Bouncy Boy Toy ("The Only Novelty Dildo That Hops!"). It fell to the floor. And then it bounced. And jumped. And boinged. The mouths of the Lady Lutherans were agape; everything seemed to happen in slow motion as the gag sex toy hopped its way across the living room and careened down the hall.

Muriel was mortified. She knew she had to say something to the ladies, but she had no words to describe the how or why of this mobile marital aid. The parishioners looked like they were in shock too, though one of the younger Lady Lutherans covered her mouth to suppress a giggle.

Then they heard a crashing sound.

"GODDAMN IT!" yelled Sven from the next room.

Hearing her husband take the Lord's name in vain snapped Muriel back to attention and called her back to action. Muriel quickly led the group into a discussion of the Holy Trinity, which easily segued into a group talk on the ultimate fate of certain celebrities they deemed to be big time sinners. The ladies considered the perceived moral shortcomings of singers

Miley Cyrus, Julie Andrews, and Pat Boone, and whether, at death, any of them would ever be embraced by the arms of Jesus. Then it was prayer time again.

When the ladies' prayed their last prayers and everyone said goodbye Muriel stormed off into the den. "Sven, this is the last straw! I'm going to go downstairs and tear that son of yours limb from limb!"

Sven was even angrier. But not at Martin. Instead, he gave Muriel a fierce look and hollered, "You'll do nothing of the sort, you harlot!"

"What the heck has come over you, Sv-"

"Leaving your pleasure toy to bounce around like that! And breaking three of my Union ships!"

"Sven, sweetheart - that ding dong is not mine, it's –"

"Pastor Yarborough's, isn't it?!" His veins bulged from his neck and forehead. He grabbed what was left of his U.S.S. Merrimack model and threw it at the wall, smashing their old wedding photo and sending shards of glass all over the floor.

"What in St. Woden's name did you do that for? Svenny, have you lost your mind?"

"No, but you have lost any morals you had left! You and the Pastor fornicating! And leaving it for me to watch!" Sven grabbed the TV remote and showed her the porno that had been left in the DVD player. It was the usual stuff – a young female with a tiny waist, outsized rubbery boobs, a pube-less pubis, and a bleached ass, was engaged in coitus with a fat, old, hairy man with an elephantine schlong that was vaguely erect. But a bobble head of Muriel had been Photoshopped on the bleached-assed starlet's face, and Pastor Yarborough's head was comically pasted over her sex partner's parched and withered face.

With surprising force, Sven pushed Muriel out of the den. She ran upstairs to her bedroom to cry. How could her own husband believe such vile things about her? She didn't know much about pornography, but she sensed that Martin must have had something to do with this.

Once she got her tears out of the way, she thought of another way to get even with that good-for-nothing-allegedly-molested son of hers.

She waited until the following afternoon to hatch her plan. She knew that Martin would be making his weekly trip to the bank, to deposit what she called his "prize" for winning the "molesting lottery." Sure enough, at exactly half past three, she heard Martin's side door open and close. She watched through the front blinds as he walked out and headed down the street.

Muriel rushed to the garage, where she found a hammer, some nails, and some plywood. For years she'd taught classes on making Christian-themed birdhouses, so she was pretty handy with carpentry, just like her Lord and Savior. With a spring in her step, she traipsed downstairs and nailed all the doors to Martin's room shut and affixed plywood over all his windows. She went so fast that she accidently drew the hammer down on her thumb, causing a bloody mess all over the front stucco. By the time she staunched the bleeding, the front of the house was covered with blood and looked like a crime scene.

In her rush to lock Martin out before he came back from the bank, Muriel didn't hear the cries within the room as she furiously pounded nail after nail. Sven had been inside his son's room rummaging around for more Pringles. After a half hour of his yelling for help, the old man tried to break through the wall to escape, causing severe pain to his shoulder, a hole in the drywall and structural damage to the house. Still unable to fit through the support beams, he broke off one of the stripper poles in Martin's room and used it as a battering ram to break through a small window that Muriel had nailed shut with plywood.

Meanwhile, Martin, flush with cash, headed for home. He had just crossed the street toward his house when he saw a figure break through the window. The guy's face and clothes were covered in white dust from the drywall.

Martin was just about to call the cops when he realized that this man in whiteface was his father. The Sasquatch-shaped hole his dad had left made Martin bust up.

Sven ran back through the front door of the house yelling, "You're a harlot, you pastor hussy! You shameless, fornicating pastor strumpet!" The neighbors slammed their windows shut.

Martin decided to sit on the curb across the street and watch the show unfold. He laughed so hard that he almost choked when he saw his dad chasing his mom out of the house with a broken ship-in-a-bottle. Muriel barely made it into her rusty Ford Taurus to speed away.

When she left and the whole scene was over, Sven sat on the stoop and wept. Martin stopped laughing.

VI

Martin hesitated at first, then walked over to the front porch to sit with his dad. Seeing old Sven, his stoic, but ineffectual father, collapsed, broke, and sobbing, made Martin feel sick.

"Dad, are you ok?"

Sven turned away. "Yep."

"Are you sure?"

"Yep."

"Dad, is there anything I can do?"

"Nope."

Martin was tempted to put his arms around his dad, but that would have been weird and uncomfortable for both of them. Since there was nothing he could do for his father, Martin crawled through the Sasquatch hole and went back to his room. Assessing the damage to the wall and to the stripper pole, Martin called Lavonne, his Tuesday lover and a journeyman carpenter, to come over and make the necessary repairs. Within minutes she was there, with tool box and drywall mix in hand.

Then Martin walked upstairs to check on Sven. He found his dad in the den.

Sven was there hurrying about, trying to bring some semblance of order to the room after the bouncing toy incident.

"Hi Dad, I brought something for you."

Sven looked up, accepted the Pringles can from Martin, and nodded. The younger man was just about to walk out when Sven said, in a voice even softer than usual, "Son, please come back."

He turned around to see his father holding up a bottle containing a replica of The Golden Hinde, the ship used by the explorer Sir Francis Drake. Sven had told him the whole history of the vessel, though Martin hadn't seen the model in ages.

"Ingrid gave this kit to me the night before she left," said Sven. He held the bottle up to show Martin the carefully crafted details of the ship's hull and sails. "I think she would've liked how I put this ship together."

"I'm sure she would've been real impressed, Dad." Martin remembered that his sister had given Dad the explorer's ship as something meant to be symbolic of the momentous journey she was about to take.

"When you two were little you used to sit here," Sven said, pointing to an overstuffed ottoman in the corner. "You and your sister would always want me to tell you about the ocean, ships, whales, the world and all that…" Sven's voice trailed off as he peered out the window, perhaps towards the sea that lay miles and miles away.

Martin was at a loss for words - he didn't want to leave, certainly not now that his dad was opening up to him for the first time in a long time. Maybe, ever. But Martin was afraid that he couldn't handle his *own* emotions if his father kept talking about Ingrid.

"That was before your blasted mother joined that blasted church. *They* killed her. Your mom and Pastor Yarborough killed my daughter!" Sven throttled the bottle as if it were the clergyman's neck and then held the bottle to the table as if he were about to christen it. Martin gently pried the bottle out of his father's hands.

Martin, of course, was devastated when his sister was murdered. He had never wanted her to go on that church mission to Africa to begin with, not only because of the dangers present in that part of the continent, but also because he detested the church that sponsored the mission. The church that had almost destroyed his life.

Martin recalled the time when, just before she was to leave, Ingrid sat at the dinner table with the family and expressed second thoughts about going on the trip. She said she wasn't sure if this was what God was calling her to do. She wasn't even sure if *she* wanted to do it either. But Mom convinced Ingrid to go out there to witness for the Lord, to save heathen souls. Muriel said she had prayed about what her daughter should do and that God had personally told her that Ingrid should go. And Martin remembered that Dad had said nothing to Ingrid except "do as your mother says."

But, sitting here with his father, Martin didn't feel like getting into an "I told you so" speech. Following his sister's death, Muriel's seemed to go on much as before, but Sven never recovered from the grief. If only his sister were here now, Martin thought. Maybe, things would be different.

"Dad," said Martin, "I'm not going to pretend that I was in favor of Ingrid going, but," he searched for the right words, "I don't know if it's really fair to say that Mom caused Ingrid's…" He choked up. It had been five years since they'd shipped her body home and laid her to rest but now it seemed like just yesterday. Without anything more to be said, both the old man and his son sat there looking away from each other, softly crying.

The phone rang. Sven shuffled to the kitchen and pick up the corded, rotary phone. He said hello, listened for a short while, then hung up.

"That was your mother," Sven told Martin. "She said she'll be staying with Earl and Agnes from now on." He added with a bitter smile, "She said Helga wouldn't take her in after seeing that bouncing ding dong."

Martin chortled.

"Please don't laugh, son. It's really not funny."

VII

Two weeks passed slowly with Muriel still gone. She stayed with Earl and Agnes for three days until she had an argument with Agnes about how much tuna to put in a casserole. Muriel was then asked to leave.

She ended up sleeping on a cot at Clark and Betty's place. Their flat was cramped and Muriel had some issues with Betty's casserole making too, but this time Muriel wisely kept her cooking know-how to herself.

Betty and Clark, now flush with Martin's set-up funds, were preoccupied with fixing up the new Eldertude meeting house and getting the word out about their club. With masks to disguise their identities, they went to every senior center and Applebee's in the area.

Though Muriel remained suspicious of Eldertude, she couldn't help volunteering to decorate their meeting house. She opted for a striped carnation theme, which, as she was told by a fellow candy striper who was "Oriental" (her words), symbolized the meaning of "no" in Asia. To Earl and Agnes, "NO" was at the very core of the Eldertude creed. Muriel convinced Clark not to post a Norman Rockwell-style painting depicting wholesome looking seniors in wheelchairs, walkers, and canes, all armed to the teeth and pointing their firearms at a festive group of racially-diverse teens. Instead, Muriel put up a picture of Methuselah, the oldest man in the Bible.

Within a week, Eldertude held its first meeting. It was attended by a score of distressed seniors, all angry about their cuts in benefits and bitter about their lot after what they perceived as a lifetime of hard work and playing by the rules. A few owed their lives to government benefits but nevertheless felt a duty to demonstrate against the government. At the meeting, a plan was concocted to disrupt the upcoming Seward Centennial and to stage sit-ins at City Council meetings - all in Abe Lincoln masks to avoid being recognized.

Clark went further and advocated the kidnapping of that "smirking, smooth-faced Mayor" until a list of demands for city services were met. When put to a vote, the hostage measure lost by only a small margin. Muriel voted against the measure (though she believed that Mayor Schendlein sinned like the dickens), believing that she might eventually need the mayor's help in her fight against her son.

Meanwhile, back at home Sven managed as best he could without his wife. Martin spent afternoons in the den with him, helping the old man glue up his ships and sharing can after can of Pringles. But Martin, unable to cook anything more complicated than Top Ramen on his own, and knowing that he could barely take care of himself, let alone take care of his dad, handsomely paid each of his three lovers to come over to cook, clean, and look after the old man.

The ladies, seeing how allergic their lover was around the cat Muriel had brought home, arranged to have a mutual friend, an amateur pornographer, take the animal off his hands.

Martin kept up his evening partying, but things were way too quiet round the house without Muriel. Martin found himself almost missing his mother's acerbic presence.

That, however, was before the day he received a call from Dawn Manzetti, a well-known local lawyer. She advertised herself as "The Seward Shark" around town - on buses, in high school yearbooks, and on ads above public urinals. Attorney Manzetti told Martin that a certain Ms. Muriel Kihlstrom had consulted her about evicting him from Ms. Kihlstrom's residence and that she –The Shark -was conducting her due diligence investigation. Martin told The Shark that he would've hoped her research had revealed that he was co-owner of the house, so it was unlikely, if not impossible, that he could ever be kicked out.

Then, in almost a cheerful tone, he dutifully recounted the abuse he had endured at the hands of the youth pastor and church group his mother had signed him up for, how Muriel had repeatedly refused to believe him that the abuse was going on, and how she had forced him and to go on trips with the now-disgraced and deceased youth pastor. The Shark tried to argue with him, throwing in some fancy but irrelevant lawyer words, like "res ipsa loquitur" and "promissory estoppel." Then Martin told her that Muriel had forced his sister to go on a Lutheran mission to a war-torn village in Africa, where she was killed by anti-government forces.

"So, you can 'commence your litigation' as you say" said Martin, "But I don't think Ms. Kihlstrom is going to be very happy with all the negative publicity this is will generate." The whole town, he said, would know that his mother's actions and inactions had caused his sexual abuse and his sister's death. Then he alluded to Muriel's alleged affair with Pastor Yarborough. In the end Attorney Manzetti said she now saw major problems with this potential case and, without even saying goodbye, hung up on him.

Martin took a bit of pleasure in matching wits with The Shark. But his thoughts were really with his dad, and how the old man's spirits had flagged since Mom left.

One day, while helping Sven repair the Clipper ship, the old man broke down. In a voice that sounded like it was about to crack, he told Martin that the last time he'd seen that particular model was on the fateful night with the Lady Lutherans and that "destructive, bouncy, thingamabob." Strangely though, that memory made Sven miss Muriel even more. He missed those afternoons, he said, when she'd be between volunteering shifts and would come home, make him a sandwich, and delight him with a new scheme for kicking Martin out. Sven would slowly chew his food and point out the flaws in her plans.

The sad old man looked off into the distance and let out a sigh.

As the two of them glued the last of the sails to the tall ship. Sven added, "Of course your mother can be a pain sometimes, but – and you may not believe this - she loves you. And… she loved Ingrid." Sven teared up but was determined to finish what was on his mind. "Your mother made me swear never to tell you this, but

I might as well tell you now: she carries around a lot of sorrow about what happened to you and your sister, probably even a little guilt. But Lord knows she's got her pride. Yes, she's stubborn, but she cares for you, I know she does." He took out a hanky and blew his nose. "I just wish things could go back to the way they were."

Martin was already concerned about how to take care of his dad and now, for the first time in his life, he wished his mom were there to help. In times past, Martin would practically jump for joy every time Muriel would go off to some Bible convention, but now he worried that, without Muriel, Sven would just fade away. The old man barely touched the meals Martin's lovers made for him; indeed, he was wasting away to skin and bones. He was even sleeping later in the day than Martin. Seeing his dad's feeble condition made Martin feel guilty about his role in trying to destroy his parents' marriage.

And so the next afternoon, after a long and sleepless night, Martin sat his father down and confessed that HE, not Mom had been behind the dildo debacle. He also admitted that he'd superimposed bobble heads of her and Pastor Yarborough on to the penultimate scene from one of Martin's favorite fetish porno, "The Harder They Fall, the Harder I Cum."

At first, Sven didn't believe him. That is, until Martin brought Ming in - she was a porn site developer who could hack her way in and out of anything - and asked her to show Sven how easy it was to place a picture of someone else's head on those mechanically writhing bodies. Once Sven played around with various faces (Mother Teresa, Eleanor Roosevelt, former TV personality Bob Saget) in an orgy scene, he was finally convinced that the Muriel-with-Pastor sex tape was a hoax.

But Sven was still livid with Muriel for breaking his ship model.

Martin insisted, though, that Mom had never intended to break anything, other than, perhaps, the record for Most Annoying Mother in the Universe. He tried to convince the old man that mommies and daddies should stay together for the sake of the children.

"But, Son, you're grown up now. You can't expect parents to stay together just for the sake of their 30 year old boy."

"Actually, Dad I'm 29."

Sven arched his eyebrows.

Still, he didn't protest when Martin walked him to the kitchen to call Muriel.

Betty answered the phone. She couldn't talk long because she had to rush back to the hospital, where surgeons were reattaching Clark's left pinky. An explosion occurred in their apartment, she said, while her husband made a pipe bomb for use at the grand opening of the Tran Ho Rec Center, a new building named after the biggest slumlord in town.

Betty quickly handed the phone to Muriel.

Muriel waited to hear what Sven had to say. She was relieved to know that Sven no longer believed that she was having an affair. And she was surprised to learn that Martin had come clean to him about the whole thing. The couple made awkward small talk until Martin brought Peri, Lavonne and Ming upstairs to stand by Sven and listen in on the conversation. The ladies, who had been doing tequila shots downstairs, wrote down little cue cards for Sven to say, like "I miss you", "I can't live without you", and "You're so pretty, I remember when you could stop a clock." Lavonne, who'd had more liquor than the others, wrote "Woman, I want you to come home so I can give it to you like only your man can." Sven read Lavonne's line to Muriel verbatim.

"What the dickens!" cried Muriel. She called out to Betty, "I've got to go. I 'm worried about Sven. He does NOT sound well."

VIII

Before you could even recite the 23rd Psalm, Muriel rolled up to the house. She saw Sven sitting on the front stoop – just where Martin and his ladies had strategically placed him. He looked dejected and lonely. Muriel rushed to her husband and put her arm around him. They hugged for a while, until Muriel, always embarrassed by public displays of affection, led her husband back into the house to make him a grilled cheese sandwich.

A few days later, a Dutchwoman came to the door. She identified herself to Muriel as Assistant District Attorney Van der Kloos. She spooked the H-E double hockey sticks out of Muriel when Van der Kloos questioned her about her son and why he gave a check to Clark and Betty Stapleton. In her thick and often unintelligible accent, Ms. Van der Kloos explained that the Stapletons and other Eldertuders were suspects in the shooting of a local young dot com mogul.

Muriel told the D.A. a little white lie, saying that Martin had a kind heart and that he had merely given money to the couple because they were having a hard time making ends meet.

When the Dutchwoman finally said goodbye, and Muriel closed *and* double locked the door, Martin was standing right behind her.

"Thanks, Mom," he said.

"For what?"

"For covering for me."

"Well," she said, avoiding eye contact with her son, "I just don't want you getting mixed up in anything. Not while your father still needs you here."

Martin didn't know what to say.

Muriel broke the embarrassing silence – and a potentially emotional moment, by adding, "But remember, if, God forbid, anything happens to your father, you're out on your bum, buster."

He looked into his mother's eyes. "You know, Mom…I forgive you."

"For fibbing to that unholy Dutch witch? I'm just glad that I left Clark and Betty's before the police raided their whole apartment and arrested me too."

"No, for the Youth Group thing. And…for what happened to Ingrid."

Muriel's eyes welled up. "I'm not asking for your forgiveness."

"Well, I'm not doing it for you."

She wiped a tear with her apron and hurried away. He could've followed after her and said something to really rile her up. But what was the point? It's not like her pride would ever allow her to say she was sorry for what happened to him and to Ingrid. If Mom really felt any sense of guilt, he finally realized he'd never hear it from her. And if she didn't feel any guilt, well, he'd need to live with that too. For years Martin had been told during his court-ordered therapy that, by trying to punish his mother, he was only punishing himself. Now, for the first time, deep down, he truly *understood* that.

Martin was about to head back to his place to run a few miles on his treadmill, part of his new fitness kick. First, though, he went to the den to check on Dad. Sven stood there with a broad smile, admiring his newly-rebuilt model ship. Martin looked around and noticed that the den was now spotless: Muriel must have swept out all the remnants of broken ship bottles, shattered picture frames, and plastic chunks from the broken marital aid.

With his wife back, Sven was now in much better spirits. He had regained most of the weight he'd lost in his wife's absence and seemed to have more energy. Martin sat down next to him and held the ship's mast while his father glued it to the hull. Sven excitedly recounted some legendary naval battles and told Martin, for the first time, of his harrowing but also unforgettable experiences as a young seaman on board an aircraft carrier.

"I could tell you some salty stories about what went on below deck," Sven said with a sly laugh.

"How salty?"

"Salty, son, real salty…" Sven's eyes wandered over to his C.S.S. Virginia and held it up to the light, examining each detail. Then he looked at Martin and grinned, "Yep, being at sea is a real humdinger."

"I'll bet. Hey Dad, why don't you come down for tonight's party? The Wednesday folks will be here and I've told them a lot about you; I'm sure a lot of them would love to hear about your Navy adventures. You can come down early, and leave before it gets, well, 'salty.'"

Sven laughed and said he'd think about it.

When nine o'clock rolled around, Sven did join the party. The Wednesday crowd gave the old man a big cheer when he entered the room. Within minutes,

Martin came out of a little cubby with Peri, with whom he had just shared some "quality time," and gave his father a hug.

Peri grabbed a moist towelette from her purse and dried her privates in order to present her new pole dance and fire swallowing routine.

Martin called Candace and Harlan and, for the first time, invited them over to party.

Jesus H. Fuck, the nitrous tank guy, and Khang, tapped another keg of hand-crafted German beer as the festivities continued. Blair's parents arrived and parked themselves at the roulette table. Soon, they were tumbling dice and downing daiquiris with a group of circus clowns who were on parole.

Martin enjoyed Peri's performance but his eyes really lit up when he saw Officer Gonzalez enter the room. He gave her a kiss on the cheek and made her a Dirty Martini. The officer told Martin that she had just come from a glass blowing class at the local community college. She told him about some of the courses she had taken there, including a sailing class.

"They even teach sailing there?"

"Yeah. Actually, they do it over at Wells Fargo Lake.

Sven's passion for the sea had rubbed off on Martin, so the next day the young man cabbed over to Seward Junior College to sign up for "Sailing and Seamanship 101."

He started his first class the following week. Martin found that he loved the freedom of sailing despite the fact that he now had to get up at an ungodly hour and had to be fairly sober in order to concentrate on not capsizing the boat. Martin discovered that just getting out of his house every morning to sail was a major step for him.

He had long worried that his molestation settlement, which allowed him to not work and helped him maintain his core values of hedonism and debauchery, also thwarted his ambition. Worse, it made him almost afraid to live.

Within a few weeks Martin was seaworthy enough to bring his father along. Sven loved being out on the water, feeling the warm sun and cool breeze across his face, as Martin deftly maneuvered the rented dinghy around the artificial islands in the lake that were paid for and named after their corporate sponsor. Sven told his son how much being out there reminded him of the summers of his youth spent sailing on the Great Lakes with his own father.

As for Muriel, she mellowed - to a degree, anyway. She still schemed of ways to get Martin out of the house, but instead of acting on them, she simply wrote her plans in her diary, waiting for the inevitable day when Sven would be gone and she could finally rid herself of her son. But it's not as if she was wishing her husband away. During their separation, Muriel realized how much she adored her husband, warts and all. And she discovered, during her stay with Earl and Agnes and then Clark and Betty, that others were not as receptive as her sweet old Svenny to her constructive advice. He not only needed her, but, unlike so many others she helped, Sven truly appreciated her.

Fortunately, she was welcomed back to church after prayers were held to forgive her for the dildo debacle. The gossip about Muriel's alleged affair with Pastor Yarborough disappeared after he was discovered bathing naked in the baptismal font with another man and was asked to leave the church. The Lady Lutherans also resumed their weekly prayer group, though at another house. Sadly, Muriel and Sven decided to cancel their Monday bridge club, since most of the other members had become so radicalized by Eldertude that they could talk of nothing other than leading a bloody senior revolution.

Muriel and Martin now live in a kind of détente; their relationship has evolved to one of benign neglect. Occasionally, Muriel still carps about her son, but her criticism is less caustic, and borders on self-parody. And fortunately, at the very least, the two are united in their love and care for Sven.

IX

When Martin's 30th birthday came, Sven bought his son two cases of potato slabs. Muriel even made Martin's favorite strudel an gave him her favorite inspirational book, "I Was Touched by the Nail Scarred Hands." Lavonne came over in the morning to teach him some woodworking, and Ming dropped in an hour later to give Martin his first computer hacking lesson. Peri – a certified chef before she found her true calling in stripping, came over at lunch time to begin teaching Martin some rudimentary cooking skills.

Martin wasn't ready to do anything radical, like getting a job or going to college, but he now made a conscious effort to expand his vistas by getting out of his comfort zone. To that end, he decided to introduce a fourth woman, Officer Gonzalez, to his roster of lovers. She came by last night when her shift was over to play their special game of sexy cops and robbers. She also gave him some juicy gossip which he shared with Mom about the ongoing police investigation of Eldertude.

Outside the Kihlstrom family residence, Martin idled his new hybrid convertible Mini Cooper, a birthday present to himself and a self-reward for reinstating his license. A trailer was hitched to the vehicle, hauling another present he gave himself: a catamaran. He gave two toots on his horn. "Come on, Dad, are you ready for some sailing?"

With a spring in his step, Sven got in the car. They waved goodbye to Muriel and drove off into the morning sun.

NOT WITH *MY* DAUGHTER

Chad paced the floor, nervously waiting for Kaitlin's date to arrive. He already had enough on his mind, what with that new ballbuster at work, and piles of bills to pay. And now he had to deal with some pimply faced yob he didn't know putting moves on his teenage daughter. Upstairs, he could hear that damn sonic boom-throbbing bass music blaring from the bathroom where she'd been primping for God knows how long. She called that noise, what was it - Rubstep? Dubstep? Dubyastep? All he knew was that it sounded like the same shit that got him so rattled yesterday that he stabbed his pen into his palm. Again.

At times like this, Chad wished his ex-wife hadn't made him quit smoking because *dammit,* a cigarette would've calmed him right now. But, of course, there were no longer any smokes in the house. Instead, he bounced around from one end of the living room to the other, shaking his head, and thinking of what he'll tell this potentially young punk: *you better treat my girl with respect, and God might have ten commandments, but I've got eleven so you better -*

The doorbell rang. He walked deliberately to open the door, already extending his hand with an alpha-male handshake, something he'd learned at a business seminar. Chad looked up to find a tall young man in a blue beanie with a cheerful, almost beatific smile. The boy's clothes, heavily-starched Chinos and checkered button down shirt, were comically baggy.

"You're Ray, is that right?" Chad shook the boy's hand as he leaned in with his shoulder. "I'm Chad Tucker, Kaitlin's father. She'll be down in a bit but in the meantime, have a seat and let's get acquainted, shall we? "

Ray turned to sit down on the couch. From the back, where his beanie didn't quite cover his head, Chad could see no trace of hair on the kid. *So the kid is bald*, thought Chad, *that's just typical of the things Kaitlin keeps from me.*

"Yes, I'd love to get acquainted," said the young man in a calm voice. The kid had penetrating eyes and a kind of quiet confidence; he had none of the awkwardness or false bravado that Chad was used to seeing in teenage boys. *Wait, maybe this guy's older, some old creep who preys on underage girls. Of all the guys she could've dated in Seward!*

"Ray!" Chad demanded, "How old are you?"

"I just turned 17 last week."

Chad tightened his face to give the kid a stern look, a look that he would've used on his subordinates, if he had any. It was a look designed to show he meant business.

"I'll get straight to the point." To emphasize, Chad pointed his finger at the young man. "I'm going to make this crystal clear: my daughter means the world to me. She's all I have left now and I will do anything, and I mean ANYTHING to protect her. If you hurt her in any way, if you so much as lay a finger on her…" He hadn't really thought this thing through. "Well, you know what I mean."

The boy was unfazed by Chad's vague threat. Ray spoke calmly, "Sir, I can assure you I would never use violence against any human being. That's just not in my nature."

"Good, good." Chad took a breath and continued. "AND, what I also want to make absolutely clear is: no alcohol, no drugs of any kind, no speed racing. Also, you need to respect Kaitlin and…" Chad wasn't sure how to phrase this part.

Ray leaned his head toward Chad in what to the older man recognized as an active listening position. "And?"

Chad squirmed a little. The fact that the boy was so polite and surprisingly mature for his years made The Talk even more difficult. "And there will be no, uh," He looked toward the ceiling. "Funny stuff. Yes, no funny stuff with my daughter."

"No humor?"

"No *fooling around*."

"And, sir, what does that term mean to you?"

Chad looked into Ray's intense blue-gray eyes. *Is this kid just fucking with me? Does he really not know what fooling around means?*

"OK," Chad tried to explain, "No 'fooling around' means no, um, sexual activity of any kind. Period. And I already mentioned no drugs, right?"

Ray sat back, put his head back and closed his eyes. He looked as if he were seriously contemplating a universe of implications in the older man's words. It took a full minute before Ray's lips began to move. But no sound came out. It was as if Ray was channeling some higher power. Chad prayed it was the God of Celibacy.

Finally, Ray said, "I think I understand where you're going with this, and can I certainly appreciate the passion in which you express your love for your daughter. I think we can both agree that Kaitlin's a dynamic young woman with a bright future ahead of her, Chad."

"Damn straight." *Wait - where did this kid get off calling me by my first name?* He felt like telling the boy that from now on, it's "Mr. Tucker" or "Sir" to you, but restrained himself.   No sense in overplaying his hand.

"Also," Ray continued, "I wonder if you and I have gotten off on the wrong foot. As the loving father of such a beautiful young lady, you have every right and every reason to suspect the worst from one of Kaitlin's potential suitors. But my spiritual beliefs preclude me from ever being under the influence of any drug, including alcohol. While I do not oppose these substances on a moral level, I find that their use interferes with my practice of meditation and is inconsistent with the level of consciousness that I strive to maintain."

Ray rolled up the sleeves of his shirt and put his hands behind his head. Chad thought the boy was staring at him, but he realized that Ray's eyes were almost looking right through him. Chad was about to look away when he saw the boy's bare arms. Ray was even skinnier than he first thought. And he had the whitest skin Chad had ever seen. It was like a Canadian's arm after just getting out of a cast. It finally dawned on Chad that Kaitlin's date had probably gone through chemo. Hell, maybe he was STILL going through it. Chad was tempted to ask the boy about his illness, but decided against that, for now. No sense in coming across as a softy. *Too bad though*, he thought. *Hearing the boy's story might have given me some inspiration. God knows I could use some now.*

Ray sat forward, leading the older man to do the same. Chad felt like the kid was using some matching and mirroring techniques, like the kind he'd learned about in a sales seminar, but even if Ray was being manipulative, Chad couldn't help following the boy's lead. Ray suddenly crossed his legs, manspread-style, so Chad crossed his legs too.

"Now, as far as sexual activity is concerned," said Ray, "I'm afraid that my sexual life, just like yours, is not a matter of anyone else's concern. Kaitlin told me that was one of the core beliefs you espoused during your last marriage."

Chad shifted in his chair. "Well, yeah my wife said she was cool with it."

"Until she left you." Ray's tone was neutral. No hint of blame or sarcasm.

"But, Ray, you have to know, that's only part of the story: she not only left me, she cleaned me out too." Out of the corner of his eye Chad saw the foyer.

It brought back the painful memory of an angry Miss Piggy (Chad's name for his ex-wife) charging out the door, suitcase in hand. A suitcase filled with jewelry, cash, stock certificates, and bonds.

Ray gave the older man a sympathetic look. "I'm very sorry to hear about that. I wish that I had some personal experience to share with you that could help you with your pain." Ray put his hands together, mulling over this conundrum. Chad recalled that his own father used to do that, though usually while mulling over options for his son's punishment. Chad waited for the boy's response. He hoped that Ray could offer at least a kernel of wisdom. "Well, Chad, at the risk of sounding cavalier, you know the old saying, 'someday, we'll look back on this and laugh'? Why not laugh about it right now?"

"I've been trying to," Chad said, looking away. He was ashamed to be talking to anyone about his troubles, let alone some teenage boy. But he didn't have anyone else to confide in. He would never burden Kaitlin with his problems. She wouldn't be interested in them, anyway. And Kaitlin would be especially unsympathetic now that she was making noises about moving to Idaho to live with Miss Piggy and her latest female lover.

"I've been really trying to let go of my feelings of resentment, Ray, and I've been working on my anger issues. But now all I'm feeling is, I don't know, shame, I guess."

"Well, that's at least a start. Have you tried owning these feelings and standing in front of a mirror and fully accepting them?"

Chad's eyes became diffused. He struggled to find words for the emotions bubbling up from deep within his broken psyche. "I'm trying to accept my feelings but sometimes I get so god damned – excuse my language – overwhelmed." He buried his face in his hands. Oh God, he hoped he wouldn't start blubbering right then and there.

There was a long silence. Chad hoped Ray would break it. Instead, the young man just sat there looking at him. It seemed to Chad that Ray wanted him to continue. "Listen, Ray, I'm really sorry about giving you such a hard time when you came in."

"That's OK. And perfectly understandable, given the stages of grief you're going through."

"Thank you, really, THANK YOU, for acknowledging that. Listen, everything feels so hard right now." Chad lowered his voice so there was no chance that Kaitlin could hear him from upstairs. "I mean, money, dating…"

"AND raising a teenage daughter," Ray said with a twinkle in his eyes.

Chad laughed. "And, yes, there's THAT.
And…" A look of anguish came over his face. "It's bad enough that I have to compete with Jeff, this co-worker from hell, the guy everybody thinks is Mr. Hot Shot Salesman. But now I have this new boss, and she's a bitch."

"Perhaps it would be more constructive if you didn't refer to a woman using a derogatory term," said Ray, adjusting his blue beanie over his bald head.

"OK, you're right, sorry. But this b-, well, this lady, she's always dogging me at work, and they say we'll all be downsized soon, and this fucking woman is now calling me 'Chad The Irrelevant', and saying I'll be the first piece of dead weight to go when the firm trims the fat." His eyes welled up. "I don't want to be irrelevant…"

Ray leaned over and put a hand on Chad's shoulder. "You're not irrelevant, Chad. You're very relevant."

"But there's another thing. It's my daughter…." Chad covered his eyes but tears still trickled down through his fingers.

Just then Kaitlin came downstairs. With her cream colored skin, wavy brunette hair, bright red lipstick, and shapely figure - accentuated by her tight, red dress - she looked stunning. Like Hedy Lamarr or some other 1940's starlet.

She saw Ray hugging her father and rocking her old man gently back and forth. She sighed. "Dad what's wrong?"

Chad looked to Ray and whispered, "What should I do? Should I tell her?"

Ray answered without missing a beat; maybe he'd been through these lectures with his dates' parents a thousand times before. "Think about your outcome. If you want closer emotional intimacy with your daughter, then you should tell her everything that's on your mind."

Chad took her by the hand. "Sweetheart, I love you. I'm sorry I've been so on edge lately…" He turned to Ray, who nodded approvingly. Chad gently clasped Kaitlin's hands. "I know I haven't been the best dad, especially in the past few years. I know it's no excuse but I've had a lot going through my mind. Sometimes I wonder whether I can still keep on keeping on. But I do. For you."

Kaitlin looked confused and embarrassed. "Uh, OK, Dad. Thanks for sharing." She signaled to Ray to get up and get ready to leave.

She pecked Chad on the cheek. Then she gave Ray a slow, soulful kiss. "Dad, we won't be out too late. Unless we end up at Ray's for the night."

Chad lovingly put a coat around his daughter's shoulders and opened the front door for the couple. "You two have fun tonight." He whispered into Ray's ear, "Do you think we can continue our talk later some other time? It's really helped."

"Of course, Chad," said the young man. "When I find some free time I'd be happy to do what I can." The teens took off.

Chad went to the kitchen, grabbed a can of Coors out of the fridge, and sat down at the table. He wondered when they'd be back. He had so much he wanted to talk to Ray about.

THE DIRECTOR'S CUT

I
Monday

"What do you mean which park? *Central* Park, near the duck pond, like we talked about. The video's set up and I've been waiting here for almost an hour." A brisk autumn breeze whipped up a whirl of leaves and candy wrappers. Seamus Diamond shivered as he felt the chill through his sweatshirt, a threadbare garment which barely covered his large frame and even bigger belly. He squeezed his cellphone between his shoulder and his ear, leaving his hands free to check the depth of field of his shot once more. "Are you on your way?"

"Sorry, no can do," said Meghan. "I guess I forgot. I had a late night last night and I'm kind of hung over." She laughed. "No, I'm REALLY hung over."

Meghan had flaked on him before but at least she'd always called to cancel. Seamus didn't want to push his erstwhile actress too hard – after all, she would now be working for him for the umpteenth time without pay. And he didn't want a blow up with her about what she was doing last night and *with whom*. Still, the scene he wanted to shoot was important: it was the penultimate scene in what would be his 50th short film.

He felt this film was equally important for Meghan's acting aspirations.

"C'mon Meghan, there's only about an hour of light left. Just grab a cab and get over here. I'll pay for it. Look, it'll only take a few minutes and we can wrap this baby up. It'll be a pisser, I promise."

"Look, Seamus, I've been doing some thinking lately and, don't take this the wrong way, but being in your little films isn't a good use of my time anymore."

"What do you mean? What's a better use of time than making cinematic history?" He tried to put a smile in his voice. "Remember, it's all just you and me. Like…Ingmar and Ingrid, Warhol and Edie Sedgwick."

"Edie died."

"So what? All of them died. Everyone dies."

"Seamus, we're not making any history. We ARE history, as far as I'm concerned."

"But Meghan, remember everything we always talked about?" He scratched at his beard, trying to think of something to say to persuade her. "You want to act, right? "

"Sure, but…all I'm saying is that you're a good guy and all, it's just that, c'mon, it's time to grow up. I mean, you're pushing thirty by now."

He was silent. He didn't want to remind her that he was thirty two.

"Anyway," she continued, "I've found a new director who's got some big plans for me, and, I'm sorry, but face it, Seamus, you'll always be that stock boy at a bodega, living in a hovel in Queens."

He felt a lump in his throat. "Meghan, that's not true. You know it's not true."

Technically, it wasn't: Seamus had lost his stock boy job two months ago after wrenching his back hauling boxes. But it would take more than getting fired from some shitty day gig to shake his confidence. Hell, it would even take a lot more than his hundreds of rejections from the film industry.

For Seamus, it wasn't about becoming the next sellout director. His passion was making art. With his latest short film, that's just what he was doing, at least in his mind. He wasn't about to let Meghan's stubbornness, or the fact that they broke up six months ago, stop him.

"C'mon, Meg, I'll make it up to you, it'll just take a few minutes."

"Goodbye, Shay. I'm going back to sleep." Seamus heard a distant laugh, a man's laugh, on the other end. She hung up.

Seamus let out a long sigh. Then he went back to mapping his shot. Why not? He had never let things like unreliable actors or ex-girlfriends stop him before. He would just do some background shots this afternoon, go home, edit a bit, and then place a Craigslist ad for an actress to replace Meghan.

Adjusting the camera on his shoulders, Seamus focused on some interesting angles made by the shadows around the opening into a pedestrian underpass.

Just then, two tall figures, a man and woman, emerged from the tunnel and walked by Seamus. His camera followed them. Peering right into the lens the guy said, "If you assholes keep following me, I'm gonna shove that thing right up your sphincter."

Seamus took his eyes off the viewfinder and looked at the man. Was he serious? The guy was tall and thin, but broad-shouldered. He was also handsome, despite his pockmarked skin, and dressed like some cowboy hipster: black snakeskin boots, black jeans, a black leather vest, and a black cowboy hat. He looked like the sort of self-satisfied douche bag Meghan would like.

Seamus did a double-take. *Wait*, he thought, *I know this dickhead! It's Troy Todd!* Seamus had gone to film school with the man now known to the world as T. Eduardo Todd, an A- List director whose entire oeuvre consisted of movie remakes and sequels. He had his arm around a leggy brunette, a Bollywood starlet type. She was the kind of bimbo who was surely working her way up the economic ladder by dating famous directors, before settling down to a series of successful, yet unfulfilling marriages to billionaire industrialists.

"Hey, Troy, I mean T. Eduardo, how are you?" said Seamus with his toothy smile. "Remember me? Seamus Diamond? We were in film school together?"

Though Seamus and Eduardo had worked on a few projects together at N.Y.U., the man clearly had no idea who Seamus was. For Director Todd, film school had been ten years, and a shitload of sequels and remakes ago. Seamus had only been able to attend for two semesters before being forced to quit for financial reasons.

T. Eduardo feigned interest in Seamus with a "Yeah, sure, Chief. Sorry, bro, I thought you were the pa-pa-raz-zo." He stretched the word out. Todd didn't bother to introduce Seamus to his lady friend. She looked bored and complained to her strategic beau that they had to hurry to get crosstown for dinner.

"So what are you working on now?" Seamus asked.

"Don't you read the trades, my friend?" His tone suggested that everyone should be aware of what the great T. Eduardo was up to at any given time. "It's a sequel and a remake of *Ferris Bueller's Day Off.*"

Seamus would've liked to ask how a remake of that '80s classic could also be sequel, and, more importantly, why anyone would even attempt something so unoriginal. But he'd been told a millions times to watch his motor mouth. But in T. Eduardo's favor, he'd actually done some interesting French New Wave-inspired work at N.Y.U. So maybe his newest film wouldn't be *too* bad.

"I'm working on a new film myself, a short, actually," said Seamus.

"Coolio," said the A-Lister, while feeling up his lady friend's skirt. She didn't slap him. She just giggled.

"Can I show you my work sometime?" asked Seamus. "I'd like to get your opinion."

"Sure. Why the hell not?" The famous director took out his cellphone and scrolled through his contacts. "Here's my assistant's number," he said, holding up the phone so that Seamus could write it down. "Call her and maybe she can set something up, buddy."

Seamus wrote the number down, thanked him, and gave him a business card with Seamus' online video links. "Great running into you," said Seamus. He turned to the woman, who had already begun to walk away and said, "And great meeting you too." The woman said nothing and did not look back.

T. Eduardo slapped Seamus on the back and said, "Sure thing, Amos. We had a good time, good time."

The A-Lister and his girlfriend left, cackling to each other as they walked on.

Seamus' cell phone rang. It was Shannon, so he let the call go to voice mail. He loved his sister - she was like a mom to him. But he did NOT want to be nagged yet again about going out to Long Island to see her and the retarded, er, "special" people at the adult residential facility that Shannon managed.

It was finally getting dark, but Seamus still needed a couple more shots before heading home. He turned the camera back on and zoomed in on the pedestrian tunnel. The graininess of the stone work against the graffiti was perfect. He tried to read the scrawl: "Chris X, Spuyten Duyvil."

"Spuyten Duyvil, what a crazy ass name for a place," Seamus said, to no one in particular. "Ah, those fucking Dutch!"

Slowly and carefully keeping a steady hand, he kept the camera rolling as he walked toward the tunnel.

II
Lights, Camera, Mayhem

Seamus took a dozen steps inside the narrow cave-like walkway and found himself in total darkness. He fumbled with his camera, and after a moment, he managed to find the switch to turn the strobes on. A beam of light revealed four scowling eyes peering right at him. He could just make out the outline of two young men sitting on the floor only a few feet away. They had the aggressive look of those raccoon-sized rats Seamus had seen in the bowels of Grand Central Station, the ones who showed no fear - only a vague look of contempt for mankind.

"What the fuck?!" someone growled.

Seamus smelled something acrid – these guys were smoking something, but it definitely was not tobacco or pot. In a flash, the toughs jumped up to confront Seamus. Though the two of them were a few inches shorter than Seamus (who was six foot three and 260 pounds), they looked menacing enough. One punk, apparently unfazed by the November chill, donned a wife beater tank top. The other had no shirt on at all. With the camera's lights on them, their faces grew even more intense and malevolent. But Seamus wasn't particularly scared. At least not at first. He had a friendly personality to go with his bearded, babyish face and big smile, and he had a knack for making friends with just about anybody.

"Sorry, guys," said Seamus, stopping to put his camera down. "I was just finishing a shot. I didn't see you there."

The teenage malcontents circled around him, peppering Seamus with such questions as: what kind of shit-fuck were you filming?! Are you some kind of director? You ever made any films we saw?

"Probably not," answered Seamus. "I do shorts – you can see them online. But someday – knock on these fiberglass cave walls - I'll get to direct feature films."

The bare chested punk pointed to the camera. "How do you use that thing?"

"It's pretty simple, actually," said Seamus. "You just press this to let it roll –"

"Hey Big Shot Director, what's this for?" asked the kid in the wife beater, putting his fingers around the lens.

"It's for the zoom. Careful –"

"How 'bout this one, Spielberg?" demanded the shirtless guy, pointing to the aperture ring.

Seamus gave a deep belly laugh. "'Spielberg'! I like that! I love his work, but actually, my films aren't nearly as sentimental."

"Hey, what's your name?" the wife beater tee guy asked, in a slightly, friendlier tone, "So if, like, we see your name in lights someday."

"I'm Seamus. Seamus Diamond. I'm half Jewish, half Irish, and half genius." He grinned a toothy smile and extended his hand, "Pleased to meet –"

Suddenly Seamus felt a sharp stab in his palm. The punks jostled him and wrested the camera away. The camera's lights bounced around the tunnel before its bright beam pierced into Seamus' retinas, nearly blinding him.

"Yo Spielberg," said the shirtless punk as he dropped trou and mooned Seamus, "Film dis!"

To Seamus, everything from then on was a blur.

He heard one guy bellow, "Hey, fat fuck, how you like it now when someone's filming YOU?"

The other guy spoke yelled into in Seamus' ear. "See how fucking annoying people who take pictures can be?" Seamus felt a SLAP! to his face. "Smile, fat fuck filmmaker, and get ready for your close-up, 'cause you're about to get your ass kicked!"

Next came a volley of punches, kicks, and head butts. To Seamus, who was grunting and groaning through it all, the assault seemed to last for hours. In truth, its duration lasted two minutes and twelve seconds. Then, the two punks bailed, taking the camera with them.

Seamus lay in the dark tunnel all alone, retching and coughing, half conscious, and not even fully aware of what had just happened.

III
Wrap

Seamus lay on the cracked pavement for at least an hour, too bloody, sore, and stunned to move. He figured that at any minute someone would walk by and maybe call the cops or an ambulance or something. But no one came. Just as well: he was mugged five years ago and remembered what a waste of time it had been talking to an officer who didn't really care and was just there to fill out a pointless report on a crime that they all knew would never get solved. Seamus didn't want anyone to call an ambulance, either: his insurance had lapsed when he lost his job, and he knew, from when his mom became terminally ill, just how much emergency services and even a single night stay in a hospital could cost.

Except for the soreness in his face, lower back, stomach, buttocks, and the pain in his hand, he otherwise felt alright. He was well enough, at least, to hobble over to the subway and catch the train home. Emotionally, though, he was drained. The day had been a waste, with Meghan flaking and T. Eduardo's Hollywood Brush Off. And then, for an encore: the shit-kicking of his life. Now he'd have to tell his roommate Kyle that the camera he'd lent Seamus had been stolen. Kyle would undoubtedly be pissed and Seamus would be forced to use his own amateur-grade gear from now on.

When Seamus got back to his apartment building there was a note in the lobby saying that the elevator was out of service. Not again! With great pain, he practically crawled up the four flights of stairs to reach his place. Once inside, he was relieved to find the lights off. That meant he could wait until tomorrow to tell Kyle about his camera. Seamus went into the bathroom and washed his bloody face, feeling the sting of the warm water on his broken skin. He brushed his bloody teeth, and then popped two painkillers and a sleeping pill. He plopped on his bed to try sleep it all off.

But he couldn't sleep. He was troubled by the things Meghan had said. He had already felt bad enough about his unrealized and increasingly unrealizable dreams. But she didn't have to rub it in. No one was more frustrated than he was about always getting "just this close" to a major feature film deal, only to have a new team of producers come in to shelve it or some random act of God screw the whole thing up. To Seamus, a recovering Catholic and a lapsed Jew, God's so-called random acts were nothing more than Holy terrorism.

He tossed and turned as he stewed about his years of failures – like losing agents and having the numerous scripts he'd written on spec end up in some trash bin (maybe a floating barge?) where all dead scripts finally end up. Sure, he could focus his career on podcasts, podisodes, and YouTube, where he already had his own channel. But Seamus's dream was to write and direct features for the BIG screen. And on film, *not* video! He'd tried Hollywood, but his contacts in the major studios told him not to bother unless he brought them a script involving vampires, zombies, hit men, WWII, Satan, clowns, or hookers with hearts of gold. Even Jane Austen remakes, he was told, better have at least a few horse chases, a high body count, and, for extra points, a sassy black dude sidekick. Then, after giving up on the big studios, he was rejected by all the major independents. That's when he turned to online crowd-funding sites, but he could never raise enough money to turn his full-length film ideas into reality.

He'd never admit defeat to anyone else, least of all his sister, but the events of the past few months – like breaking up with Meghan and losing his job - had thrown him for a loop. Seamus' thoughts turned to his mother and her cautionary advice: "Life is hard and they treat you like a whore." She was even more negative about his movie aspirations. Shannon was now a lot like that, too.

But with Seamus' dad - when he was alive – well, that was different. By the age of four he'd entertain his father with his little stories and fantastical ideas for movies. Young Seamus would detail the sequence of these imagined films almost shot-by-shot, too. So, for his son's tenth birthday, Leonard gave Seamus his first video camera. A few days later, however, tragedy struck: Leonard Diamond, beloved father of Seamus and Shannon, and not-so-beloved-ex-husband to Maeve, dropped dead of a heart attack, He was only 41. Maeve, until the end of her days, claimed there was a connection between Leonard's gift and the man's death. For years, Seamus poo-pooed this, as well as most of her neurotic theories. But now, when he reflected on all the heartache he'd experienced trying to make his films, perhaps she wasn't so crazy after all.

Maybe Mom had been right all along about him changing careers, he thought. For years she had told him that only one in a million ever makes it in the entertainment industry, and "Shay, you ain't even one in a thousand." On her deathbed, in fact, Maeve's final words to Seamus were: "I love you, but cut the shit. Get a real job."

It's not that Seamus lacked talent. He had plenty of that. And not just by his own estimation, but in the opinion of his film school professors, who admired not only his originality, but also the sincerity and earnestness in his work. Nor did he lack ambition or a good work ethic. How else could he have finished 49 shorts? And how else could he have written dozens of scripts, all while working those soul crushing day gigs?

But now, with everything going wrong at once, Seamus wondered - if there really is a God, maybe this is His way of telling him it's time to call it quits. But then what? After giving up his lifelong dreams would he just have to get some dumb ass job and eke out the remainder of his existence?

More importantly, was his life even worth it at all? He'd been despondent enough when he turned thirty. Now, two years later and two years older, and still without any hope for his career, he was even more depressed. Seamus knew he probably wasn't thinking straight, but it dawned on him for the first time, that maybe, just maybe, suicide was the best alternative to this life of abject misery and failure.

Seamus tossed and turned some more before finally nodding off.

IV
Tuesday

When Seamus awoke it was still dark. His cellphone's clock read six p.m. He'd slept for more than sixteen hours! He checked his voice mail - there were a dozen message, all from his sister Shannon, and all along the lines of "where the hell ARE you?!" Damn! He'd forgotten that he was supposed to have headed out to visit her today. He called her.

Shannon picked up on the first ring. "Well look who finally decides to call? Seamus, are you OK?"

"Yeah, sure, I'm alright." Seamus tried to sound as chipper as a guy who'd been beaten the night before, and hadn't yet had his morning coffee, could sound. The last thing he wanted was to have to get into what had happened to him the night before. He didn't want his sister to worry about him, nor was he in the mood for her to tell him to stop lugging that damn camera around and forget all that "movie malarkey."

He covered the mouthpiece and yawned. Then he tried to sound, well, maybe not perky, but at least, awake. "I'm sorry for not getting back to you, but I just woke up."

"Just woke up?!" said Shannon. "The sun's been down for over an hour and you just woke up? Oh, I get it, a late night with a lady friend?" Shannon laughed.

Seamus chose his words carefully. "There *was*, shall we say, an incident with a young lady in the evening, as a matter of fact," he said, technically not lying to his sister. "But look, Sis, I'm pretty beat. Do you mind if we take a rain check 'til tomorrow?"

"I guess so. The main thing is I'm glad that you're alright, I was really getting worried, Shay. But, yes, PLEASE come tomorrow. I'd love to see you. Plus, I want you to meet two new special people who just moved here: Christopher and Steve. I told them all about you and they're all excited to meet you because they want to make movies too."

"Retards making movies?" said Seamus. "Tell them it's been done."

"You're a regular laugh riot," said Shannon, without a trace of humor. "OK, Seamus, see you tomorrow. And bring your film equipment so you can give everyone a demonstration. I told them that you're a big-time director and you couldn't make it today because you were too busy. So play along. And don't screw things up, OK? My guests get agitated when I tell them that something's going to happen and then it doesn't."

They said their goodbyes and hung up. Seamus realized that he was starving, so he headed out to the bodega down the street to pick up what for him would be his breakfast: an irradiated hot dog and a pint of milk.

On his way out of the store he was accosted by a tall, gangly geek of a man. The guy jumped off a motorcycle and ran toward Seamus. An equally lanky dweeb sat in the motorbike's side car.

"De Directeur!" the first geek yelled in a harsh and surprisingly high voice. "Excuse me! De Direkteur, De Regisseur Fat!" Seamus didn't know whether to fight or flee. There was also a third possibility, which was to just bust up over the guy's comical accent. "The Dutch are not the fucking ones!" the geek screamed.

The sidecar dweeb took out his camera and zoomed in on Seamus.

The walking geek screamed even louder, "Hey fat fuck film maker, *you* are the fucking one!"

Then he kicked Seamus squarely in the testicles. Seamus fell back, dropped his meager groceries, and doubled over in pain. The crotch-kicker ran back to the two-seater motorbike. He revved it up, hopped a curb, and the two geeks rode off.

After the sharp stab of pain in his groin had begun to subside, Seamus wondered what the hell had just happened. He collected his milk and his sad looking hot dog from the pavement and limped home.

When he returned, Kyle was there. So was Kyle's girlfriend, B.J. Kyle had been his roommate for the past year and had studied film for a time at U.S.C. He had long, stringy, blond hair, and a long, skinny frame. The dude looked like your average bro, save for his most distinguishing feature: he had no butt. Presumably he had a rectum, or some other apparatus for elimination. But no matter how tight Kyle tried to buckle his belt, his jeans always sagged down to his pubis, and way past his non-existent ass.

Kyle began dating B.J. six months ago. When Seamus had once asked her why she called herself B.J., she said, "It's not what you think," but would elaborate no further. She was a young woman with a petite and cute figure, small boobs, and straight, horsehair thick, rubella-style hair. She preferred to wear "thriftsters" - thrift store hipster clothes, and had adopted an East Village just-stepped-in-dog-shit expression that Seamus found annoying but also strangely attractive. Since she'd been dating Kyle, she pretty much lived in their apartment too.

Seamus was about to ask them how the porn shoot had gone (Kyle did lighting, and B.J. did sound for any paid film gigs they could get). But as soon as they saw him, Kyle said, "Man, you look like shit. Hey, B.J. doesn't he look like shit?"

B.J. looked at Seamus' cuts and bruises and agreed that Seamus indeed looked like shit. "What the hell happened to you?" she asked.

Seamus told them about last night's beating and about the groin kick from the crazy Dutchman. About

how the Dutchman called him a "fat fuck filmmaker" -
just like the punks the night before.

"And, Kyle, the other thing is, I'm sorry, but
those two punks last night snagged your camera. They
must have grabbed it at some point while they were
kicking and punching me. And I think they filmed it -"

"Whoa," said B.J. "They filmed your ass-
kicking?"

"I think so, I mean the camera's lights were on
me, I think the whole time. I'm not totally sure, though.
Obviously I had my mind on other things." Seamus felt
the swelling in his cheek where he'd caught a
particularly nasty blow.

"Let's see if we can find this beating online
somewhere," BJ said. She opened her laptop and
searched while Kyle did the same on his tablet. Seamus
grabbed his smartphone and did his own Google search.
Then he typed in "fat fuck filmmaker ass kicked" and
there it was!

The three of them watched the clip from the
night before: some arty shots going into the tunnel and
then 2:12 of gruesome violence. Kyle and BJ were
ecstatic.

"Dude!" exclaimed Kyle. "That's got to be your best work yet. That almost makes up for the loss of my camera, which was insured, by the way. Awesome career move, bro!"

"Thanks for your empathy," said Seamus, holding out his bruised arm to show them the stigmata on his hand.

"Look, sorry about the scratches and all," said Kyle, "But you have to admit this clip is fresh. Who's kidding who? The timing, the lighting…"

"And oh, the horror," said B.J., said in her best Colonel Kurtz voice. "That, and the absurdity."

Kyle said, "And even the… I guess you'd call it, acting."

Seamus grimaced.

"Yeah," added B.J. "You've got to post this on your channel."

"Maybe put it on a million channels," said her boyfriend.

Seamus' first thought was absolutely not. Then he remembered all the things that had stirred around in his head last night while he lay in bed, such as the realization that he was ready to make radical changes in his life. Seamus uploaded the clip.

No sooner did he do that when someone posted a link to the clip: it was a new video called "Fat Fuck Filmmaker Gets Ass Kicked in Queens" by The Mad Dutchmen. Sure enough, it was the testicular thrashing from just a couple of hours ago. Seamus posted that clip on his online feed as well.

"Ooh, this is good," said B.J., reviewing the Dutch crotch-kick.

Kyle said, "We've got to get this stuff out there!"

"Yeah, way the fuck out there!" agreed B.J.

B.J. excitedly told them that this was *true* cinema verite, not like some fake reality show. Nor was it played out, she said, like those stiletto heel-puppy-crushing videos. Sitting side by side on the couch, the three of them blogged and uploaded the clips to every social networking and video posting site they could get their clickers on. B.J and Kyle's enthusiasm didn't surprise Seamus, he knew that they were sick of doing sound and lighting for what they called "boring, four-on-the-floor" porn shoots. They were always looking for a new, and more lucrative, gig. And so, they pressed Seamus to let them film more videos in the same vein.

"I don't know, guys," he said. "Putting aside for a moment my extreme pain, who would really would want to watch this stuff?"

B.J. said, "I'm sure that plenty of people would pay to watch you get the shit kicked out of you."

"I know I would," joked Kyle.

Seamus said he'd think about it. Although he hated to give up control of his scenes, he did like the element of chance that the amateur cinematographers a.k.a. thugs had inadvertently brought to the work. It was kind of an *I Ching* of violence. Plus, he allowed, there was something to be said for letting the story unfold naturally and in real time, all the while viewing – and being part of the action - from varying POVs. Seamus' disassociated and analytical view of his own beatings did not surprise his roomies: though Seamus was largely an autodidact, he was also well versed in film theory, criticism, and the semiotics of the medium.

He popped a couple painkillers to ease his throbbing nutsack and went off to bed.

V

Wednesday

The next day, Seamus woke up, showered, grabbed his own video gear and trained it out to Long

Island. He de-trained at Huntington and exited the station just as Shannon drove up to the waiting area.

As soon as he got in the car, she saw his bruises and looked worried. But Seamus cut in with a "don't ask" look. She didn't. They drove off through wooded greenbelts, past slate covered diners and White Castles.

Soon they were at Shannon's workplace, The Edelman Center for Special Adults. Christopher and Steve, two new middle-aged guests who happened to have Down's syndrome, were already waiting at the door. They hugged him.

The moment Seamus began lecturing Christopher and Steve on the rudiments of acting, he forgot all about his aches and pains. His new students were eager to learn, too. Seamus set up his camera and soon he was pacing between shots and making on-the-spot creative choices. Seamus directed the two men in various scenarios: Batman & Robin, Abbott & Costello, Romeo & Juliet, Hall & Oates.

These guys were willing to do just about anything. He'd try them in horror and fantasy genres later, but for now, why not get their feet wet by doing a crime show? Isn't that how Richard Belzer learned how to act?

"Listen up," Seamus said. "You two will star in a new show –"

"What's it called?" interrupted Christopher.

"It doesn't have a name yet," said Seamus.

"All shows have names," observed Steve.

"Well…" Seamus fiddled with his beard. "OK, I've got it! *Special People, Special Detectives.* Wait, or maybe *Down's Syndrome Looking Up!* But let's not lose focus on the minutiae right now."

"The what?" asked Christopher.

"Never mind," Seamus answered. "OK, here's the set up: you're two detectives who just happen to have Up syndrome, I mean, Down syndrome."

"OK," said Steve, without conviction. Christopher looked equally confused.

"You know," said Seamus, "Private investigators. P.I.'s. Private dicks." Christopher and Steve both grinned, ear-to-ear. "You take on white collar crime cases. And you have a special talent for solving complex money laundering schemes. Your chameleon-like skills allow you to go undercover, like, deep in the inner sanctums of Wall Street. Zurich,

Tokyo, even the Chicago Cattle Market. Basically, any air-conditioned white collar environment, in order to root out corruption."

Seamus paused for effect, and then looked them squarely in the eyes. "You two will play heroes! And, because your clients pay well for your services, you're both filthy rich!"

His actors beamed.

"As detectives, you hug people. A lot. And through that hugging you get clues. Sometimes it's physical evidence, like a strand of hair, a wallet, or a sock. Sometimes you get emotional clues too. Some suspects break down crying in your empathetic embraces. With the right hug, some of these thugs even confess right on the spot."

He asked his actors to hug each other. "Hugs for thugs! Hugs for the thugs!" the two men chanted. Then, without prompting, Christopher and Steve ran around hugging every resident in the house.

Seamus spent the rest of the day like this, writing simple dialogue, running scenes and basically having a blast filming his newly-conceived show. Then he did some down and dirty editing on his laptop so he could show the piece to all of the residents.

The guests gave the boys a standing ovation. The actors took a bow and then pranced around like Reagan after he acted in a war film and began to believe he was really a war hero.

To Seamus, Christopher and Steve may not be actual heroes, but these Down Syndromers were pretty good guys. They were the type of special guys who you'd like to sit down and have a special beer with. And, Seamus respected their acting abilities. When he asked them to play junk bond brokers or pork belly futures tycoons or go undercover as special architects, they were surprisingly convincing. (This was unexpected since neither guys had any prior training as actors, not because of their so-called disabilities.)

On the drive back to the train station, Shannon told her brother, "I'm really glad you came out and yes, I'm glad you were able to make the residents happy."

"But?" Seamus knew his sister all too well.

"But I don't appreciate you making fun of them."

"What are you talking about?"

"You know damn well, Shay. This whole *Up Syndrome* thing –"

"Actually, its official title is now *Down's Syndrome Looking Up*: *Special People, Special Detectives.* And I think you're missing the point – the show is all about demonstrating how special people can do far more than non-special people think they can. Maybe they can even do *more* than we un-special, half-chosen/half-unchosen, people can do. It's like that Devo song: they have jobs, wear hats, and bring home the bacon."

"The song is called 'Mongoloid' and that term is way out of date."

"Whatever. Anyway, Mongoloids, I mean, Down Syndrome people, can solve even the most sophisticated international financial crimes."

Shannon rolled her eyes. "Oh, pleeeeeez."

Seamus changed the subject. "You know, I'm not 100% sure of my feelings right now, but I think I might have a crush on Brenda." Brenda was one of the younger and prettier special residents.

"Don't even joke about things like that!"

He chaffed at his sister's attitude. He had come all the way out to Huntington just to help her out. Seamus actually enjoyed today's just for the hell of it filming, something he hadn't done in a very long time. So what was Shannon's fucking problem?

At the station, he got out of the car quickly, said a curt goodbye and boarded the train.

VI
Train and Vein

The car was packed when he got on, then emptied out after a couple of stops. That left Seamus alone to muse over what he'd filmed today. *Down's Up* was fun and funny, a new creative direction for him, something loose and unpredictable. Definitely a departure from his work over the last five years, which tended to be non-linear in its storytelling and usually featured philosophical and meta-textual themes. Kind of like a David Mamet screenplay, without all the cussing and Social Darwinism.

At the next stop there was a delay while the engineers uncoupled the last three cars of the train. Just as the doors were about to close, a young man came on board. He immediately spotted Seamus.

When the train began to move, the guy walked toward Seamus, calling out, "It's you! That masochistic director guy!" He came within ten feet of Seamus before the train suddenly stopped and then lurched forward. The guy lost balance and leaped into the air.

But he quickly recovered by twirling around a passenger's pole and then grabbing the rider straps with both hands. Finally, he topped it off with a couple jazz dance moves.

"Ta da!" said the man, who froze in place as if he were waiting for applause.

Good save, thought Seamus. That was cute, but he was not in the mood for a shit kicking right now. Seamus was about to tell the guy to come back tomorrow, but he didn't want to be rude.

"My name is Cal Gilroy," the man said with a friendly smile. "That's my stage name."

Seamus smiled. "Pleased to meet you. I'm –"

"I already know! You're the – sorry - Fat Fuck Filmmaker."

"I prefer the half Jewish, half Irish, half genius, Seamus Diamond." They shook hands. Cal explained that he was a struggling actor who graduated from SUNY Stoneybrook three years ago and now commuted into Manhattan five nights a week to hone his craft at an actor's studio.

"Hey, Fat Fu-, I mean, Seamus. If you ever need an actor, anytime, just give me a call." Cal ripped out a sheet from his notebook and wrote down his contact info.

"A lefty, huh?" observed Seamus.

"Yep. Born and raised."

Hmm, thought Seamus. *Maybe I AM in the mood for a beating after all.*

He adjusted the monitor on his laptop and flipped on its webcam. "As a matter of fact, Cal, you can be in a film, right now, if you want."

"I can?"

"Sure. All you have to do is beat me up. But it's got to look real."

The actor looked like he thought Seamus was pulling his leg, so the director pantomimed what he wanted by punching himself in the face, *Fight Club*-style.

"You want me to hit you? Right here?" Calvin looked around to make sure there was no one else on the train. "Um, OK." Then Cal confidently added that if Seamus wanted him to ride a horse or do swordplay, and do it in several foreign accents, he could pull that off too.

Cal paused. "Sir, what's my motivation?"

"Your motivation? Here's your fucking motivation," Seamus raised his voice. "You left-handed loser! You left handed pansy, but hetero, fruitcake! I'd never waste money paying a left-handed actor 'cause everyone knows they can't act. Hell, southpaws can barely walk. That's right, you're not getting paid by me and you're angry about discrimination against your type. You know, the left-handed loser type. THERE'S your goddam motivation."

The director searched for more ammunition to fire up his actor, but his mind froze. After all, other than having large and unnaturally white teeth (which Seamus assumed that Cal, as an actor, would be proud of) the actor was just some average-looking white guy. Yes, that's it!

Seamus got up in Cal's face and yelled, "You fucking Caucasian! You left-handed Caucie asshole! Caucie! Caucie! Caucie!"

That did the trick. With the webcam still on, Calvin found his motivation, pummeling Seamus with an impressive display of dirty punches and roundhouse kicks. By the end of it, Seamus was left with a bloody nose and a torn sweatshirt. The timing could not have been better: by the time Seamus reached his stop, he had already stanched his bleeding with a discarded *New*

York Post, gathered up his gear, and obtained the actor's signed release.

Cal gave Seamus his head shot as they said goodbye, adding, "If you need any more violence, remember, I'm your man. Take a look at my vita on the back - I'm trained in all manner of stage combat, including knife throwing."

Seamus promised to stay in touch, hopped off the train and headed home.

Seamus couldn't wait to show B.J. and Kyle the latest footage of violence. Kyle gave it the thumbs up. B.J. loved it too, adding that she was impressed by the realism and the details: the bloody nose, the rolled up newspaper and Seamus' seemingly real and painfully palpable reaction.

Seamus smiled modestly. "That wasn't due to any brilliant acting on my part. Cal really had a strong right hook."

Though Seamus was humble about his acting abilities, he wasn't modest about what he regarded as a new genre of masochistic films. As he talked, he became grandiose, comparing himself to the old-time hunger artists - the ones people would pay to watch starve themselves, just like in the Kafka story of the same name. The twist here, he told his roommates, was that people weren't watching some boring, slow-action starvation. Instead, these were fast paced videos of a man being brutally AND entertainingly beaten.

All this talk got B.J. excited. "Shay, your new direction is much fresh! Much fresher than those Rwandan and Oxfam snoozers. And way more fun to watch than Sally Struthers and Alyssa Milano balling their eyes out to that annoying 'Arms of an Angel' song."

"Actually," said Kyle "I think that had to do with animals dying in shelters."

"Who the fuck cares, Kyle?" she said. "My point is that all that over-the-top tear-jerking shit is a bore. But Shay's exciting and fun-to-watch beatings – man, these are good. There has got to be a way for us to make some money from them."

"Yeah," said Kyle, "But we've got to find a way for people to pay for our clips."

What did he mean "our clips"? thought Seamus. He was the only one who was literally and figuratively taking all the punches. But, what the hell: if he could make money somehow, he'd take Kyle and B.J. along for the ride, too. Besides, he and Kyle were short on the rent this month, so any money they could generate now would help.

Kyle did have a point, though. Seamus knew that they had to break through the age-old internet conundrum and find a way to monetize his shtick.

After they uploaded the train beating clip, Seamus said, "I think I know how to drive fans – and ad money – to our site.

He had them set up his video cam in their living room and let it roll. Seamus ranted against as many people as he could think of. His conscience wouldn't allow him to criticize racial minorities or women. Instead, he focused his venom on New Zealanders ("Aussie wanna-bes"), Prius drivers ("self-righteously slow drivers clogging the fast lane"), and Methodists ("a WASP-y denomination for serial adulterers").

When he was finished, they uploaded the clip, which he entitled, with mock pretension, "A Filmmaker's Manifesto."

Seamus then took a couple painkillers and headed for bed. He watched part of Salvador Dali's razor-blade-in-the-eye film in bed on his laptop for inspiration, before dozing off for the night.

VII
Thursday

It was early afternoon when Seamus woke up. Emotionally, he was starting to feel better now that he had an exciting project to work on. True, he found that he needed at least twelve hours of sleep to recover from each of his beatings. But his physical pain was a small price to pay - he was finally starting to get noticed!

To prove it to himself, Seamus went online and found thousands of new subscribers to his video channel and even more followers on Twitter. There were over two hundred links to blogs and other sites that mentioned Seamus' name and his work. Folks either loved him or hated him, but for the most part, the critiques on contemporary culture sites and cinema blogs were positive.

Some were even glowing. One writer spoke of Seamus Diamond's work as a post-modern snapshot into the zeitgeist of despair. Another self-proclaimed cultural critic described Seamus as a fetishistic iconoclast intent upon breaking down the fourth wall, "a luminous meme signifying cultural catharsis." A group of French semioticians and film theorists also took note: they wondered if Seamus Diamond was the true love child of Baudriard and Jean Luc Godard, a young man born with Foucault's pendulum around his neck. A German site named Seamus as the younger generation's latest meta-Lady Gaga of Suicide. The chatter on the blogosphere was not confined to esoteric sites either. By now, a few mainstream media outlets and aggregators were starting to pay attention too.

Just before sunset, Seamus walked out of the house and headed over to the Army & Navy store he frequented. Last night on the train, the over-zealous method actor had accidentally ripped Seamus' favorite sweatshirt in the melee. (Who knew, thought Seamus, that this average white man could reach down and find such rage deep from within?) After shopping and finding something he liked even better - a heavily discounted Trayvon Martin-themed hoodie with Skittles printed on the front - Seamus paid the clerk and walked out.

Immediately, he was accosted on the sidewalk by a flash mob of angry Methodists. Seamus knew they represented that denomination, not just because of their pale skin and drab clothes, but also because they marched to and fro with placards saying "Methodists' Lives Matter." The group of two dozen or so screamed and shook their fists and cellphones at Seamus. But, to his dismay, no one laid a finger on him.

Seamus realized that if he wanted more attention – and more ass-kicking - he'd have to up the ante; a few inept beatings and the occasional crotch kicking would not nearly be enough to keep Seamus Diamond's videos trending online.

When he got home he found Kyle and B.J. sitting together on the living room couch, engaged in parallel play as they each plugged away on their own digital devices.

Kyle looked up at Seamus and smiled. "You're blowing up, bro."

B.J. added, "Yeah, you're getting some major action on the socials."

"That's awesome." said Seamus, "And thanks, guys, for spreading the word. But now, my friends, I've got some BIGGER and BETTER ideas!" They were all ears. He told them to get the camera ready while he went to his bedroom to get dressed for the filming.

Seamus came out donning a fake beard (a relic of Halloweens past) and a robe, which he fashioned from an old sheet.

"I'm going to be speaking on camera as the Prophet Mohammed," Seamus told them.

"Mohammed?" B.J. laughed. "I thought you were supposed Fidel Castro." She reached into her purse and pulled out a Post-it note and wrote, "Hello, My Name Is: Mohammed."

Seamus stuck it on his robe.

With the camera rolling, Seamus as Mohammed intoned against infidels, specifically singling out Zoroastrians, Shakers, Quakers, and Confucianists. Then, departing sharply from the teachings of the Koran, he said that Jesus was an abomination to the holy ones. He attempted to prove that by twisting up all of Jesus' parables ("Then Christ fed his disciples with the body of Lazarus, lightly sprinkled with a couple dashes from the faith of mustard seeds. But, Jesus, who the hell eats a dead body – and with mustard seeds?") Finally he delivered what he called his "Spermin' on the Mount", which consisted of him masturbating to a makeshift cross.

When Seamus called "Cut!" Kyle and B.J. just stood there awestruck.

Finally Kyle piped up. "All I can say is - fucking brill!"

"You're downright sexy when you get dangerous like that," purred B.J.

B.J. calling him sexy – that was music to Seamus' ears. But the "dangerous" part? He reflected on what he'd just taped and immediately felt regret. The last thing he wanted was rioting and senseless murders because of this clip. Plus, that whole dressing up as Mohammed thing was getting played out. It had been done to death. Literally.

"Hold it," Seamus told them. Kyle paused the footage. "We can't use this, guys. This is wrong."

B.J. said, "But we can always C.G.I. the name tag and make this thing look older and more authentic."

Seamus shook his head and explained his reasons for not wanting the video to get out. Despite their protestations, Seamus stood firm. In place of the offensive Muslim gag, he suggested recording a rant against veterans of volunteer wars. The ones, he said, who feel entitled to free medical care and college grants. The ones who waste our tax dollars fighting elective wars which have nothing to do with protecting our freedom (unless one considers low-priced gas a "freedom.") The ones who actually make it more unsafe for Americans to travel around the world. These self-aggrandizing warriors, he said, cry that "freedom isn't free" while expecting military discounts, pats on the back, and Canadian style welfare. Seamus said that he'd read somewhere that if we cut only one seventh of the U.S. military budget, we could give free college tuition to every student in America, free health care to all its citizens, and feed every starving person in the world. And, he alleged, we'd STILL be spending more on defense than every other nation in the world *combined*. So, said Seamus, "we should draw down our overseas troops –"

"Woah, woah, woah!" screamed Kyle, "You can't say anything against our troops. That's like knocking, I don't know, disabled children or something."

"KYLE'S FUCKING RIGHT!" yelled B.J., "ARE YOU TRYING TO GET US ALL KILLED?!"

"No," said Seamus, "I mean, not *you* guys." Then he added, "Anyway, I don't really believe most of that stuff." He laughed; it was amusing to him to think that his personal beliefs had *ever* had any bearing on his rants.

Seamus said he had an even better idea. He ripped his beard and robe off and instructed his crew to let the camera roll. He improvised a long diatribe against "those child buggering Minnesotans and their Saskatchewan cohorts." Then came his critique of architects ("They're nothing but yellow dog embezzlers who dare to play God"), and finally a rant against "that saccharine pied piper of the 'Me Generation'" James Taylor.

They uploaded the clip and Seamus retired to his bedroom for the night.

But then Seamus tossed in bed, unable to sleep. Something was bothering him, and it wasn't just James Taylor. Nor was it the dull ache in his hand where he'd been stabbed in the park, though that still hurt. *Is this is what a stigmata feels like*? He was reminded of a pamphlet found on the subway once called "Touched by the Nail Scarred Hand." Jesus had died at what – age 33? Well, Seamus was now 32. So maybe he could get a head start on Christ, at least in the crucifixion department. Why not? This whole ass-kicking video thing was pretty tame in comparison to the shit the self-proclaimed Son of God allegedly had to put up with. But at least Jesus was famous. As for Seamus, nobody cared him and his films before; sure, he was now FINALLY getting some recognition, but only by getting assaulted and by insulting people who didn't deserve it. But if the only way for him to get some attention for his art was to hurt and to get hurt, then what the hell was the point?

Still restless, his thoughts turned again to ending the whole thing – both his filmmaking dreams AND his life. And to end it all in a BIG WAY. That gave him another killer idea, so to speak. He turned on a light, scribbled some notes in his notebook, popped a Sominex, and drifted off to sleep.

VII
Friday

Seamus woke up feeling good. Not being beaten the day before had allowed his body to begin to heal. He was still cut and bruised, but his chest no longer looked like a bruised banana. But what really helped elevated his mood was his epiphany last night. He opened his notebook to read his scribbling from the night before. Then he added more details to plan of death and world domination: Seamus would dare people to kill him and he'd go all over the city followed by cameras to film his assassination in real time. The "assassin cams" were to be posthumously edited into a pre-autographed video special collection box. Everything would be designed and edited according to his detailed specs.

Of course, the thought of the pain of ending his life in such a violent way scared him, but dwelling on the imagined finality of death also gave him a sense of peace. He knew he couldn't face living a long and unhappy *and* unsuccessful life, but he could at least hold on for a few more days.

Merely making the choice to be assassinated, however, did not mean that he could now just sleep through the gig. There was so much work to do! And, being the control freak that he was when it came to his craft, Seamus was determined to choose the time and place of his death. He knew he'd have to stir up enough "interest" – i.e. intense hatred – to get the job done. To do this, Seamus spent the afternoon responding to angry posts and laudatory Tweets. Then he gave a dozen interviews to bloggers and vloggers.

Seamus went out for a walk to do some thinking. But by now it was hard for him to walk around in public without getting spotted as an emerging internet celebrity. Some haters – mostly Minnesotans and Methodists – would yell at him. But most people, admirers and critics alike, simply mobbed him and asked for his autograph. And every would-be sadist and/or attention whore now angled to be in one of his videos.

He walked by the neighborhood bodega, the scene of the Dutch crotch-kick. Just the sight of the parking lot alone made his testicles ache. Toward the back, near a decaying Datsun pickup, he spotted an unkempt gentleman he'd seen many times before but never had really noticed. The gentleman had a cardboard sign with arcane and tiny lettering upon which he detailed his many conspiracy theories. The one that caught Seamus' eye (and he had to get up real close to read it) was a screed about John F. Kennedy. Apparently, the real "facts" were that JFK was actually assassinated by Nebraskan marijuana farmers who were opposed the gold monetary standard and were tired of being crucified on a cross of gold. This gibberish gave

Seamus an idea. He turned around to go home, nearly stepping on the poor gentleman.

When he got back he made a series of phone calls to custom car rental agencies. Then, he checked out the schedule online for all the farmer's markets in the metro area. He woke Kyle and B.J. up and instructed them to get the film studio – their living room, that is – ready, and to fire up the camera.

Once everything was set up, Seamus delivered another diatribe. This time he attacked those "lazy-ass" farmers, with their Farm Aid concerts, handouts, and Federal subsidies. He said they were "social parasites" who were paid not to grow anything, while spending their days running Nigerian-inspired online scams. Then he intoned against all the N.R.A. gun-toting closet cases who would "suck their own dicks if only they could find them."

Finally, Seamus made his big announcement: "This coming Sunday, on the 25th, I'll be hitting all the farmers markets in town – with my CAR. And the car you'll find me in will be a 1961 convertible Lincoln Continental, just like the one President Kennedy was shot in during that fateful ride in Dallas. Sure, the J.F.K. shooting was a major event, but, folks, this is the Big Apple! We can do assassinations bigger and better than that!"

He rattled off a list of all the groups he had previously denigrated (just in case they had forgotten), and then dared his audience to "awaken the homicidal giant within. Be a fucking man – or woman - and come take me out." He urged everyone to watch, too: there'd be cameras placed all around the vehicle and his assassination would be webcast in real time, from every possible angle. Seamus told his Web audience that watching his death, his public punishment, would be cathartic, and would undoubtedly lead to a more positive public discourse.

He insulted his viewers once again, and then thanked them for watching. "Make Kennedy proud and blow my mind like Oswald." He added, "Lee Harvey, not Patton."

When Seamus yelled "Cut!" his audience of two gave him a standing ovation. Kyle had two thumbs up.

B.J. smiled and turned to Kyle, "See! I told you Seamus is half-Irish, half-Jewish. And *all* genius."

VIII
Saturday

The next day was a whirlwind of activity. In the morning, the three of them cabbed it out to Sheepshead Bay to rent the Lincoln. They drove that boat of a vehicle home, cranking Brenda Lee tunes on its non-historically accurate 8-track tape player. To their amazement, they found a parking a spot on their block. There, they installed webcams and microphones throughout the cabin area, trunk, and hood, all designed to give a 360 degree view of the proposed murder in 5.1 surround sound.

When they got back to the apartment, Seamus storyboarded how the scene should go down. He walked his crew through several scenarios, taking into account a number of gruesome details, such as where his head would fracture and still stay in frame, depending on the caliber of the firearm used. Having spent his whole life in the States, Seamus had naturally envisioned dying by gunfire. But he tried to take into account other possible methods of homicide, such as knives, bombs, fire, electric shocks, and poison darts. And, with more and more people owning private drones for protection (and for other dubious reasons), he had to plan for death by drone too.

Seamus had specific ideas for the story arc. That's why he decided to prerecord his narration. He wanted the lighting to be perfect too – there would be no "60 Minutes"-style silhouettes in *this* film. Nor did he want the detritus of his brain and other exploding organs to be obscured by poor production values, like some drunken selfie. Seamus was also adamant that he did NOT want the stark lighting of Kyle and B.J.'s porn shoots, which he said made everyone look like they were copulating in an Arby's. So he gave Kyle his nearly maxed out credit card and sent the buttless man-boy to a lighting rental facility in Long Island City.

Their apartment was beginning to look like a campaign office or a war room, with maps and charts all over the walls. B.J. sat on the couch next to Seamus and got to work spreading the word of tomorrow's Filmmaker Assassination Day to every online media and social networking site she could find. Seamus sat beside her, concentrating on his narration script.

Suddenly his phone rang. It was Meghan. As in, Meghan the Flake. "Hey, Mr. Big Shot, it's me!" she said. "I've been watching you online and I've got to say WOW you've got bigger and brassier balls than I ever thought you had." She paused. "And…I was wrong, I just wanted to tell you that. You're not some two-bit film school dropout. You're really going somewhere with your life."

How Seamus had longed to hear her praise!

"Don't worry," she added, "I'm not going to try to talk you out of your big day tomorrow," she said, "Even though I don't really want you to die." Seamus' eyes misted. "But I know you well enough to realize that I can't change your mind once it's made up." He swelled with pride; what she said was true: he *was* determined, and more than a little bullheaded too.

"Shay, honey, I'm just wondering if I can come over so you can maybe interview me. You know, as Seamus Diamond's girlfriend, the one who knew him best."

A week ago he would've gladly had her over. But now Seamus had a sense of purpose. And he had too much self-respect to give in to her shit. "I'm sorry, Meghan," he said, "But I'm in the middle of something important."

"Oh, alright… but if you DO live, then promise me you'll come to see a scene I'm doing, OK? It's with your friend Cal."

"Cal?"

"You know, he said he was the Caucasian who beat you up on the train the other day. Anyway, it'll be at that stinky yoga joint & theatre in the East Village. Lots of people are showing new work there."

He remembered that Randy, one of the actors in his last short, had recently e-vited him to the very same performance. But, even if Seamus lived past this week, the last thing he wanted to see was another yam-in-the-ass performance art piece.

Seamus was about to decline, but luckily for him, another call came through. It was an unidentified

number but he didn't care. "Meg, I've got to take this."
He hung up with her and took the call. "Hello?"

There was a long pause. It sounded like a
robocall. Then he heard an officious voice: "This is T.
Eduardo Todd's assistant. Please hold for Mr. Todd."
Seamus waited. And waited. He was about to hang up
when T. Eduardo finally got on the line. The A-Lister's
voice was tinny, as if he was trapped in a bathysphere
somewhere 20,000 leagues under the sea. The famous
director obviously had him on speaker phone.

"Seamus Diamond, my friend!" T. Eduardo
said. "I've finally found you, bud! You're the man!
You're a legend, Chief!"

Seamus didn't know what to say. If his former
classmate and now Mr. Bigshot had called him even a
few months ago, maybe Seamus would have felt
different about talking to him. But now Seamus was
busy and was in no mood for Hollywood bullshitting.
"T, it's great to hear from you but –"

"I'm going on the record, brother," T. Eduardo
said, "That I always knew you were a genius! Bringing
a new voice to the ass-kicking genre?! That blows my
skirt up, Champ!" The famous man told Seamus how
he had been following Seamus' every move online. T.
Eduardo told him that, should he survive the
assassination tomorrow, he might get a deal with T.'s

new production company. "I'm expanding a little outside the remake/sequel genre, Scout, and I want to talk to you about a new project that maybe we can work on together: it's a film musical based on the comic strip *Broom Hilde.*"

Seamus had already heard about this ill-conceived project from a Hollywood bottom-feeder he knew, though he didn't want to mention that. All Seamus could say was, "That's why they pay you the big bucks." He wasn't kidding either: Seamus had read in the trades how T. Eduardo had earned $20M alone from "It's a Good Life, Bro", a sendup of "It's a Wonderful Life" in which an angel earns his wings by helping a teenage virgin get laid.

Just to fuck with the famous director before hanging up, Seamus pitched what he thought was one of the stupidest concepts ever. "I've got another one for you: it's a cross between 'Vincent & Theo' and 'Ocean's 11.'"

"Talk to me, talk to me."

"It's about two pickpockets who ply their trade in an art museum. After years of pickpocketing there, they learn to love art. The thieves then buy up all the paintings by some living artist and conspire to drive the price of her art up by killing her."

"Nice."

"And I'm thinking that, now that '80s lightweights like Michael Keaton are making a comeback, how about going bold and casting Judge Reinhold or Joe Piscopo?"

"That is sweet! You got it all, my man," said T. Eduardo, "Art *and* Commerce, Guns *and* Butter!" He added that he had the perfect choice for the artist too. "I'm buds with Xchecka, you know the artist with the buzz right now?"

"I don't think so."

"You don't? You've GOT to check her out, my friend. She paints real reproductions of famous works - like the one by that guy who did "The Last Supper" - except Xchecka gives it a modern spin by giving Jesus and the Apostles smartphone and painting Google glasses on the Mona Lisa. You know, to show how things would've been different back then if everybody had been wireless. How cool is that?"

Seamus rolled his eyes but all he said was, "Too cool for words."

"Let's hold that thought - I'm insanely busy right now, bro, so we'll have to take a rain check."

Seamus agreed and was just about to say goodbye when the line went dead.

He had just gotten back to work on his narration script when Kyle came running in and told him the exciting but terrible news: Kyle just heard that a man who was thought to be the "guerilla filmmaker and provocateur" Seamus Diamond had just been stabbed to death!

But Seamus, of course, was very much alive - though with any "luck" he wouldn't be around for long. He grabbed his boom box and tuned in to one of those "you-give-us-ten-minutes-we-give-you-the-world" news stations. The newscaster reported that the police had arrested a murder suspect in this apparent case of mistaken identity: some unhinged upstate farmer who'd happened to be visiting the city to watch the sixth revival of a 9/11-themed musical, had recently become obsessed - *and* incensed - by the incendiary words of "the controversial Mr. Diamond." The man killed someone he mistook for Seamus.

Silent Tammy, a former reality show star, had also taken credit for the murder. But authorities concluded that she was not connected to the killing or to Seamus Diamond, other than the fact that she had answered Mr. Diamond's Craig's List ad for an actress and that he failed to respond to her. The victim, Sebastian Ludwig, was described as a "chubby and uncoordinated" - a struggling musician who was on his way to Manny's to buy a guitar strap.

Seamus was horrified! This was exactly what he did NOT want to happen: some innocent person dying because of him. What in God's flippin' name had he done? How self-absorbed – no – selfish, he had become! When Seamus had made the decision to off himself, why hadn't he just done it quietly and in a place where no one else would have been hurt by his pie-in-the-sky plans of self-destruction? Why hadn't he'd just gone into his bedroom and quietly killed himself, maybe with the seeds of an organic apple or with a Japanese hand tool? Like in the old days, when the Greatest Generation ended it all without a big hoopla, *and* without trying to make some sort of statement. Christ, he wished he'd never bought into all this fifteen minutes-of-online-fame crap.

His phone rang again. This time it was Shannon. "Seamus, my God, I'm hearing some crazy things about you? Are you alright?!"

"Uh, yeah,"

"What is this I'm hearing about you trying to get yourself killed? Listen to me, Shay. I'm worried sick. And Christopher and Steve are worried too!" Her voice cracked. "Even Brenda, your retarded, I mean special, hottie is in tears. She's banging her head against the wall right now! Seamus, this is all a joke, right? Tell me it's a joke."

"Yes, Shan," he said. He wasn't lying, "It's all a sick joke. Anyway, I don't want any more people getting hurt. That's why I'm calling off my assassination."

B.J. and Kyle overheard Seamus and scowled.

"Oh, thank God," said Shannon.

"Sis, you don't have to worry about me." Seamus saw B.J. and Kyle waving their arms, trying to get his attention. "I'll call you back later."

No sooner had he hung up when B.J. yelled, "Were you joking?"

"Yeah, Seamus," Kyle cried, "What are you thinking? You're not really serious about calling off your suicide tomorrow, are you?!"

"Yes, I am," Seamus replied. He looked out the tiny porthole-sized window in the kitchenette. He thought of that hapless, dumpy musician who had died because of him.

"Seamus, goddamit!" Kyle angrily threw his moldy plate of pad thai against the wall. "We've rented the car and I just got the motherfucking lights! We've announced your death to the entire world and now you're making us look like flakes!"

"Kyle's one-thousand fucking percent right," said B.J. "This is *very* unprofessional!"

"And this," Kyle told Seamus, "Isn't all about YOU, you know." They watched the Thai food slowly drip down the wall.

Seamus ignored them. He went online and posted a news flash: due to the unspeakable tragedy that occurred today, he was indefinitely postponing his martyrdom. With regret, he wrote, his suicidal campaign would not resume until "the world is a better place."

B.J. and Kyle slumped on the couch and stared sullenly at Seamus. But fuck them, Seamus didn't care. Couldn't these two self-serving parasites understand that an innocent person had just been killed because of what the three of them had been doing? No, all these two cared about was getting ahead in the industry at all costs, and to hell with anyone else.

Having to look at these two amoral money-grubbing sphincters made Seamus realize he couldn't stand one more minute inside his apartment. So, without any further consideration, Seamus just upped and left.

Once outside, Seamus walked and walked, ambling aimlessly for blocks. He had no idea where he was going, but just knew he had to get away. Filled with rage and pumped on adrenaline, Seamus actually ran, something he hadn't done in years.

When he stopped to catch his breath, he discovered that he *did* have a destination after all. He'd go back to Central Park, near the duck pond, and maybe, with any luck, he'd find those thugs in the pedestrian tunnel who'd started this whole sordid mess. And, with still more "luck", they'd finish the job they started and put him out of his misery for good.

Seamus found The Tipsy Tramp, a liquor store on Second Avenue, and bought himself a fifth of cheap gin, the strongest drink he could afford with what little scratch he had left. He wandered over to the tunnel near the pond and looked around. There were plenty of sleeping Mallards, but no sign of the drugged out punks. He sat down, drank from the bottle, and waited. Still, they were nowhere to be found.

Wallowing in his alcohol-fueled self-pity, Seamus thought about his wasted life, his failures, and his family. His father was long gone, and his mother died three years ago, just after moving to a shithole

called Seward. What would they have said if they saw
him now? Seamus knew what his mother Maeve
would've said: "This is what happens when you're
doing your silly movies and not working a real job."
He laughed bitterly – as if the killing of an innocent
person today was the natural consequence of his
misguided directorial dreams. But, in a sense, it was.

Now he was really feeling the effects of the gin.
Seamus stewed about how things had now gone from
bad to worse. He railed that he had no friends, no
girlfriend, no parents, and no job. His already meager
savings had dwindled to 82 bucks. And his career?
What a joke. All the public wanted to see was Seamus
Diamond getting the shit kicked out of him. They
didn't want to see any of the 49 shorts he was really
proud of – films that touched upon larger themes that
interested him, like freedom, duty, guilt and
redemption.

He was feeling deep, existential pain so he
chugged down more liquor. Hang it all! There was no
point in living now. Why wait to be killed by some
nutty gunman or some freak like Silent Tammy? Why
not just drink until he blacked out? Hopefully, for him,
he'd die of alcohol poisoning - or choke on his vomit.
So he drank some more.

As he gradually lost consciousness, he began to
feel at peace. His resentment toward his mother,

Meghan, and Shannon started to fade, too. It wasn't their fault that they couldn't share his dreams. And though his dreams turned to shit, he realized that he'd done the best he could with his life. And now his life was just about over.

His thoughts turned darker, murkier, cloudier. He gasped, heaved, and upchucked. Then he drifted off into a numb unconsciousness, somewhere between sleep and death.

IX
Sunday

Seamus woke up twelve hours later to the blinding noon day sun. His clothes reeked of piss and vomit. His head was pounding from the booze and from sleeping on a concrete floor. But he was alive! *God,* he thought, *if you're out there, WHY?* Seamus squinted, looking towards the heavens. It must be a good omen, he thought. Maybe a sign from some belligerent deity that last night wasn't his time to go!

He noticed what a beautiful day it was: the air was crisp and the kaleidoscope of brilliant fall foliage was dazzling. He knew he still couldn't last much longer the way things were going, but, just for this *one* day, he felt alive, truly alive! Yes, it really was a sign: a signal from the gods for Seamus to get home. To get home and find that Lincoln, and drive and drive…all the way to his demise. From now on, he promised himself, there'd be no more senseless deaths, unless one counted his own. Look out world, Seamus said aloud, the director's assassination was on again!

With his feet bruised and blistered from yesterday's death march, Seamus limped over to the subway. He reached for his wallet to buy a token and found that it was gone. Someone must have rolled in him in his sleep. Oh well, he'd have to hoof it back home. By the time he reached the bridge, he was already out of breath, so he thumbed a ride.

In spite of his disheveled clothes and unkempt appearance, a man in a VW stopped to and invited Seamus to get in. Excitedly, Seamus told the driver all about his brush with death, his resurrection, how he planned to be murdered today, and that this time no one else would get hurt. After a few minutes of Seamus' excited talk, the driver had enough of this yakking and pretended to take a call on his mobile phone for the rest of the drive. Nevertheless, the man kindly dropped Seamus off at his apartment and, not knowing what else to say, told him, "Hang in there, man. Maybe you'll get lucky today and someone will kill you."

Seamus thanked the driver and the man sped off.

He ran inside and excitedly grabbed his video gear. That's when he noticed the sign on his bedroom door, written in Kyle's distinctive chicken scratch: "Dear Seamus, you've peaked. We've moved. Have a nice life."

Dammit! He'd have to manage the cameras himself. He ran downstairs and around the block to where he'd parked the car. Seamus got in, fired up the Wi-Fi, and went live with the webcams.

With the wind in his face, he barreled down F.D.R. Drive in the Lincoln convertible. "OK, folks," he narrated into the mic he'd mounted on the steering wheel. "I'm heading over to the farmers market in the Village. I'm ready, you bastards." He pulled a megaphone out of the back seat. "Come on all you candy-assed commie Cubans, you triple-murdering Texas Teamsters, and you lapsed, lap-dancing Catholics! I'm ready to be offed, J.F.K. style!"

Ten minutes later he reached the first farmers market. Unfortunately, nobody even noticed him. He drove around the square a few times before giving up and hitting the next one. Again, there was no assassin in sight. Not even a scowl or a frown or even a wave of acknowledgment. With his megaphone he yelled, "Hey, sissy farmers! Why don't you grow a set of balls and shoot me?"

Still, no one even bothered to turn around. He hit every market on his list, all with the same result: no one cared.

By the end of the afternoon, Seamus was crestfallen. He felt like crying. Maybe Kyle and B.J. were right: maybe he *had* peaked; maybe his fifteen minutes of virtual fame were over. Or maybe he'd never had his fifteen minutes to begin with. Sure, a few thousand people noticed him over the past week, but his videos had never reached the escape velocity necessary to go viral. He was worse than being a has-been – he was a never-was.

By the time he stopped at a red light on the West Side Highway, it was all over. His whole journey, quixotic as he now realized it had been, was all in vain. He had decided to give up his life for his art, for some amount of recognition, for a validation of his lifelong passion, only to find that nobody gave a flying fuck. Seamus broke down in a torrent of tears, the wellspring of 32 years of despair.

When the light turned green he remained hunched over the wheel sobbing and shaking. Horns honked, people yelled at him to move, but he was oblivious. Finally, a cop came by. The officer called for backup, and when the officers arrived, they pulled Seamus out of the car, his hands clutching the steering wheel for dear life. With lights flashing and sirens blaring they took him away.

X
Post Production

Seamus spent eight weeks in a psychiatric ward. There, they pumped him full of drugs, told him that "happiness is a road, not a destination", and made him join a 12-Step program.

He's been out now for four months. To better help in his recovery, he's joined an online support group for has-been and never-been celebrities. Twice a week, Seamus logs on and shares his experiences with a dozen other self-described "throw-aways", the jetsam and flotsam of our popular culture. He's since learned that suicide artists - those who kill themselves to highlight a cause or to get attention - are a dime a dozen. Rather than getting the huge media coverage they craved, their lives – and deaths – are mere digital blips on a virtual radar screen. Detritus in the dead links of cyberspace.

For now, Seamus finally has a paid gig that he enjoys: he's the Artist-In-Residence/Janitor in Shannon's group home. Seamus still has his ups and downs, but for the most part he's made peace with his life and with his art. He's knows now that he'll never quit. So long as he's got a video camera and a computer he's determined to make his films, and he doesn't care anymore if anyone watches. Well, actually he still does, but not enough to kill himself over it. Someday he'll go back to Central Park and finish his 50th short, and then who knows?

Late in the evenings, while the other residents are asleep, he works on new scripts for the more high-functioning residents. In the works: a new vehicle for Christopher and Steve, in which they'll play retarded brothers who inherit their dad's billion-dollar company and become Trump-like tyrants who make their employees kiss their special asses - or risk being fired.

Today, Seamus is filming the final episode of *Down's Up.* This time, Christopher and Steve's characters have flown to the Cayman Islands to investigate an alleged Ponzi scheme. They hug the suspect, Clogg Van der Dyke, a Dutch investment banker played by Brenda, and as they do, they surreptitiously rifle through her purse. Voila! The secret bank deposit book! Now they can track down all the ill-gotten gains and return them to the innocent investors. Shannon's even in on the act – today she plays the bank's VP, who, after a few gentle but insistent (and investigative) bear hugs from our heroes, breaks down and confesses that she's in thick with Van der Dyke, and that the two of them have been laundering money for years. The crowd of Cayman

Islanders, played by the rest of the residents, erupts in cheers as the villainess is taken away in handcuffs.

Seamus yells, "And cut!"

LOVE & OTHER HATE CRIMES

"Ladies and gentlemen of the jury, the evidence will show that Bubos Boutros, a proud and upstanding pillar of the taxi driving community, did not kill his passenger when -"

Kurt Planck was putting the finishing touches on his opening statement when the intercom rang. He picked up and heard that familiar crackle of static and gravelly coughs.

"I know you're busy," said Madge. "But –"

"Are there any messages?"

"Oh, nothing urgent, a Guy Moulton, wondering if we can settle his Mom's estate and –"

"Nothing from any of the witnesses we're trying to locate?"

"No, Kurt, but –"

"Well, thanks anyway."

"Kurt, I'm trying to tell that there's a news crew downstairs. They'll be mobbing you all the way to the courthouse so I thought maybe you want to go out the back way and I'll have driver ready for you." She was always on top of things. That's why Kurt kept her working there ever since he put out his shingle a quarter decade ago. That, and the fact that this chain smoking, crusty old woman was a kick in the pants.

"Thanks, Madge," said Kurt, "But it's ok." He took off his granny glasses and cleaned them with the flap from his crisp, white shirt. "I'll hoof it. I could use the fresh air. Anyway, I'll just 'no comment' it the whole way if I have to."

"Better leave now then. And, Kurt?"

"Yeah?"

"Good luck." He thanked her and hung up.

The quickest way to court was out through the front door and straight up Grant Street. He had exactly twenty-five minutes to get to the courthouse, go through security, and check in with the court clerk before the judge took the bench. He looked in the mirror, adjusted his tie, did a final trim on his salt and pepper beard, and was just about to bolt when he got another call. This time on his cell.

"Hi Daddy."

"Rachel! Honey, it's great to hear from you, but I've got to run, the trial's about to –"

"No, Daddy, this is important. PLEASE!" She was crying.

"What's what wrong, sweetheart?" Maybe she'd broken up with yet another boyfriend or gotten another bad grade. She was bright - a junior at Georgetown (his alma mater) and valedictorian of her high school class - but ever since she started her junior year she could never seem to focus on her school work.

"Daddy, I've...been taken, I mean, I've been kidnapped."

"What?! You've been what?!"

"Kidnapped, and they said -"

"Wait. Hold on. Is this a joke?"

"No, Daddy listen! They told me –"

"Kidnapped! Honey, are you okay?"

"Right now I am, but I'm so scared! These men who are holding me say it's about your trial. They have some demands."

"Demands?" Kurt was still reeling from an all-nighter going over testimony and writing his trial brief, so he was slow to process anything she was saying. But he could tell his daughter was in real trouble.

"Who's holding you?!" He put on his stentorian lawyer voice and demanded, "I want to speak to whoever's holding you RIGHT NOW!'

"No, Daddy! There's no time!"

Kurt heard the sound of struggle on the other end and a man's voice took over.

"She's right, there's no time," said the man, in a voice that sounded garbled. Kurt didn't know if the guy had some electronic effect on his voice, or whether he was just making that distorted sound with his mouth. "If you want to see your daughter alive," said the man, "You'll follow our instructions to a t."

"That's right," said another man, who sounded like he'd just picked up on another line. This guy's voice was lower. But it too was garbled. "And he means to a *Capital* T!"

Poor Rachel sounded terrified, so these guys couldn't be messing around. Yet the kidnappers both had dairyland accents – over-pronouncing their "R's," for example - that made their threats come across as comical. Kurt was in no mood for games - or comedy.

"Now, look here," Kurt said, "What the fuck is going on and who the fuck are you?!!"

"You can call me Mondale. And the other fella, just call him Humphrey. Got that pal? Now YOU look here. You do what WE tell you counselor. If you don't, or you go to the cops, or you tell ANYONE about this, then…" He made some sound Kurt couldn't make out.

"Wait, what was that?" asked the lawyer.

"Mondale, just made an 'I'm-gonna-cut-her-throat' noise."

"Understood," said Kurt.

"Yeah, well it *better* be understood, Counselor," said Humphrey. "We want your client to lose big time. We want him executed or at the very least, sent to the slammer for life. And it's got to be done by Thursdee, or Fridee at the latest."

"I can't -"

"And this is how you're gonna do it," Humphrey continued, "You'll conduct the lousiest legal defense in the history of this state."

"But I can't do that. No honest lawyer – "

"*Honest* lawyer?" Humphrey laughed.

"OK, no *real* lawyer would ever throw a case," said Kurt. "And there's no physical evidence tying Boutros to the crime. And he simply had no motive. "

"Don't try to lawyer your way out of this," said Mondale, "Or your daughter is toast."

Kurt could hear his poor Rachel, his only child, whimpering in the background. He shuddered to think of where she might be, maybe tied up in a crack house in Foggy Bottom, or bound in the back of a trunk and driven to some Midwestern hideaway. Or maybe she got kidnapped while visiting Minnesota or Wisconsin? He never knew these days where she'd be traveling or where she'd be calling from.

"So here's what's gonna happen," Mondale continued, "We will be monitoring your actions on their closed circuit TV. And we'll be texting you, so keep your phone on for your next instructions. At every court recess we'll call you and tell you what to say or do next. So don't be a big fucker, got it?"

"I want my daughter on the line right now!" demanded Kurt.

"Well you can't have her right now," said Mondale. "Let's just say she's *indisposed*."

"Remember," said Mondale, "You do what we tell you and she lives. Otherwise…." There was silence, followed by a low, guttural sound. He must have been trying to make another throat-cutting sound. Then the line went dead. Kurt tried Rachel's cell again, but it went straight to voice mail.

He walked to the courthouse a little faster than usual. Kurt was already pumped up for trial. Even after all his years of practice, he still got sweaty palms and butterflies in his stomach, though he didn't mind them – to Kurt, they just meant he was getting geared up for battle. Normally, he wouldn't have been nervous about trying this case or avoiding the press as he strode to court. But now, with his daughter's life seemingly on the line, his heart was pumping like when he was a young attorney going into a courtroom for the first time. As Kurt did a fast clip down the last few blocks he managed to stay a few steps ahead of a local newswoman who he recognized from a case a few years back when he successfully represented some molested Lutheran boys.

Kurt made it to the David L. Roth Justice Center and was just being strip-searched to get into the courthouse when his cell rang again.

"Sweetheart," said Kurt, in a whisper, "Is that you?" All he could hear were her muffled cries. He winced as one of the guards probed Kurt's anal cavity, looking for contraband.

It was Mondale. "Yes, it's me, my little fruit of my loom."

"Fuck you. I want to talk to my daughter."

"In time," said the kidnapper.

"Yeah, Sweetheart," added Humphrey, "Rome wasn't built in a frickin' day, you know?"

Kurt ignored him. "Rachel? Baby, listen to me-"

"No, it's still Mondale, my sweet Honey-Buns."

"Where is my DAUGHTER?!"

"Relax, little lamb chop," said Humphrey. "We gave her a sodee and a cheese stick and she's now sleeping like the dickens. She's all tuckered out from a long night last night, if you know what I mean –"

"Goddamit, now you listen here, if you hurt my daughter-"

"Now YOU listen here. Something WILL happen to your darling honeybee if Mr. Boutros is not found guilty. So you better skip your opening argument and let the D.A. get on with her case. And there will be no objections from you to the prosecution's witnesses."

"But I can't just *not* make an opening statement! And I can't just sit there and say nothing if the prosecutor's questions are out of line. It'll look funny. The judge will declare a mistrial if I don't."

"And if you let this go to a mistrial your little Rachel's dead."

There came the sound of struggle at the other end. Kurt thought that the two dairyland goons were fighting each other for the handset. Eventually, Mondale came on the line. "Alright, Fancy Lawyer Shorts, do your little statement to the jurors, but it better not be any good. Understand?"

There were more signs of struggle on the line. Humphrey came on and said, "Remember to leave your phone on – in silent mode – since we'll be texting you with suggestions while we watch along on the court's TV. We'll call you at the lunch break to rate how you're doing. And we'll give you a prognosis on whether your little angel's gonna live." The line went dead again.

Kurt took the steps up to Courtroom C32, a dingy, institutional looking room with fake wood paneling and no natural light. He checked in with the bailiff.

"Are both parties ready to try the case?" Bailiff Mary Carl asked. She was a tall and broad-shouldered woman with errant sprouts of facial hair. He said he was ready so long as the prosecution was ready.

If Kurt hadn't been so upset he would've laughed seeing the junior District Attorney they had chosen for the case. This was not the experienced D.A. who handled jury selection last week. This prosecutor was young, with a cheap, puffy, Supercuts hairdo that that made her look like a cross between the Bob's Big Boy hamburger icon and the imprisoned former Illinois governor Rod Blagojevich. The way she shuffled through her documents and dropped loose papers made her seem frazzled and unprofessional. When Kurt approached her side of the table and introduced himself, he noticed that she could barely speak English. Her name was Misty Van der Kloos. She was Dutch.

Kurt was well aware of the affirmative action policy at the D.A's office: as a white male he was unable to get hired there when he got out of law school, despite having graduated 2nd in his class. But in Kurt's experience, many of the affirmative action-hired lawyers were decent attorneys, despite their often limited English skills, and he certainly had no problem with giving a boost to historically oppressed minorities and women.

Still, Kurt wondered why someone from Holland would be considered a protected class worthy of getting a leg up. Maybe it has something to do with Holland's dykes, he mused. Or maybe Ms. Van der Kloos was transgendered. After all, her voice was low and her face was stubbly. Whatever she or he was, was fine by Kurt.

Still, the fact that the D.A.'s office would choose such a low-level prosecutor, who probably hadn't tried anything before except simple drug cases, to a murder trial signaled to Kurt that either they thought the Prosecution's case was a slam dunk, or that their case stunk.

To Kurt, it must have been the latter. The evidence against his client was circumstantial at best. And no one could even pinpoint a motive for the crime. Kurt was surprised that the D.A. had even gone forward with the trial and had not at least offered some sort of plea deal.

Not that Bubos Boutros would have accepted one. Mr. Boutros, a cab driver, had picked up the victim, Boris Putachev, a man with a criminal history and ties to the Russian mafia , at the airport one night.

Boutros drove the man where he wanted to go: a seedy part of town near the Coolidge & Taft projects. There, Putachev was shot and killed. The ballistics report confirmed that the bullet had come from outside the cab, where it had punctured the rear window before coming to rest inside Putachev's head. The bullet landed on the dashboard, next to Boutros, along with tissue from the victim's brain. Toxicology reports determined that the defendant appeared to have been drugged; when the police arrived at the crime scene the cabbie was found lying down on the front seat, with an unregistered firearm in his hand.

It was obvious to Kurt that some less-than-sophisticated mobsters had put a hit on Putachev and were trying to frame Boutros for it. That would explain why those geeky cheese heads who were holding Rachel right now were so insistent that the cab driver take the fall. Perhaps these goofballs' lives were in danger too and, fearing for their own safety, were forced into kidnapping Rachel. Or maybe the Russian mob hired Minnesota dweebs like this to avoid attracting suspicion.

After an hour or two of waiting around for the judge to take the bench (judges are typically fashionably late while they take personal calls in their chambers), Bailiff Carl ordered everyone to rise as the Honorable Britney Levine took the bench.

Judge Levine sat down, and, with a gunshot-like CRACK! banged down her gavel. Then she ordered the jurors in.

Ms. Van der Kloos began by presenting the State's case. She rambled on about what a scumbag Mr. Boutros was: he had fallen behind on his child support payments (when he was hospitalized following the shooting); he had committed two traffic violations in the last five years; and he was an émigré from Canada, a country Attorney Van der Kloos claimed to be on the U.S. terrorist watch list. Luckily for Kurt, the Dutchwoman didn't connect the fact that his client grew up in the Middle East before coming to Canada and eventually emigrating to the U.S. Naturally, Kurt was worried that the man's Arab roots might have further jeopardized his defense.

Ms. Van der Kloos then delved into her own unsubstantiated theories of the case. She told the lily-white jury that this man, a foreigner, had, by driving a taxi, taken away an American job. Kurt noticed that the fact that she was evidently also an immigrant - from a hash smoking, dyke-filling and windmill tilting country, and was undoubtedly a recipient of affirmative action - didn't faze her. But it hardly concerned Kurt either, who was used to his opponents making self-serving legal arguments. Or, what laypeople who have no knowledge of the law refer to as "lying."

All the same, Kurt couldn't believe how unprofessional and prejudicial the D.A.'s opening statement was. She opined on topics that were not supported by any evidence that the judge would allow the jurors to see. Then she went overboard by not only attacking Bubos but all "der suck scum cab drivers." Luckily for Kurt, Ms. Van der Kloos' thick accent and mangled English was almost impossible to understand. Hopefully, he thought, the jurors would have no idea what the hell she was saying.

"And so, lady and gentiles," she continued, "We're going to show how Master Boutros drove taxi and took away American jobs, and he owned a foreign car too, a Toyota –"

Kurt instinctively jumped up. "Objection, Your Honor!" In his mind, he practically had yelled that out, but his voice was naturally soft spoken, so he didn't sound out of line. That was one of his greatest assets in court – while most blowhard litigators spent their time loudly bloviating, Kurt rarely spoke more than he had to, and when he did, he came across as measured and reasonable.

Just then, Kurt received a text: "Do not object to that idiot or you know what will happen to your little schnookums…"

"Counsel," said Judge Levine in an annoyed tone, "On what grounds are you objecting?"

"What? I mean, pardon me, Your Honor?"

"Mr. Planck, what is the basis for your objection?"

"I'm sorry, Your Excellency," said Kurt, "The defense withdraws its objection." He quickly sat down.

Of course, Kurt had moral qualms about failing to give his client a good defense. But he rationalized that, not only would his silence save his daughter, but in the end, his client would get a new trial with a new (more effective) lawyer, once Rachel got released.

The Prosecution aka "The People" brought out its first witness. He was a man known simply as "Pappy" and he claimed to have no last name. Even on Van der Kloos' direct examination, this alleged eyewitness admitted that his eyesight was weak from glaucoma and his memory hazy from the cannabis brownies and crème de menthes he'd ingested on the night of the attack. Nevertheless, Pappy testified that from his apartment window on the 12th floor of a building a couple blocks from the crime scene, he saw a yellow cab and a taxi driver. He claimed he saw someone throwing out something that could have been a body bag.

But then Pappy revealed that what he allegedly saw actually occurred two days before Putachev's murder. Still, Ms. Van der Kloos opined to the jury that the prior incident shed light on the defendant's *modus operandi* of probably dozens of other unreported murders. Pappy offered, without being asked, that he was glad that someone believed him, since he had a string of priors, including convictions for fraud and perjury.

When it came time for cross-examination, Kurt was about ready to destroy this witness. That is, until he got the kidnappers' text: "If you ask anything more than what kind of marijuana he uses, your little Honey Bee is dead."

"Counselor, you may proceed on cross," the judge instructed.

Kurt sauntered up to the witness. "So, you stated that you use medicinal marijuana. Is that correct?"

"Yes, Sir" replied Pappy. He wore dark glaucoma med-specs, the kind you get from the eye doctor after they squirt pupil dilating solution into your eye. He looked like a senior citizen from a '1970s New Wave band; a guy who would burst into singing "My-My-My- My Sharona" at any moment.

"What type?" asked Kurt.

"What type of marijuana, sir?"

Kurt nodded.

"Well, sometimes I like Train Wreck, sometimes I toke Hindu Kush, Green Whacker, Sour Diesel, and even Supreme Barry White, when I can get it, and I also like –"

"Thank you. I have no further questions." Kurt sat down. Bubos gave him a quizzical look.

The prosecution then brought its next witness, a former immigration supervisor from the Transportation Security Administration. Field Officer Barbi Spaccia testified that Mr. Boutros was probably an illegal alien who had overstayed his Canadian visa, since he failed to produce his passport to police on the night of the incident.

"In der opinion, T.S.A. Spaccia," Ms. Van der Sloot asked, "Do North American illegal immigrants make more crimes during trade tensions between the U.S. in A and her Canada country?"

Planck was about to jump up and object to this unbelievable leading, prejudicial and compound question. And he was also about to move the court to strike Ms. Spaccia's testimony from the record since her opinions lacked any foundation as to how Spaccia would have specialized knowledge of crime statistics or trade matters. Kurt also wanted to add that the record should reflect that his client was a naturalized American citizen, not an illegal alien. But then he felt a vibration his pocket and reached in to view the text: "Sit down, counselor, or your little Sugar Tits gets it in the foot."

Ms. Spaccia answered the D.A.'s question. "Yes, in my experience as an officer AND as a single mother of two small children, I know that Canadians commit 75% more crimes in the U.S. when there are trade tensions at the border."

"Are der trade tensions at border?" Van der Sloot asked. Of course, Kurt could've objected to this question as well, but he bit his tongue.

"From my regular and uninterrupted viewing of Fox News," the witness responded, "No other reasonable conclusion can be drawn."

"So, in opinion of you, Mizzy Spaccia, would der Butroz defendant have been more likely or less likely to commit very bad murder like he does during dis period of trade tensions?"

The judge looked at Kurt, expecting him to object. Instead, Kurt only shook his head.

"He'd be more likely to commit murder," answered the witness. "82.3% more likely."

After a few hours into the State's case, the court took a short recess. Kurt's client confronted him. "What's going on?" Bubos asked. "Why are you letting these clowns go on and on making these outlandish statements?"

Kurt had no good answer. But he was skilled attorney and was trained to at least make something up, or, as they say in the law biz, "thinking on your feet."

Kurt told Bubos, "Because, letting these fools speak only shows that we don't take these kinds of unsubstantiated allegations seriously, and neither should the jurors. Let's just give the prosecution enough rope and let them hang themselves." Bubos didn't argue with his lawyer, though, he still looked confused and fearful. "Besides," Kurt added, "Wait until you tear into them when I put you on the stand."

"You're really going to let me testify?"

"Of course," said Kurt.

Bubos was now beaming.

In the weeks before trial he had been insistent upon taking the stand in his own defense. As any defense attorney knows, that's a risky move which can open up a can of worms during cross-examination. But Bubos was adamant that he wasn't guilty and that he had nothing to hide. He was dead-set on waiving his Fifth Amendment rights in order to show the jurors that, despite his time in Canada, he was a loyal citizen of the United States. He wanted the jury to see him as he saw himself: a simple man just trying to scrape out a living for his family by driving a cab. And, he wanted the jurors to understand that he didn't know Putachev and certainly had no reason to kill the man.

Significantly, at least from the defense's point of view, Putachev had not been robbed. In fact, the police and the coroner discovered that the victim still had several thousand dollars in cash in his wallet as well as thousands more in two body cavities at the time of his death. Given the victim's criminal background, the defense's view was that Putachev's death was clearly a mob hit and, and Bubos had no history of any involvement with organized crime.

The prosecution's next witness was Richard Richards, an organizer for a Canadian solidarity group. He testified that, two decades ago, while they were both students at the University of Toronto, Mr. Boutros assisted Richards in a "Buy Canadian, Not American" school campaign.

"But isn't der United States the protector and close ally of Canada country?" Ms. Van der Kloos asked the witness.

"Sure," replied Richards, "But – "

"And," Van der Kloos continued, "Doesn't Canada exist because of the kindness of her American peoples and her top-shelf government?"

"Well," said Richards, "I don't know if –"

"What you mean you don't know?!" She theatrically cocked an eyebrow. "Master Richard are you terrorism itself?"

"No, ma'am."

"Thankee. No further questions," said the Dutchwoman. She sat down.

Kurt rose. "Your honor, I have a few questions for the witness." Then he looked down to see his cellphone vibrating with an incoming text, saying "No! You have no questions! For your Sweet Pea's sake."

"Actually, your Honor," Kurt said, "I have no questions." Kurt sat back down. The witness was excused.

Bubos gave Kurt a look that Kurt knew from twenty years of trial work meant, "Why didn't you rip that witness a new one on the stand?"

To underscore his point, he whispered in Kurt's ear, "You're supposed to be my lawyer. Why didn't you rip that dick-fuck a new asshole?"

Kurt sought to reassure his client. "Now, Bubos," he told him, "Who's going to be swayed by some pro-Canada thing you did years ago?" Actually, Kurt knew that there were enough xenophobes in the City of Seward that some folks could conceivably be biased. Why, the civic leaders were wary enough of North Dakotans or Episcopalians, to say nothing of our "dark neighbors from the north," as the local newspaper regularly referred to British Columbians. Some of these pinheads were probably on the jury right now, despite his best efforts to get rid of them in voir dire.

But the last thing Kurt needed was to tell all that to Boutros and have a scared client. Kurt had learned years ago that not only was it impossible for frightened clients to work effectively with their lawyers, but juries and the media tended to view scared defendants as cowardly - and therefore guilty. If a defendant is really innocent, the thinking goes, then he or she has nothing to be scared of. On the other hand, if defendants look too relaxed in court - like they could cut this gig by phone - jurors view them as hardened criminals. Sometimes you couldn't win either way, especially when the victims were white and their families were allowed to caterwaul on the stand about how much they miss their dead little Caucasian. Kurt knew that it was much easier to get a defendant acquitted if the *victim* was a minority; though in Seward those kinds of crimes seldom made it to trial.

D.A. Van der Kloos next brought Raskolnikov Avilov, an expert witness to the stand. Mr. Avilov, an online professor of communications at the University of Phoenix, claimed that there was currently an epidemic of crimes in Canada against Russian nationals, and that this particular murder seemed consistent with this anti-Russian animus.

Planck was almost forced to do a cross-examination by the angry look of the judge; whereupon he got Mr. Avilov to acknowledge that he was paid by the prosecution to testify and that he did not know any of the particulars of the alleged crime in question.

Avilov also admitted that last year he had been a paid expert for the defense in a famous case involving a school shooting – this time by a teacher, not a student; the teacher had become a darling of the right wing media because she was a political conservative. She had blamed the teacher's union for making her snap, and in the process wounding several teachers and middle school students. The teacher was ultimately acquitted and the jury's verdict had been extremely controversial.

During Kurt's questioning, Avilov also conceded that the Russian mafia was active in Seward. The witness allowed that Putachev's death could have been caused by any number of Russian mobsters to whom, it had been established before trial, he owed money.

Kurt was pleased with the testimony and his performance until he sat down to the defendant's bench to see a text which read "That's enough of the smarty pants lawyering. Alive Daughter = Shut the Fuck Up, Counsel."

Next, the Dutch D.A. trotted out Olga Levechev, a self-proclaimed expert in the field of cabbie-on-rider violence. In Ms. Levechev's view, which she said was backed up by her research in the Cayman Islands and by repeated viewings of the movie *Taxi Driver* ("I spent years examining its meta-text"), cabbies are five times more likely to kill than members of any other profession. Even dentists. And when cab drivers kill, which Ms. Levechev said almost a third of them do at one time or another in their lives, 97.4% of the time they kill their passengers. When D.A. Van der Kloos finished her direct examination, Planck declined to ask anything of Ms. Levechev on cross.

Immediately, he received a text saying "Good job. Keep it up counselor @ # Keep Rachel Alive. Ha ha."

After four days of this grueling testimony, it was finally the defense's turn to bring its case. But somebody – perhaps Rachel's kidnappers or their mafia bosses - managed to scare away all Boutros' witnesses. Judge Levine put out a bench warrant to locate all fourteen of the subpoenaed witnesses, but none were found before the end of the trial.

Reluctantly, Kurt put his client on the stand. Boutros told the jury that twelve years ago he had become an American citizen; that he had always treasured his citizenship, and that he had endeavored at all times to be a good American. He testified that he'd never seen Putachev before. Boutros said that he had stopped at an ATM at the victim's insistence, whereupon the cabbie walked over to the gas station to urinate. By the time he'd cleaned up some dried feces off his shoes (the men's room was at a Shell station) and got back to his cab, he felt a sharp stab to his neck. Then he immediately blacked out. The next thing he knew, he told the jurors, he was in the hospital. All he could recall about the Putachev was that the man seemed nervous and agitated. And the victim had mentioned to Boutros several times on that fateful night that he was certain that criminals were following them.

Boutros was about to go into detail about the drive that led to the ATM, a drive that included getting side-swiped by two cars along the way. But Kurt's cellphone – which he had left back at the counsel's table - started to vibrate like crazy. The phone rocked back and forth and looked like it was going to explode. Then, in a booming sound that seemed far out of proportion to the phone's size, it fell on the floor with a SMACK!

There was a long, silent pause in the courtroom, before Judge Levine slapped down her gavel so hard she broke its handle. Then she fined Kurt $1,000 for having his cellphone on in court and to replace the cost of her gavel. Then the judge adjourned the court for a half hour when her own cellphone rang and she took a social call from her son.

Thus ended Kurt's direct examination. Misty Van der Kloos attempted to cross-examine Boutros, but because of her poor English language skills and his thick Middle Eastern-meets-Canuck accent, neither could understand the other. Luckily for Kurt, Boutros' cross-examination ended after twenty minutes and without him saying anything damaging to his case.

Had Kurt been able to do his lawyering on all cylinders, he would have laid into Misty's rebuttal witnesses, two police officers, for their bungling of forensic evidence, such as not taking the accused's blood sample after he told them he'd been drugged. And Kurt would have pilloried the policemen for ignoring evidence that the victim was a known member of the Russian mafia; a man whose life had recently been threatened by other mobsters. And Kurt would have introduced into evidence the fact that Mr. Boutros had no prior criminal history and no motive to kill his passenger.

Instead, Kurt was forced to sit on his hard, wooden bench and listen to the barely coherent D.A. as she let the officers ramble on.

Next, Van der Kloos brought a jailhouse snitch to the stand. The only positive outcome, from Kurt's perspective, was that each of the prosecution's witnesses offered differing, but equally illogical and mutually inconsistent theories as to why Boutros allegedly committed the crime.

And so it went for the rest of the trial. For the next two weeks - which easily would have stretched to four weeks had Kurt been able to conduct an effective defense - he looked like a fool in court. And his incompetence was on display in front of an ever-growing audience on Court TV. Planck's ineffectiveness and inattention to the court's proceedings, his failures to probe the gaping holes in the prosecution's case, his withdrawn objections - all of his bungling went viral. Millions of people around the country (and in China, where the government had made the trial an example of the corrupt American judicial system) were now watching to see what this imbecile of a lawyer would do next to hurt his client's defense. Though Kurt had tried to tune out the media chatter, he knew that he was becoming the butt of jokes not just by local folks, but now by late night TV comics.

After the first week of trial, even Judge Levine called both attorneys in to her chambers to ask Kurt if he was feeling alright. The kidnappers made sure they could hear the exchange by requiring Kurt to stay connected via his carefully hidden phone. Kurt told the judge (with one eye on the incoming text: "NO FUNNY BUSINESS!") that he felt perfectly fine. He added that an unorthodox case like this requires an unorthodox defense. The judge gave him a stern look and said that, as an observant Jew, she would not tolerate anything unorthodox in her courtroom. Kurt looked up at the judge to see if she was joking. She was not.

Meanwhile, back in his holding cell, Bubos was fuming. He'd been told that Kurt Planck was the best lawyer in town. But if Planck is the best, how bad can the worst be? Even that nitwit clog-wearing prosecutor was out-classing his lawyer. And why was his good-for-nothing high-priced suit of a lawyer spending so much time texting instead of paying attention in court?

Kurt was aware that Bubos was rapidly losing confidence in him. That's why, at the next court recess, Kurt pleaded with the kidnappers to curtail their all-too-frequent texts. This constant real-time critiquing of his performance by Mondale and Humphrey after each objection he made, or each cross-examination he dared to undertake, was so distracting that his incompetence could make the jury sympathetic to his client, Kurt said. Mondale and Humphrey were somewhat persuaded: they agreed not to communicate as often, if only to prevent Kurt's client from walking.

But only an hour later, during a break where Kurt ran to take a dump in the stall-less and vandalized men's room, the kidnappers called again. While Kurt sat there with his pants down, politely doing his business, they put Rachel on the line. She gave her dad a quick hello, and then threw him for a loop by asking his advice about some small claims case she was involved in - some nonsense about suing her ex-boyfriend to return her undergarments. Of course, he loved to hear his daughter's voice, but he wondered why Rachel would call him with some problem that was completely out of left field when there were more serious *and* life threatening matters at stake. Maybe she too just wanted to hear his voice?

Kurt offered whatever legal advice he could in connection with the small claims suit: save all your receipts and emails and everything that can prove that the underwear was hers. When Mondale took back the phone, Kurt grumbled to him that these irrelevant distractions were taking his mind off this most-important trial. Furthermore, they were making him look even more scatterbrained and unprofessional.

Mondale disagreed. "I don't think you look nearly stupid enough."

"What do you mean?"

"You don't look dumb enough *yet* to ever see your little lollipop again." Mondale hung up, leaving Kurt with his pants down searching for some toilet paper. As is usually the case in courthouse bathrooms, he found none. Luckily, someone had left a sweatshirt on the floor so he grabbed it and used it to finish his business before getting back to the courtroom for the next session.

At five o'clock sharp, the judge ended proceedings for the day, leaving Kurt to pick up his briefs and head to his office, while his client was escorted back to his jail cell for the night.

On the first week of trial, only a half dozen people, mostly print journalists, would be outside waiting as Kurt exited the courthouse at the close of the court's session. Gradually, though, more and more news crews came and joined with the ever-growing crowd of demonstrators, counter-demonstrators, and court junkies. It was a madhouse to get in and out of the security gates. And as Kurt walked from his office to the courthouse each morning, he was stung by their jeers. There were scores of Pro-Canada demonstrators, who chanted "Justice for all and not the few, America's courts are kangaroo" as well as "Canucks Go Home" counter protesters. And there angry looking Russian women carrying signs saying "Bubos Killed Boris." Kurt mused that if they weren't pro-prosecution picketers, perhaps they were Black Plague conspiracy theorists.

The circus-like atmosphere surrounding the trial, along with Kurt's daily public humiliations, made his job especially miserable. Throughout the years, he had often defended the legal system to its critics (which included Rachel) by saying that, while the system may imperfect, it's still the best one we have.

But these days he'd wake up every morning disillusioned, thinking how much he'd rather be doing a million other things than practicing law. That's why, he told Madge, he couldn't wait for the trial to end so that he could go back to building and flying ultra-light aircraft and playing guitar, just two of his favorite pastimes. Tossing and turning in bed each night, Kurt realized that, not only was this trial by far the worst one he'd ever worked on, but his enjoyment of the practice of law was rapidly eroding. And so was his respect for Seward's judicial system.

At last the time came - and not a moment too soon - to conclude the trial. The D.A. gave her closing arguments, holding the floor before the rapt jurors for over two hours. In her barely comprehensible syntax, she reiterated what little evidence she had found that she could twist around to make Kurt's client look like a fanatical terrorist and sociopath.

As to Kurt's closing argument, the kidnappers didn't want him to give one. He prevailed on them, though, by saying that failing to give a closing would undoubtedly trigger a mistrial, which the kidnappers didn't want. As a compromise, Mondale allowed Kurt to make the closing argument, provided he wear the striped suit he'd worn years ago when playing the lead in a local revival of *The Music Man.* (Was poor Rachel tortured to reveal the existence of that costume?)

In the end, Kurt, decked out in his garish garb as "Professor" Harold Hill, did a weak summation of the case, noting that while "my client may be bad, he's probably not THAT bad."

As expected, the jury took only a few minutes of deliberation to read its verdict: Bubos Boutros was guilty ("with a capital G", the forewoman noted) of murder in the first degree. The forewoman apologized to the judge for taking as long so long to deliberate.

"We reached our verdict in a matter of seconds," the juror told the visibly pleased judge. "So we spent most of the time discussing whether the defendant's counsel could also be found guilty."

The judge smiled one of her mirthless smiles. She excused the jurors, thanking them for taking the time out of their lives to perform such an honorable duty. (In truth, none of the jurors were self-employed, so they were thrilled to be paid by their companies to just sit there and to receive their per diems and the free lunches that were the perks of jury duty.) Judge Levine adjourned the proceedings and set the sentencing hearing for the following day.

Kurt could barely look Bubos in the eye when he assured his client that they would appeal. Bubos was led away in cuffs as he alternated between screaming, "It's an injustice! An injustice!" and singing "America the Beautiful."

Hoping to avoid the dangerous crowd, but still attempting to keep some semblance of dignity, Kurt dashed out of the courtroom. Once outside, he practically ran to his office.

Kurt had just plopped down at his desk and rolled up his sleeves when Mondale called. Without much enthusiasm, Mondale congratulated him for the outcome of the trial and for following instructions well. Then he put Rachel on. Her voice cracked with emotion as she thanked her father for saving her life. Kurt did his best to hold back his own tears.

Then Humphrey grabbed the phone. "Counselor, or should I say Music Man, ha hah, your little doll face won't be playing 'Seventy Six Trombones' any time soon."

"What does that mean?

"It means, your little Rach- Rach isn't out of the woods yet."

"WHAT?!"

"There's been a change of plans. If you want to see Rachel again you better make damn certain that Boutros gets the death penalty."

"But that's impossible," said Kurt. "The prosecution didn't even ask for that. That means that the most my client could possibly get is life imprisonment."

"Don't give us any of your legal mumbo jumbo," said Mondale, "We want that bastard to fry in the electric chair."

"We don't use the electric chair here," said Kurt. "We're more 'civilized', I if you want to call it that: we're a lethal injection state." He loosened his tie, a noose that felt like it was slowly tightening around his neck. "The only way capital punishment could happen is if the judge declares a new trial AND the D.A. reinstates her charges to include the death penalty."

"Let's get this straight, counselor," Mondale said. "We don't care if it's the firing squad, the guillotine, or death by chocolate. Just make sure that dang cabbie is killed!" Kurt heard his daughter moaning as the kidnapper hung up.

Kurt immediately got to work that night preparing an *ex parte* emergency motion. He didn't have much hope, but he'd do his best to convince the judge to throw out the verdict and declare a new trial. In support of his motion, he argued that the jury had been erroneously allowed to hear prejudicial statements from so-called eye witnesses about Canadians. Furthermore, he argued, the prosecution should never have brought its unqualified "expert" to testify about violence committed by cabbies. Finally, Kurt cited case law that shielded cabbies from disclosing their past criminal history as persuasive authority.

Bright and early the next morning, Kurt filed his motion. Unfortunately, Judge Levine arrived two hours late and appeared to have woken up on the wrong side of the bed. Without apologizing for making everyone wait, she said she had been in her chambers talking to her son on the phone. All the ass-kissers in court smiled at the judge. Whatever she and her son had talked about had apparently made her even more cantankerous than usual.

Levine glared at Kurt as he made his argument, covered her ears to avoid listening to more, and, in one swift hit of her broken gavel, denied the motion. Judge Levine further admonished Kurt by adding: "Mr. Planck, you are a loose cannon, a pool without a fence. And right now, counsel, you're a ship out of water."

D.A. Van der Kloos, at first slow to pick up on the judge's mixed metaphors, turned to give Planck a smug grin. Then she piled it on. "Your High Holiness, is it der court's belief that Mr. Kurt is now a boil on these judicial buttocks?"

Judge Levine let out an uncharacteristically genuine laugh and nodded her head.

Kurt was exasperated. All he could think of was his poor Rachel being killed by these Minnesota goons! Fast on his feet, Kurt made a motion for a mistrial.

"On what grounds?" intoned the judge.

"Uh, Your Honor, I'd be happy to lay out our argument. But can I just ask for a short recess to confer with my client?"

The judge reluctantly agreed, and gave him fifteen minutes to be back in the courtroom. "Otherwise," she said, "You better bring your toothbrush because you'll need it when I send you to the Big House." This was a common threat by jurists to lawyers, but usually made to first-time lawyers in court.

Kurt thanked the judge. But instead of conferring with his client, he took his phone into the restroom to wait for the kidnappers' call. He expected that they would have watched the denial of a new trial on TV and would undoubtedly have something to say about it.

He didn't have to wait long.

The phone rang and Mondale was on the line. "So, Mr. Clarence Darrow, what do you have in mind now to save your poopsy-doodle's life?"

"I'm sure you've heard that I've made a motion to declare a mistrial," replied the lawyer. "I know you didn't want that, but this is the only hope we have left to get a new trial and the death penalty."

"Alrightee then. On what grounds are you asking for a mistrial?"

"What grounds? I don't know yet. Maybe there was some juror misconduct."

"Well," said Mondale, "That redheaded Juror Number 8 was criminally beautiful. Does that count? Heh-heh!"

Planck had grown to hate Mondale's Midwestern humor, particularly when so much was at stake. But he tactfully ignored the joke. Kurt scratched his head.

"Wait, I've got it!" he said.

"Hey," said Mondale, "Our Johnny Frickin' Cochran just got his first idea." Kurt heard Humphrey laugh. He thought he even heard Rachel laugh too. But surely that was just a figment of his imagination.

"OK, here's what I'll do, I'll fall on my sword; I'll declare my own incompetence. I'll say I'm impaired – I don't know, mentally ill, or something. And then I'll remind the judge about every wrong move I made during the trial."

"And that'll take days, let me tell you," added Mondale, with a corny Midwestern guffaw. "Don't forget to tell Grinch Levine that you've fallen madly in love with Juror Number 8."

Humphrey got on the line. "Hold on, counselor. This hogwash won't work. All you'll get, even if you're lucky, is a new trial. That'll just get you the same result. What you need to do is make the judge and the D.A. hate you and Bubos enough to re-charge him with the *death penalty*. So you just make darn sure you piss off EVERYONE."

When Kurt re-entered the courtroom, that's exactly what he did. He was rude to the bailiff and flipped off the D.A. When Judge Levine took the bench, he refused to call her "Your Honor." Instead, he called her "Judge", which, for some unknown reason, judges hate. Kurt told the court that he'd been incompetent and that he'd given ineffective counsel. When the judge told him to be more specific, Kurt, with a pained face, was forced to recount every bone-headed move, every lapse in judgment, and every verbal blunder he'd made throughout the two week trial.

Then the judge ordered Kurt to turn around, face the court's cameras and repeat to the packed courtroom everything he had just said. With a red face, he did so. She then had him stand in a corner with his nose to the wall, while the judge asked the defendant whether he agreed with Attorney Planck's assessment of his own incompetence. Bubos said he not only agreed, but did so wholeheartedly. Bubos added that he could come up with at least a dozen more examples of Planck's malfeasance, but the judge said that wouldn't be necessary.

In the judge's effort to appear to be fair and impartial (she was up for re-election this year) she rubbed her hands together and pretended to consider Kurt's motion. Then, after a short pause, she summarily ruled against him. She noted that while Planck's conduct was unprofessional and bizarre, it was not enough to overturn the verdict. Then she ordered monetary sanctions in the amount of $50,000 against Kurt to "deter him from bringing further unmeritorious motions before this court." Pursuant to court rules, any sanction of $10,000 or more had to be reported to the State Bar, so Kurt was forced to disclose his judicial spanking.

Kurt was angry, but hardly surprised. He knew that the judges in Seward were becoming sanctions crazy in order to raise money for a new courthouse. But he didn't care about the money, he cared about Rachel's life! Kurt was frantic. He desperately needed to find a way to free his daughter, but he'd run out of options. Sure, he could appeal the decision. But even if he won, that could take months, even years for a new trial. And the kidnappers had made it clear that Rachel didn't have much time.

As he fretted, Humphrey called to say that Kurt had only a couple more hours left before Rachel would be "erased." Before he could say anything, Humphrey hung up.

Kurt walked back to his office to think, but he couldn't sit still. With Rachel's life hanging by a thread and with no clue as to how to save her, he paced the floor and wrung his sweat-drenched hands. What was going on?! He'd done everything these dairyland assholes told him to do and still they wouldn't release his daughter. He was used to dealing with clients with unrealistic demands (like the client who wanted him to sue the police to get his "8-ball" of cocaine back), but Rachel's kidnappers were on a whole new level. He wished law school had prepared him to deal with idiotic, but dangerous, goons who kidnap your only child.

It was horrific for him, facing this ordeal alone. But Kurt was glad that Rachel's mother hadn't lived to see their child in danger. He was also glad that he and Kay had finally made peace with each other years after their divorce, and not long before the plane crash that killed her three years ago.

He felt fortunate, too, that in the two years since Rachel started college, her bitterness toward him - she had long viewed as a workaholic and absent father - had subsided.   Last year, they began Skyping each other every Sunday; Rachel was just as likely as he was to initiate the call. Though Kurt worried about her safety, living as she did in a sketchy area off of Capitol Hill, he was pleased that Rachel wasn't the rebellious party girl and shit-starter she once was.

Though her grades this year had been spotty (she had taken an internship at a TV station, which took up almost all her free time) her overall GPA was good. A few months before the trial she had told her dad that, after graduation, she was even thinking of law school. Kurt was happy to hear that, though he was surprised. He had great faith in his daughter's intelligence and her ability to be successful in any field she chose. But he worried that her black-and-white thinking and moral indignation would be a liability in a profession in which its practitioners looked for gray areas and loopholes and were averse to any facts which could not be twisted. That's why Kurt tried to dissuade her from law in favor of other professions, like marriage and family counseling, for which he felt Rachel was temperamentally better suited. When he gave her example after example of how the quality of the legal system had markedly declined in the past 25 years. Rachel countered with the obvious response: if the system is so bad, why are you still a lawyer? Kurt couldn't recall his answer, but his explanation didn't make much sense to her or even to himself.

Now, as Kurt sat in his oversized chair at his oversized desk, squeezing a stress reliever ball while impatiently waiting for Humphrey or Mondale to call, he didn't give a damn what career Rachel chose. He just wanted her to be happy and SAFE. He buzzed Madge. "Any messages?"

"No, Kurt, like I told you, I'll let you know if it's something important."

"But I just saw a call come in."

Madge coughed and wheezed. "That was just some crazy lady who wants a free consultation. Something about her son getting mixed up in some internet thing with a Congressman. Like I said, I'll buzz you if it's urgent."

"Thanks, Madge."

He hadn't told Madge about the kidnapping. He was afraid to. He knew she'd be fearful and upset, for she too had watched Rachel grow up, and he knew the two were quite fond of each other. But few things in the office ever escaped Madge. The legal secretary and smoking chimney could sense that something serious was going on, for her tone toward Kurt, though raspy, was especially calm and reassuring.

Kurt tried to relax . He reclined, put his feet up on the desk, and tried as best he could to not even look at his phone. His eyes wandered to the frames on the wall. Next to his diplomas and his law license, were pics of Kurt with his ultra-light planes and of him shaking hands with various politicians. There were photos of Rachel: as an impish three year old with chocolate cake smeared all over her face; as a second grader in pig tails, smiling a gap-toothed smile; Rachel after she won her sixth grade spelling bee; and Rachel, in a gown and tassel, proudly smiling with her arms around her dad at her high school graduation. He studied her pics until he couldn't see anything more through his veil of tears. Though Kurt wasn't a religious man, he briefly considered dropping to his knees to pray that his only child could be spared.

Finally, the phone rang. "Counselor," said Humphrey, "Your darling Sweetpea has something to tell you."

Kurt cleared his throat and waited. He had no arguments left, no deals, threats or pleas. He was defeated. He just wanted to hear his daughter's voice, perhaps – God, no! – for the last time.

"Don't you want to talk to her?" asked Humphrey.

"Yes," Kurt said, in a voice just above a whisper. "Please. Put her on."

"Hi Daddy!" said Rachel, sounding like her old chipper self.

"Rachel, honey, I love you."

"I do too!" She was almost giddy. "And I've got a nice big surprise! Look straight ahead. No, a little to the left. There, on the wall. A little lower, next to that corny-assed 'justice is blind' scale."

He was confused, but did as she said. And there, right in front of him was a miniscule camera! "Hi Daddy!" she yelled through the phone, "I can see you!"

He examined the little device. Where the hell had that come from and why hadn't he noticed it before? Had these goons been spying on him the whole time?

"Daddy, the whole world can see you!"

"What?" Kurt's fingers smudged the spycam's lens. He wiped it off with his shirt.

"I said the world is watching!" She put him on speaker phone. On the other end of the line, somewhere in the distant background, he thought he heard the sound of a crowd. And the crowd was laughing. My God, just how many kidnappers WERE there?

"Smile, Daddy. Smile like you're on - what was that show? Candid Camera! Oh, and I've got some good news: I'm safe! Mondale and Humphrey, they're actually friends of mine. Their real names are, well, never mind that. But guess what? You're about to be a star because - are you ready? Drum roll please! Welcome everyone to … *Face Yourself!"* Kurt heard audience claps and generic TV theme song music with cheesy electronic drums.

"Honey, I'm sorry," Kurt said, peering his huge eyeball into the camera. "I'm not following any of this."

"That's OK, silly! I'll have to make this quick since we only have thirty seconds on commercial break 'til we're back live, but I've been hired to be on this new reality show! Isn't that exciting? And the great news is that I wasn't kidnapped – the producers set the whole thing up. I'm safe and sound and it's all for the show! Isn't that great?"

Before Kurt had a chance to answer yes - *and* to ask her what the bloody fuck she was thinking putting him through all of this emotional turmoil - she was back on the air. Rachel told her viewers that they'd be cutting to another segment, but told her father to stand by for later. It wasn't until Madge rushed into Kurt's office to have him listen to the radio promo for *Face Yourself* that he fully grasped what was going on. The announcer teased viewers to tune in Sunday night for the premiere, in which "an unhappy and emotionally distant lawyer is made to face himself and see who he really is" - in front of millions of people.

Madge lit up a cigarillo and told her boss that, while she usually hates reality shows, this one sounded good. "Well done, Mr. Planck," she said, blowing smoke out her nostrils. Madge gave him a congratulatory hug, before retreating to her office.

If Kurt hadn't dropped his cell phone in all this confusion he would've realized that the show had cut back to him and he would have heard the audience go "ooooh!"('80's audience style) when they hugged.

Rachel gushed, "You're seeing only the first of many breakthroughs now that Kurt Planck is confronting himself!" Rachel turned the show over to the main host, Dr. Angela Schussel, M.D., a psychiatrist and purported expert on self-actualization through accurate self-knowledge.

That Sunday, the debut episode of *Face Yourself* featuring "The Emotionally Stuffed Lawyer" aired. It was too painful for Kurt to watch, but Madge saw it and told him all about it.

Though he wasn't totally on board with Dr. Schussel's diagnoses, Kurt had to grudgingly admit that the show's premise was good: to get people to confront the truth about themselves, by any means necessary, so that this self-knowledge can lead to profound changes in their lives. And, in the process, make Dr. Schussel and Rachel rich and famous.

During the show's segment featuring Kurt, Rachel opined that her father had stuffed his emotions while spending years representing clearly guilty clients; this, she said, led to a bitter divorce and to his estrangement from his only child. Rachel told her viewers that a lawyer's quest for truth and justice should always begin at home. And, Dr. Schussel added that exposing Mr. Planck to ridicule and legal malpractice were necessary steps in his "treatment."

Initially, Kurt had feared that Rachel had orchestrated the fake kidnapping solely to humiliate him. But he finally came to believe that she was sincere (or as sincere as anyone in reality TV can be) when she said that she was helping him come to terms with his choices in life. Rachel insisted that she had done all this because she loved him more than anything else in the whole world.

Inasmuch as the whole debacle destroyed Kurt's career and nearly ruined his life, he grudgingly admired the fact that it was Rachel, even more than Dr.

Schussel, who had perfectly conceived the scheme. He discovered that, because Rachel had asked him for advice on the seemingly irrelevant small claims matter, everything she had told Kurt had become privileged attorney-client communication, according to the law in the state Rachel had called him from. Thus, the bulk of that communication, which was cleverly edited for television, could never be used by Kurt to sue the show's producers or its network. Moreover, Kurt was barred from testifying against Rachel's two corny cohorts, Humphrey and Mondale, who were considered *de facto* agents of Kurt's client, Rachel in the proposed small claims case.

It wouldn't have mattered anyway. The show's producers quickly donated a huge sum of money to the Renovate the Court Fund. Then Dr. Schussel donated thousands of dollars to the Orthodox temple that Judge Levine attended. To Seward's civic and judicial leaders, *Face Yourself* was a win-win for everybody.

Though the first season isn't even over, Rachel and Dr. Schussel now have two other reality shows in production. They also have a line of "True Self" brand fragrances, jewelry, and handbags. For Rachel's own contributions toward consumer culture, she was recently the subject of a glowing bio on The History Channel. Rachel's segments on celebrity flameouts who have attempted suicide has revived many a flagging career and – she's convince of this - saved countless lives.

Right now, Rachel's at the top of her game. But it's only been a few months since the trial so it remains to be seen if she can hold on to this fame long enough to brand herself an American icon.

As for Kurt, the State Bar found that:

> "Mr. Planck's performance amounted to a deception to the bench, moral turpitude, willful blindness at best and a reckless disregard for the foreseeable consequences at worst; a blatant failure of ethical duties and a *res ipsa loquitur* example of a contemptible fraud perpetrated on the People of this State."

In other words, the lawyer's governing body concluded that he sucked and was punished by being denied the "privilege" of practicing law for two years.

Today, after recovering from the shock and embarrassment of his license suspension, Kurt is happier than ever, having been freed from a profession and court system that he increasingly did not believe in. And, now that he's a consultant to *Face Yourself*, he gets to see Rachel more than ever. Rachel took a leave of absence from college and she and her father recently found a place together, a two bedroom in Long Island City, near the studio where the show is taped. Kurt was able to take Madge along as an assistant; she found a flat in the East Village upstairs from a hookah joint. Whether Kurt , had, before his *Face Yourself* therapy, stuffed his feelings for Madge, or whether he merely had succumbed to the romance of New York City in autumn, is unknown. But what we do know is that he and Madge are now dating.

When the smoke clears in everyone's busy schedules (and from Madge's incessant smoking – which Rachel is determined to make her quit under threat of making her the subject of a new episode), Kurt hopes that he can spend some more quality time with his daughter. He's planning an outing with Rachel to New Mexico in a few months where they'll be building and flying ultralight aircraft. Depending on how that goes, he hopes it will become an annual father/daughter thing.

As for Bubos, his case was appealed, this time by a new team of celebrity lawyers, all the way the U.S. Supreme Court. However, the jury's verdict was sustained. The high court, in a 5-4 decision, refused to set aside the verdict, concluding that Bubos Boutros was so obviously guilty that even the incompetent actions of his "craven and self-serving" lawyer did not prejudice him. Mr. Boutros is currently serving a term of life imprisonment in the state penitentiary.

The good news is that Bubos Boutros will be eligible for parole in eighteen years.

SORRY FOR YOUR LOSS

Dear Mrs. Blakemore:

I am writing to tell you how sorry I am to hear about your loss. Please know that my thoughts and prayers are with you and Kerry right now. Although we've never met, I feel as if I know you personally, since our paths have crossed many times throughout the years. I too knew your husband well (though, truth to tell, not all of the times we had together were what I'd call "good"). I'm sure you know how Jim's best qualities – his live-in-the moment, *joie de vivre*, I think they call it - also had a darker side, right?

Don't get me wrong, I am <u>not</u> putting Jim down! I'm not one of those ninnies saying Jim Blakemore got what was coming to him. No, he didn't deserve it. The fact is, I was disgusted (and heartbroken!) when I saw on the news what that hateful mob did to him. You and I know (or at least I do) that Jim wasn't peddling child pornography or part of some kiddie sex ring. (Of course, if he really had been a pervert and if he had tried to molest my son – OUR son - but that's neither here nor there right now - I'd have shot him too!)

But I know he was innocent. That's <u>not </u>to say that Jim never did anything wrong. I'm sure you know that he could be a real donkey's ass sometimes, so I'm not about to put a halo around his head. And, no, I'm not asking you for forgiveness for what I'm about to tell you, since it's probably too late for that. But I am sorry if my son and I played some part in Jim's passing.

To be fair, though, Jim <u>really</u> got me all riled up! What kind of father would deny his own child? What kind of man would treat a woman like the way he treated me: without a care. As if all my sacrifices for him didn't matter?! Not a *real* man. But I'll say no more about that!

And please don't blame our son either. (Let's call him "Evan".) I guess I may have put some ideas into Evan's head and he just got carried away. But all he wanted to do was to help me. Why? Because, since the day he was born it's always been me and him against the world. We've always looked out for one another. You know, we had to. It's not as if *Jim* was there for our son when he needed his daddy most. Of course, I'm not bitter or anything. Bitterness is for mediocre minds, and I am anything but mediocre!

Still, it's a shame that your husband isn't around to see how smart his son has become. Now, I don't know much about computers so I couldn't tell you exactly how Little Ev (Ha! He's seventeen now and towers over me, but I still call him little) did what he did. And those technical geeks in the government haven't figured it out yet, either. (To think that Evan's

2nd grade "teacher" Mrs. Goode said that he was dumb and he wouldn't amount to anything! She was a real "C U Next Time," if you know what I mean.)

Before I tell you everything that happened, you need to know <u>why</u> we did what we did. As with most everything in my life, the whole thing started with our Jim. You know how he'd act so important and would never be around when you needed him? How he'd just ignore you and pretend you were just a piece of dog doo that he was trying not to step on? But then he'd step on you anyway? Maybe not – maybe <u>he</u> treated YOU like a princess. But not me. I'm not complaining because I'm a positive person. But YOU spend one day in my Payless shoes and you'd know what I'm talking about! But, this isn't about "poor me." It's about moving on. I just hope that you and Kerry will find the peace that I've finally found. (By the way, I saw Kerry on TV again yesterday. What a lovely young lady! Just a friendly tip, though: she could use a little makeup!).

Even though we don't know each other personally, I do feel for what you're going through. Maybe I can offer some comfort by saying that, though times may be tough for you and Kerry right now, it's even harder for poor Evan. He has to grow up knowing that his OWN father ignored him - AND, he's got to defend Jim's memory and reputation!

Don't think it's been easy for me, either. I was practically spit on by Chad, my flaky babysitter's boyfriend, just for defending Jim. Even Guy, our next door neighbor, told me he thinks Jim was guilty as sin. And this is coming from a nut who plays with model trains! By the time you finish reading this letter you'll know that Jim was innocent too, since maybe even you didn't believe him. (I'm sure that's why he moved out before he died.) But, of course, no amount of finger pointing is going to bring him back. (Still, just where <u>were</u> the police that day when Jim was just happening to be emptying out his desk?!! It's the United States Capitol, for goodness sake. Something's fishy here, right?)

Anyway, let's all take a deep breath and I'll start at the beginning. I met Jim a few years before you, right before he graduated from Cal. I was going to Las Po – well, never mind, it's a junior college (a top notch one, though!) when I heard about this party in Berkeley. There were supposed to be a lot of cute guys there so I went out there with a girlfriend. She left when she didn't find any action (I'm sorry, but she was kind of slut!) and I was about to leave too…until I spotted the boy who would change my life. It was two in the morning and there was Jim, looking sad AND very drunk. He was just sitting on an empty beer keg and babbling to himself. You might not know this now, but he was real looker back then. He still had a full head of sandy brown hair and a sexy little butt. Oh, and, those puppy dog eyes! There was no way I could resist, you know what I'm saying? I'll spare you the details but let's just say we had the most passionate and romantic nights of our lives.

After that evening of love, I didn't see Jim again for a long, long time. Years, actually. No, he didn't just knock me up and leave – you know he wasn't the type to do that. Plus, how was he to know I wanted to raise our son by myself? I guess it's just my old-fashioned upbringing: I was raised by my own mother (a single mom too, may she rest in peace) to believe that I didn't need a man to tell me how to raise a child. Besides, at the time I had a decent job, so I thought I could do this act alone. (But then they fired me for no reason at all! So, because of Jim, we had to go on food stamps. But that's another story.)

Years went by. We moved out of state and went on with our lives. Then one morning I was flipping through the channels, and found some morning news show and - there Jim was! Right there, standing next to that (awful) Congressman Sachs who was talking about some silly town hall meeting.

I knew it was Jim alright, though he certainly wasn't that cute and sad boy who had fallen for me that night. He was balding and paunchy. And what was that, a double or triple chin? (He must've been getting fat on your food! You might try cutting down on the fried stuff, that's how I keep MY figure. Just a thought!) On TV, Jim looked arrogant and smug, like he was living the life of luxury. Seeing Jim there on the screen, I don't know why, but I knew I had to see him again. Maybe I was a little peeved that he was living the high life while Evan and I were scraping by in Section 8 housing and food stamps, but don't get me wrong, I wasn't angry. I wouldn't be a good mom if I lived my life like that, and believe me, everyone I know will tell you, I've been the <u>best</u> mother anyone could be. Even after all the guff that men have given me. And all the h-e-double hockey sticks that those hags in court have put me through. (And years ago, a FORMER friend had the nerve to suggest when I was pregnant that I should have thought about aborting our poor baby Evan! Can you imagine anything more IMMORAL?!) Anyway, Congressman Sack of Poop (that's what I call him) was saying on TV that all concerned citizens should go to the Seward Senior Center on Tuesday night to talk about issues important to them, blah blah blah.

So, I rented a car (I <u>had</u> to; mine got repo'd after Jim had left us in such dire straits) and on Tuesday night I went to over to the meeting. Sure enough, Jim was there. I could see him out near the stage, brownnosing, while that good-for-nothing Sack of Poop was shaking every hand and kissing every baby he could find. I can still see Jim standing there, with one of those old brick-sized cell phones (I know you're

NOT too young to remember those!) glued to his ear. Our Jim was barking orders into it like he was Mr. Important or something.

So what did I do? I walked right up to Mr. Important. And guess what? He pretended like he didn't even know who I am! CAN YOU BELIEVE THAT? It had only been a few years before that we'd spent that wonderful night of love making. BUT now he was playing all coy, as if he's never seen me in his life! Talk about play-acting!! (Gwen, my flaky babysitter, told me later that maybe Jim just didn't see too well. Did he have vision problems? Did he have early Alzheimer's or something? You'd tell me, wouldn't you?)

So Jim shook a bunch of hands and then reached out to me, as if I was just another of those kiss-the-fanny constituents. but just as his hand went out, he ran backstage, pretending to take a call on that big brick of a phone! How rude is that?! Oh, and, get this - now he had a wedding band! *Just when was Jim planning to tell me that he'd gotten married?!*

I tried to get through the crowd to find Jim again, but Congressman Sack of Poop kept droning on about America and the American Dream. Then, just when I thought he was done, so I could go find Jim, a bunch of goody-two-shoes with what I call helium hands started asking question after question. The typical hogwash - like repairing sidewalks, trade agreements, civil rights, all kinds of nonsense. I was just about to go find Jim when some crazy old lady started babbling about her grown up son and how she wanted the Congressman to help kick him out of her house. Sack of Poop was quiet (for once!) but Jim, with a straight face, told the nut that he'd look into the matter. (Knowing Jim, as you and I do, he just said that to shut her up, right?)

An hour went by. Then another. I checked my watch for the umpteenth time. I could feel my blood pressure go through the roof. And all this time, Jim was standing toward the back of the stage, and there was no way I could get to him. Before I knew it, it was 10:00 p.m. and I had to leave because Gwen wouldn't babysit past 10:30 - even though she'd promised to babysit until midnight.

So, after all that - renting a car, getting a babysitter, the whole nine yards - Jim and I never even got a chance to talk. It's not like I was going to plop the whole thing about Dev - I mean Evan - on Jim right then and there. The fact is, I hadn't yet decided whether I was even going to tell him about our son. I figured I'd play it by ear.

A few more years went by and I tried to get Jim out of my mind. Of course, that was hard because I both loved and hated him so. But for a while I almost did forget about him. I met this (horrible!) man named

Enrique. He and I had a child, who I'll call "Darryl." Today, Darryl is a lovable little four year old. Not as bright as our Evan, but what do you expect, considering Darryl's father? What Darryl lacks in smarts, though, he almost makes up for with his simple and pure heart. All in all, Enrique and I were together for three years before we split up last year. (Enrique knew what he did! Just because everyone's on the take and won't to listen to me does not mean it didn't happen!)

Now, Mrs. Blakemore (may I call you Caroline?), you may not know how hard it is for a single mom with no financial resources to go against the system. The police, attorneys, court-ordered shrinks – even the female ones – no, ESPECIALLY the female ones! - treat single moms like dirt. So I had no other choice than to tell Darryl and Evan that Enrique, the so-called "man of the house", was a womanizer, a liar, and a gambler. And, of course I had to break the news to them that those cowards in the D.A.'s office had refused to bring charges. (What "proof" did they need - do I look like a liar or something?)

One day I happened to be telling Gwen about my problems with Enrique. (Why not? She's always going on and on about hers, and she runs some silly advice column in the local paper) Flaky Gwen said that, if it was HER, she'd take her case to anyone and everyone who would listen - from the Governor all the way up to the President of the United States, if she had to. I'm sure you've already noticed that Gwen's not the sharpest tool in the shed, but this time she made sense. So that's how come I thought of Congressman Sachs – and Jim, of course. Yes, Jim would help me get justice against Enrique. Your husband was a caring man. At least at one time, anyway.

After that, I tried and tried to make an appointment to see the "Honorable" Sack of Poop, but of course, crooks like that never call you back. I found out that Jim was still working for the crook, but not in his local office – Jim was now in D.C. But how was I supposed to fly all the way out to Washington to see Jim? Where was a poor single mom like me going to find enough money for a plane ticket?

Well, sometimes things have a way of turning out alright by themselves. The first good thing that happened was, two weeks later, Enrique died. (It was obviously an accident and there's no way Evan had anything to do with it, but those police bums keep saying it's an unsolved murder case.) But, wouldn't you know it? Deadbeat Enrique, in life, and now in death, never provided anything for me or for the son and stepson he claimed to love.

We were often short on money before, but now, let me tell you, we were REALLY broke. But, though I've fallen prey to the falsehoods of men (what woman hasn't?), I wasn't born yesterday. (Our son tells me, in that sneering way of his, that I can be pretty clever when I need to be!) So, Evan and I started talking, and our ingenious little man went on the internet. Later, when I asked him what he'd been doing, Ev said that he'd calculated how much money -with penalties and interest - that our Jim, owed for 17 years of past due child support. I won't tell you the sum - I'm not vulgar about discussing things like that - but it was huge. In the high six figures, and, adding what they call "punitive and exemplary" damages, it's in the seven figure range. Maybe that kind of money doesn't seem like a lot to a woman of like you. You've probably never had to work like I had to, but that's a lot of dough to me! Enough money to send Evan to college and to help me buy a place and a nice car. And money left to over to pay for Darryl's trade school or training for whatever his modest talents and abilities allow him do.

Evan did his part by adding up the child support, but I came up with the idea about finding a lawyer to take the case for a split of the profits. I first tried the big shot lawyers in town – Planck, Manzetti, but they charged too much. After I went through the ENTIRE Yellow Pages and Evan looked online, all we could find was a two bit dwarf lawyer with Parkinson's who agreed to take the case on contingency. The first thing this shaking little shyster did was to front the money from the potential lawsuit to buy us all first-class plane trips to Washington. The lovely little Jewish

lawyer would've come with us too had he not been too
shaky to get through airport security.

Now, I'm sure you're asking yourself, what
were we going to do when we got there? Well, I'll tell
you. I'm sure you can tell by now that I'm a very
mature person. The time before, when I went to see Jim
(at that town hall thing, remember?) I was just going
there to be friendly. BUT SEVEN YEARS LATER,
SEVEN LONG YEARS OF SCHLEPPING THE KIDS
TO BUSSTOPS, OF UNPAID BILLS, TV DINNERS,
ABUSIVE BOYFRIENDS AND FLAKY
BABYSITTERS, and this time I was more than a little
peeved at Jim. I was angry! Who wouldn't have been
teed off at him after all he had put us through?

Now, before we even got on the plane, Ev had
really done his research. He found out everything he
could about his dad: Jim's address, social, bank
account numbers and balances Our brilliant son even
found Jim's medical records online too! And, even
though I told him that it wasn't necessary, he pulled
your medical files too. (Which reminds me, there's a
mole on your back below your shoulder that looks like
it's getting bigger. As your friend, and soon to be part
of the family, promise me you'll have it looked at,
OK?)

After a bumpy and scary flight, we finally
arrived at Reagan's Airport (the BEST president ever,

right? I'm no racist – in fact my shoe shiner is black – but I still think white men make the best presidents! There. Someone has to say it!). So by the time we got out of the airport, it was late afternoon. We quickly had to figure out where to meet Jim. Going to your house wouldn't have worked, since it wasn't your day to volunteer and you'd probably be home. (Ev looked at the schedule on your cell phone and found out you help with the Red Cross on Monday and Wednesday afternoons. Good for you!) But even if *you* had been out, Kerry would have been getting home from school any minute. (This was before she told you she hated you and moved out to live with Jim's mother. Helpful hint: you really need to get a more secure email account!) I called Jim's office and found out that he was still at the Capitol that afternoon.

So I took the kids with me and grabbed a cab to the Sam Rayburn building to get to his and the Congressman's office. Once there, I politely asked to speak to Jim. Some young hussy - a megabuck donor's daughter, no doubt - told me that Jim was in a meeting and that I'd be better off making an appointment. SHE SAID THAT TO <u>ME!</u> CAN YOU BELIEVE THAT? TO ME!! So, I was real nice, and said, that's fine, but we'll wait. She said maybe we could schedule something for next week. No, I said, we're only in town for today, we'll wait here, and would you please be so kind as to let us know when his meeting is over? The floozy huffed and puffed even when I smiled at her and said that we'd just like ten minutes of Jim's time.

I'm sure this harlot could see how sad-looking we were. Especially four year old Darryl, who was so cute and docile. Still, though, we were forced to sit in the waiting room for an eternity. I was hoping that my sorry-sacked Darryl would melt the heart of even this intern or whore, or whatever underling she was, but she looked like the type who hated kids. So we waited there for about an hour. Darryl and I played Fish or some other silly game (even though Evan was playing CHESS by that age, for goodness sake!).

Meanwhile, Evan slowly paced around pretending to be talking on his cellphone. All the while, though, he was looking over the strumpet's shoulder as she PRETENDED to work. (She wasn't fooling anybody!) In no time, before you could even say "deadbeat dad," in fact, Evan picked up the password to the office's internet system!

FINALLY, after what seemed like an eternity, Jim finally sprang out the door of his office. Of course, our Mr. Big Shot had a smartphone in *each* hand. He spoke to the little tart, telling her that the Congressman's plans had changed on account of some emergency and that Sack of Poop and Jim had to get to airport right away.

Your husband started to exit the office when I cried, "Jim! Jim! Look, sweetheart, we're all here! We've been waiting for you! Just give us a few minutes of your time!"

"I'm sorry ma'am", he says. (Like I'm a madam in a whorehouse? As if he doesn't even know who I am!) "I can't meet with you now. There's some urgent government business I need to attend to."

What a bunch of hooey, right? Jim was just about to run out the door when little Darryl ran to him, wrapped his arms around Jim's leg and kept yelling "Daddy! Daddy!" Now THAT got Jim's attention! But not enough to stop him from blowing us off and running out the door. So there was another instance of Jim's rudeness And I can tell you that Jim's response really hurt little Darryl's feelings, because he thought – and still thinks –that Jim is his daddy too. (It's a long story, but basically one time, just to make Darryl feel better, I told him that Enrique, the lying scumbag, wasn't his real father, and that Jim WAS. What else would a good mother do to console her younger, developmentally delayed, son?)

Anyway, like I said, Jim treated us like scum and tried to run out the door. I'm not criticizing him – after all, he was (and still is) the love of my life. I'm just telling you about his uncivilized behavior so that you know the state of mind we were all in at the time.

Here, we'd come out all the way from - well, never mind - just to see Jim. Here I was, a woman who was far from just an acquaintance, and with a toddler who could just as well be his son too. So I stood up and looked right into Jim's eyes.

I told him, in a voice only he could hear, how upset we were that The Great Jim Blakemore won't meet with us because of some silly "government business"?! He can't meet with his soulmate? He doesn't have time for his children, who are standing helplessly before him. And my eyes were saying please talk to us, just give us five minutes of your ever-so precious and all important time!! You left us so poor that we had to use some of the money you owe us in child support just to fly here to see you!!

BUT don't think that I'd ever be so uneducated as to yell at Jim from across the office or right in front of everyone, especially that bimbo receptionist. (Oh, and *please* tell that me Jim wasn't boffing her!) The problem though was that Jim just pretended he didn't hear me. Then he ran out of the office, mumbling something about getting to the airport.

And so, Caroline, you can understand now how Jim put me into one of those infuriated states – you know, where your face turns beet red and your head's about to explode. (Did he make you angry like that too?)

By the time we made it back to our hotel I was really steaming. Evan was so upset by Jim's insensitivity that he was shaking. And, our son started throwing things around the room and talking like a crazy person. He even got mouthy to me and asked, "How do you even know Jim is my biological father anyway?" and, "Mom, it was just a one night stand years ago, so why are you still obsessed with this man?" Ha! As if a seventeen year old boy could ever be an expert in the affairs of the heart. Well, I did my best to calm Evan down, but my own blood pressure was skyrocketing. I really thought I was going to have a stroke or a heart attack, or both. I yelled, I screamed. I must've called our Jim just about everything in the book. And I may have even let out a few cuss words too, who knows?

I said to Evan, did you see how your father treated us? I think I may have even yelled something to Evan about how his father had leered at Darryl like a dirty child buggerer. I felt so dirty after that ugly scene at the Capitol that I went for a hot shower. I left the two of them in the bedroom, where Ev was on his in laptop, while Darryl lay at the foot of the bed, watching one of his stupid shows.

When I finished up in the bathroom, Evan showed me what he'd been up to. I guess that something about what I may have said about Jim leering at Darryl sparked something in Evan's impressionable (but GENIUS) mind.

What Evan did was this: I don't know all the technical gobbledygook, but it had something to do with Evan cracking the security code at Jim's office. And then Ev bumping cellphones with Jim. Like I said, I don't understand much of it really, but that's how come the kiddie porn ended up on Jim's work computer, his laptop, and his cellphones. All from our brilliant but mischievous son! Now, at the time, Evan did try to explain to me what he was doing. But honestly, after that miserable afternoon at Sack of Poop's office, I just needed to tune everyone out, unwind, and watch some reality TV.

So after that, I didn't think anything more about Evan's computer hacking. The next morning we packed our bags and flew home. (Another bumpy ride!) But, I guess that sometime during the following week, Evan later said he secretly sent more child pornography to Jim's computer. And this is where I think Evan maybe went too far: he "borrowed" your husband's email and cellphone accounts, and sent out all those disgusting emails and texts and made them like they came from Jim.

To be fair, when Ev sent all those disgusting pictures of naked boys and girls, he had no way of knowing that Jim's address book contained the emails to nearly every Congressman, Senator, and Cabinet member in Washington and that the kiddie porn would, by mistake, be sent to all of them.   (But De-, I mean, Evan, where did you get those dirty pictures? Is this something Grandfather Clark showed you? And what were you thinking, dragging your father's name through the mud, causing a bunch of wackos to kill him? How are we supposed to get child support now? Did you even think about that?!!)

But Caroline, let's not give little Ev a complex. He's *not* the only person in the wrong. Why, he told me that the government's computer protection was a joke and that the system at Jim's office was just daring for someone to hack it.

It's just too bad that the few good people accused of being pedophiles are viewed as *guilty* until they prove themselves otherwise. I guess you, me, and Evan learned something from that.

Though none of this is really MY fault, I do feel bad that everything got so out of control. The federal charges, Jim losing his job, the melee, the murder. I cry every night thinking about our poor Jim (do you, Caroline?) Maybe if that two bit lawyer hadn't talked me into going to D.C., Jim wouldn't have made me so angry, and Evan wouldn't have done what he did, and none of this would've happened. But, there are no do-overs in life, right? Besides, I'm the kind of person who takes responsibility for her actions and that's exactly what I'm teaching Evan. WE ARE BOTH SORRY (AREN'T WE, "EVAN"?!!) FOR WHAT HAPPENED. WE'RE SORRY THAT WE COULDN'T SAVE JIM FROM THOSE HOOLIGANS (AS IF ANYONE COULD!) MOST OF ALL, I'M SO SORRY THAT I COULDN'T HAVE SPENT MORE TIME WITH JIM, THE LOVE OF MY LIFE. AND NOW IT'S TOO LATE!!

In my heart, though, I was with Jim every step of the way. And it pleases me to know that deep down, and to the very end, Jim knew it too.

Caroline, I regret that I cannot see you or reveal our identities. At least not right now. I'm sure, as a mother, you know that you have a duty to protect your children first!

But, since some of our actions may have gone a little too far, I guess I shouldn't say anything more now than: we are very, very sorry for your loss.

Please know that we'll *always* be there for you. And, don't worry, we'll be checking in on you and Kerry from time to time.

With Sympathy and Years of Regrets,

Another Grieving Mother

HAPPY BIRTHDAY – I'M STILL DEAD!

I

"Guy! Have a good day planning!" Joan called out from her bedroom.

"OK, bye, Mom. I love you!" Guy Moulton closed the back door and fired up his boxy sedan to get to his job at the Seward Planning Department.

On his way there, he thought about what to get her for Mother's Day. He prided himself on the thoughtful gifts he'd always given her – like the laptop he gave her last year – and he was determined to up the ante this time around. He adored his mom, the only parent, indeed, the only family member he'd ever known.

Though he'd left home for four years to attend college, earning an engineering degree, circumstances (no job prospects, a failed romance) brought him back after graduation to Seward, back to Mom and their modest bungalow. The whole arrangement was intended to be short term, but neither of them had ever found a good reason for him to leave. He liked living there and he liked his job - one his mom, a former city employee before going on disability, helped him get.

And he was largely satisfied with his solitary life of building model train sets and long distance running.

As usual, Guy made it to work ten minutes early. He smiled at the mousy girl whose cubicle he passed by every morning to get to his own. Then he sat down and put in a solid day reviewing plans for city improvements, analyzing engineering data, and writing reports. It was the kind of detail-oriented work that some find boring, but he found it challenging, or at least not unpleasant. When the clock struck 5:30, he cleared his already tidy desk and headed home.

When he got home, he expected Mom to be plopped on the living room couch, knitting him yet another unneeded scarf, and complaining of her numerous ailments. The Praise the Lord Channel would be playing in the background. She would have asked him about his day and he'd give her his one sentence synopsis. Then he'd go for his eight mile run. Later, Mom would have dinner ready, usually something involving Hamburger Helper or, on special occasions, baked ziti. Once Mom had served him, she'd join him at the kitchen table. He'd scarf down his reheated food while she'd tell him about her day, often in excruciating detail. There'd be a rundown of all the soaps she'd watched, who she had seen visiting the next door "hussie" that day, and what time Mom had eaten each of her meals. She'd also offer a few bad jokes, usually gleaned from The Seward Chronicle's "Doggone Funny" column.

But tonight, when Guy came home, he found Mom reclined in her Ezy Chair, snoring fitfully. She was still in her nightgown and night cream and clearly hadn't left the house all day. At least she had her laptop by her. He was glad she was using it. He'd bought it for her so she could stay connected and mentally engaged even as her mobility gradually decreased. At first, she thought the gift was frivolous, but once he showed her how to use the computer, she was on it 24/7. Much of her time was spent writing poison pen letters to the editor of the local newspaper on any issue, large or small, that ticked her off.

To Joan Moulton, she had too much too complain about and too little time. Despite endless medical tests and the protestations by her doctors that her ailments were psychosomatic, Guy's mother believed that her end was near. She had little fear of death. In fact, she welcomed the imagined peace of it all, the relief of finally being free of her pain-wracked body. Her psychics and astrologers had assured her that when she passed away, she'd immediately be embraced by the sweet arms of Jesus.

But she was worried about her only child. For years she had lectured him, saying that he needed to start making goals and plans for the future. But Guy lived day-to-day, refusing to talk to her about anything serious. To Joan, the poor boy had gone from being a follower-type in boyhood, to being a loner in high school. Now he was almost a recluse. Who was going to look after Guy when she was gone?

This evening, after Guy roused her, Joan nagged him *again* about that young woman at the planning department -the ONLY female there who looked younger than forty. Guy once mentioned the girl to his mom and he was sorry he did. For the umpteenth time, he tried to get Mom to shut up about his co-worker by telling Joan that the girl was mousy and seemed to be even shyer than he was.

"With a little makeup, I'll bet that even the mousy girl would look alright," Mom replied. "And, maybe *her* shyness would force *you* to become more outgoing."

He rolled his eyes.

"Son, you can mock me all you want, but you're already twenty-six years and old and not only are you not married, you don't even date." He leafed through his model train catalogue, trying to ignore her.

"It's those trains, isn't it? You're spending way too much time down in the basement with that nonsense." She sighed. "That looney stuff won't get you a girl."

"No, it's not the model trains, Mom."

"Then you're gay, is that it?" He shook his head. "Look, it's OK, son, I love you. We're all sinners." She prided herself on her "tolerance" despite becoming a born-again Christian twenty years ago.

Guy was tempted to tell her that he *was* gay, just to get her off his back. But he'd feel guilty about lying to her.

At any rate, Joan couldn't be sure that Guy, if left to his own devices, would ever find a mate of any gender. And she worried that without proper guidance he'd never achieve his true potential, like becoming Chief City Planner. She knew that no one else could provide this guidance to her son, but she also knew was dying.

She had to find a way, even after death, to keep steering him in the right direction.

Desperately looking for answers, she revved up the search engines and Googled like maniac. She hoped to find a website that could deliver inspirational messages to her son after she was gone.

Eventually, she found something even better: a company that promised to send email messages and presents on birthdays and other holidays to Guy for up to ninety-nine years after her death. So, as a surprise gift to her son, Joan withdrew nearly all of her savings to sign up for the works: the Eternity Plus Plan.

For the next few weeks, Joan secretly wrote volumes of emails she hoped her son would someday read. One day he'd surely be grateful for her post-mortem mentoring, but right now, this was her secret.

One late Friday afternoon, two days before Mother's Day, Guy came home from the office to find Pat Robertson on "The 700 Club" accusing homosexuals of causing an earthquake - and his mother lying stiff as a board on the couch, her unblinking eyes facing skyward.

At the age of 63, Joan Moulton was dead.

II

Guy wrestled with his grief. Losing his dear mother left Guy with a profound sense of loss, and a frighteningly existential feeling of being all alone in the world. His mom had made her passing easier on him: using the mortuary's "pre-need services" (to use the death biz lingo) she'd pre-planned her cremation, funeral, and wake. She even referred her son to a lawyer to help settle her estate.

Her friends Muriel and Helga, as well as a dozen other ladies from the Evangelical Lutheran Church came to the service. Guy didn't invite any of his own friends, mostly because he didn't really have any. Not close friends, anyhow. As to his co-workers, he liked them well enough, but he never really clicked with anybody there. In fact, not only did he not invite his colleagues at the Planning Department to the service, he never even told anyone at the office that his mother had died.

After Joan's funeral, Guy sat in his basement. all night, and, sadly and quietly, worked on his model train set all night.

He inherited the cozy old house, which seemed enormous without his mother there. Even his home town seemed too large. A small suburb when he was growing up, Seward had since doubled in population, with low cost housing on the south side and McMansions on the north; a place with streets he'd barely heard of, teeming with people he didn't know and would probably never meet. With the requisite Starbucks, Taco Bells, and Target stores, Seward now had the generic feel of almost every 21st-century suburban town in America.

The loss of his mother had carved a massive hole in his life, but Guy knew that somehow he'd get by on his own. After all, she'd always been sick and he'd cared for her most of his life. Plus, even though he felt guilty for thinking this, in the past few years she had really become a burden. And, even though he'd have to make his own dinners and pack his own peanut butter and honey now, he relished his new freedom to do what he pleased.

Two weeks after her death, he even brought his HO-scale train set up from the basement and placed it smack dab in the middle of the living room. That's something Mom would never have allowed. There, he enjoyed his evenings watching "Mythbusters," while painstakingly building a replica of Seward, circa 1900, for his train set. Guy figured eventually that he'd sell the house and move to one of the new condos on the north side of town, or maybe even to another city. But for now he'd just stay put.

Three months passed and, before he knew it, it was Guy's 27th birthday. Since that year, it fell on a Saturday, he spent the day home and alone. Guy missed his mother – her hugs, her cake, the knitted sweaters she'd always give him, but all in all he had a good day. He took a long run through the foothills, then treated himself afterwards to a banana split. Ice cream was something he loved but a treat he only reserved for special occasions. At five foot nine and 140 pounds, there was little danger of Guy getting fat, but he wasn't one to take chances. After all, he was proud of his washboard abs, abs he'd chiseled from a daily routine of 500 sit-ups.

That night he sat in bed and scrolled through half dozen emails and texts on his phone. He was happy that his roommate from college had remembered his birthday, as had a couple other college acquaintances.

Then, a new email came in. Its subject line read "Happy Birthday! Love, Mom." He thought it was probably some Nigerian spam but he opened the email anyway.

To his surprise, it really *was* from Joan!

She explained that she was sorry she couldn't be there with him right now, but she wanted him to know that she was there in spirit:

> "Dearest Guy, before I passed, I wanted to find a way to still be part of your life, so I decided to write my thoughts, wishes, and prayers for you in messages that will be sent to you on all of your birthdays and on special holidays. It's all part of this service I signed up with. You'll also be getting presents delivered to our door, I mean, *your* door! My sweet boy, I'll never stop loving you. Even in death, I'm still your

mother. I want to gently remind you, Guy Moulton, to keep good grooming habits and get your hair cut at least once a month! And, I guess I don't have tell you, but remember to save for your retirement so you that you don't end up like me. Broke and dead. Ha!"

He smiled. Though she'd managed to pass the house on to him (along with a small mortgage, too), financial planning had never been her strong suit. Before he turned in for the night, Guy walked past Mom's bedroom door, which was still closed tight as dick's hatband, and called out "goodnight, Mom."

Early the next morning, there was a loud knock on the door. Guy opened it to find a deliveryman with a big-toothed smile and a ponytail, his brown uniform neatly tailored to show off his ripped quads and calves. He had Guy sign for a package. The attached card read:

"Son, remember when you were little and you wanted to build bridges and dams? Well, here's something you'll really like! Love, Mom."

Inside the package was a set of DVDs, a series on the greatest engineering feats in history. Guy couldn't wait to watch the first episode. He had planned to pursue a Masters in engineering so he could build massive public works. But that made him remember, with a touch of bitterness, that the main reason for him not pursuing a post graduate degree was because his disabled mother had needed him at home.

The holidays were fast approaching. This would be the first Christmas he'd have to celebrate without Mom.

Christmas Eve Day brought the usual holiday snail mail and email greetings, mostly from Joan's distant friends who didn't know that she'd passed away. On Christmas morning his mailbox was filled with Happy Holiday spam from online companies he'd once made purchases to, and from a soft-core porn site he'd once visited.

Then he saw this email: "A Merry and Joyous Christmas from Mom". His hands trembled, as if the digital message had come in a real envelope and he was about to announce the next Oscar. With a hard click of his keyboard he opened it up:

> "To my wonderful Guy - I'm wishing you all the best for a wonderful and joyous Christmas Season! Don't dwell on what you've lost this year, think about what you have left. Good health, good looks, a beautiful house, and a good job."

Suddenly there was pounding at the door. Here was the same dude - Mr. Big Smile, Pony Tail &

Ripped Thighs – bringing another present from Mom. Guy excitedly ripped open the box. It was an electric moustache groomer. He was puzzled; he rubbed his smooth face. The attached note read:

> "Son, I know you don't have facial hair, but I always thought you'd look so handsome with a moustache. But keep it well trimmed! No mutton chops like some crazy doper, or a handlebar moustache, like those drugged out baristas at Starbucks! Love forever, Mom."

It was a strange gift, but what the heck; Guy didn't have much else to do these days than to grow facial hair. So that was that: he stopped shaving above his upper lip.

For the first couple of months, Guy's scraggly mustache looked like the dying mosquito-infested sprouts from a Chia pet, but by Easter time, it was starting to look like the real thing: closely trimmed, but with hair as thick as a beaver's. His dark hair and his even darker 'stache made him look like a young Josef Stalin. Or Freddy Mercury, without the overbite.

Soon, Easter was upon him. Since Guy wasn't religious, Easter had never been much of a holiday for him. As a child he hated that his mom would drag him out of bed at 4:30 a.m. to go to the Easter Sunrise church service held at Shadowcliffs, a bleak, shadeless, gravel pit, half- filled with water. Later, as an adult, he'd humor Mom by going to Easter services at her Lutheran church, but he didn't enjoy it any more than he did singing "He is Risen" in that bleak gravel pit they called a "lake."

So, this Easter Sunday, Guy slept in. Then, he enjoyed most of the day at home building his model for the original Seward Train Depot that had been demolished a half-century ago.

That evening Guy checked his phone for messages. There were two emails: "Happy Easter and Enjoy our New Running Shoe Specials!" from an site he'd once purchased his Air Nikes from, but wouldn't let him opt out of its email list no matter how many times he'd tried.

The second message was the one he had hoped for! It was from his Mom. She wished him a Happy Easter and asked how he was enjoying his new moustache. As it was now nine months since her death, she wrote, it was now time for him to stop mourning.

The first thing he should do - in her "professional opinion as a dead mom," she joked - was to remodel the house. She advised him to get rid of the chotskies she'd accumulated over the years and to make the whole place more modern. A place that, if – no,

WHEN - he marries, a new gal would find inviting. Just don't touch *my* room, Mom warned.

With his mother's blessing to renovate the place, Guy went through all of his old stuff and had a garage sale that Saturday. For almost a whole day's work manning the table in his garage, the sale of all of her knick-knacks and old (but not "cool-old") furniture netted him only $42.50. He resolved to never have a garage sale again.

Fortunately (in a sense), he had saved up for a Mississippi steam boat cruise that he planned take with his mother. Having decided that he'd be too sad to go on the cruise without her, he opted to use the funds to buy new furniture and artwork to replace everything in the house. Then he really splurged and bought the biggest flat screen TV he could find.

Guy spent a long weekend of moving things around and mounting the TV. Finally, Guy sat down and gazed with pride at his remodeling project. Though the place now looked a little generic, with bland landscape paintings and nature photographs, it also looked fresher and more modern. It certainly didn't look like the kind of house that a disabled older woman had lived in for twenty-five years.

One thing didn't change: he kept his train set dead center in the living room.

III

August came, and so did Guy's birthday. This was his second one without Mom. Just as he was thinking of the German chocolate cupcakes she would bake for him on his special day, he got this email:

"My dearest son, Happy 28th! It's now been over a year, and I miss you and love you more than you'll ever know. But I'm in a better place. And I hope that, as you celebrate your special day, you'll recognize that you're in a better place too. Literally! I'll bet the house looks great, just the way we wanted it. And I'm sure you look very handsome with your mustache , close-cropped, I hope! I'm sure you're a real lady killer now. (I ought to know, I'm dead. Ha ha!)

"And speaking of ladies, have you asked that girl from work out yet? Don't tell me she's mousy! With the right makeover even a plain-Jane can look like a star, just like that bimbo with the big hair and the big you-know-whats in that video you used to watch."

Even though Mom was dead, Guy still felt embarrassed. *How did she know about "Beaudacious Ta Ta's"? Hey, whatever happened to that DVD anyway?*

She continued:

"By the way, I threw out all that filth before I died. What you need is a real, warm blooded *and* warm hearted girl. A girl who accepts your, you know, oddities. Someone who worships you. After all, you're a handsome young man, and that's not just me saying that because I'm your mother – that's what the church ladies said too! So, have you asked that mousy girl out yet? Just asking. And no son, I'm not nagging. How can I? I'm dead, for Pete's sakes."

Very funny. Of course she was nagging him. But he missed his mom, even her nagging. She'd always said it was a measure of a mother's love for her child. So she must really love him. So what if she was still nagging from beyond the grave? At least *she* cared.

He thought about what Mom had said about the mousy girl. Maybe it wouldn't hurt to at least get to know her.

When he went to work the next day he decided to find out a little about the young lady. Mr. Dichard, his boss, told Guy that her name was Claire, and that she was a bright, hard worker. Guy had already surmised that Claire had a solid work ethic, since she was always at the office before he arrived and would still be there when he clocked out. Guy hoped that Claire was bright, too, but since Mr. Dichard wasn't too sharp himself, the man's estimation meant little.

That afternoon, he passed Claire on the way to the water cooler. Upon closer inspection, he discovered that she wasn't plain at all. She was actually kind of cute. The fact that she was prettier than he'd thought and supposedly smart raised the stakes: Guy was even more nervous about talking to her now.

Nevertheless, he summoned his courage and went over to Claire and said hello. He introduced himself and asked her how she was doing. Claire, who had never heard him speak, looked confused.

She replied with a shaky voice, "Uh, I'm doing fine…and you?"

"Me?" He fiddled with the buttons on his overcoat. "Uh, I'm fine too."

For weeks they made small talk like that, each learning a little more about the other. Guy learned that she liked egg salad sandwiches while Claire discovered he was a peanut butter and honey man. He told her of his relatively uneventful life so far, his college days and how he planned one day to get his Master's degree, and how his mom had named him after Guy Fawkes, back when she was a Catholic.

He told Claire of his mother's death. She said she was sorry to hear that, but that everyone in the office already knew. That seemed strange. He'd never said anything to anyone there about Mom, but he figured that in today's interconnected world there was little, if any, privacy left. Claire said that in her spare time she liked to knit. He told her how he spent his hours after work engaged in his own solitary pleasures, wisely heeded his mother's advice by omitting any mention of his model train hobby.

Claire said she was thirty-one years old (another plus; he liked older women) and that her mother had died too, in a plane accident, just as Guy's father had. Unlike Guy, she came from a large family, who all lived back in Indiana. Besides knitting, her other outside interests were artistic, of sorts: she enjoyed painting by numbers and scrapbooking. She lived with her roommate Val in an apartment downtown, a few blocks from the office. She said she used to go along to social things with Val, until the girl started taking Claire to "pizza and porn" parties: soirees where wanna-be hipsters socialized while loops of vintage porn played in the background. Claire said she didn't like the parties, but not for the usual reasons: she hated pizza.

They both laughed.

Soon they were having lunch together on a regular basis, whenever work deadlines or emergencies didn't interfere. And in their line of work there were few emergencies other than the occasional copy machine malfunction or vandalized kiosk.

Time flew by and before he knew it, it was Christmas time again. Time for his holiday staycation. The office was closed for a week. Claire flew out to Indiana to see her family.

On Christmas morning Mom's newest posthumous greeting arrived:

> "Yuletide Greetings, my darling little man! I've been doing a lot of thinking and, you know how I don't like to interfere in your life, but I do hope you'll call that mousy girl today – it's Christmas, for God's sake (ha ha!)."

He'd already given Claire a "Happy Holidays" card before dropping her off at the airport. But maybe Mom was right, maybe he *should* call the girl. He rang her cell.

When Claire answered, he overheard her say to someone, "Shhh, it's the guy I've been telling you about. I'll take this outside."

Claire didn't have a whole lot to say: the family's fine, the weather's fine, the plane ride wasn't too bad. But she *did* seem genuinely happy to hear from him. She was almost giddy. She asked what he was doing for New Year's Eve and he told her he didn't know. Claire paused. She said she'd be back before New Year's.

"Well, that's great," said Guy. "You'll probably be able to get a leg up on work before everyone else comes back." There was an even longer pause. Then they both said goodbye.

No sooner had he hung up when his doorbell rang. And rang. And rang. Guy ran downstairs to get the door. It was the same UPS man, carrying another package.

"Looks like something new from your dear old mom," he told Guy, handing him the box. "She must love you a heck of lot!"

"My mother is dead," said Guy. He had meant it as merely a factual statement, but he quickly realized that it sounded curt. The man's big smile started to waver, so Guy added, "I mean, well it's complicated. Anyway, my name, as I guess you already know, is Guy Moulton."

"I'm Dave the UPS man." They shook hands. "I'm sorry, bro, I didn't mean to be nosy," Dave said. Then he added, with a whisper, "Sometimes the mail can get *pretty* interesting, you know?"

Guy had no idea what the man meant, but smiled anyway. As soon as Dave left for his appointed rounds, Guy ripped open the box. Inside was a bottle of Dom Perignon. The note attached read:

> "Here's so you and Claire can celebrate in style on New Year's Eve. Also attached are reservations and a gift card to that fancy new (well, new when *I* was alive!) shishkabob place."

Mom had thought of everything. But how did she know Claire's name? *He* didn't even know her name until after his mother died. Guy was puzzled. But here was a very expensive bottle of champagne, and he certainly couldn't drink it himself.

So he called Claire back and said, "I know it's kind of last minute, but….would you like to go out with me for New Year's Eve?"

"You mean … as your date?"

Jeez Louise, this was awkward. "I guess so. Sure, as my date." Guy filled the silence, adding, "They won't have a problem with that at the department, will they?"

"Not if they never know," said Claire with a laugh. Guy laughed too. The idea that city employees in the same department couldn't date each other, when the place was already a reality show in the making, a "Peyton Place" of trysts, and affairs, was absurd. Why, everyone knew what was going on in Mr. Dichard's office with the big boss, Ms. Gowan.

So it was agreed that Guy would pick Claire up on New Year's Eve and they'd have dinner at the Moroccan restaurant his mother had pre-booked. The gift certificate promised Baba Ghanoush! Belly Dancers! Tents! It was all a little too exotic for Guy's taste, but his mom thought it would be good, so he'd give it a shot.

On New Year's Eve day, Guy stood at Claire's doorstep. She opened the door and he noticed immediately that she had really fixed herself up. Her normally thin, straight hair – the texture of lint – was highlighted and curled. This was the first time he'd ever seen her in makeup, too. She wore a long, sexless skirt, but she also donned a tight black sweater that made him notice her ample bosoms for the first time. She smelled good, too, like the plumeria potpourri Mom used to keep around the house.

"You look nice," he told her. Claire blushed.

The two of them had a delicious and enjoyable dinner. He was embarrassed by the attention of the belly dancers and by having to stick dollar bills in their cleavage, but Guy took the whole thing in stride.

Claire told him about a party her roommate's friend was having, so afterwards they drove over there to signal in the New Year. Because of their mutual shyness, Claire and Guy spent most of the night on the front porch away from the other guests, drinking the Two Buck Chuck that some cheapskate had brought to the party. The fact that they were ill at ease with crowds brought the two of them closer together. The alcohol helped too. Claire and Guy were finally connecting, sharing their intimate thoughts and feelings. At the stroke of midnight, he popped open the Dom Perignon and they kissed. They finished off the bottle, and then made out some more.

After that, Guy and Claire began dating every week. At first they kept it a secret around their coworkers, but after a month everyone in the office already knew so there was no point in hiding it. After the third date, as was the custom in Seward, they had intercourse. Soon he was spending three nights a week at her place.

IV

Spring came again. On Easter Sunday, Guy
eagerly awaited his mother's email. He had to wait
until almost midnight, but, sure enough, it finally
arrived:

> "Happy Resurrection Day! I trust that you are
> having a good time with Claire and I'm sure
> she's a wonderful gal. But you haven't 'been'
> with a lot of women – only six."

How would she know that? He had never told
Mom about his sex life. Besides, Claire *was* his
Number 6. Guy continued reading:

> "Six gals are not enough to know whether
> Claire's the right one. Please don't be rash, like
> I was with your father. I wished I'd had a lot
> more (you know what I mean!) before I became
> a born again Christian and then died. My
> advice? Ask Denise out and see if you like her
> better. (A mother always knows these things!)
> With all my love, Mom."

Who's Denise?! Guy wracked his brain.

Just then he heard the familiar pounding at the
front door. Dave walked in, carrying a large and
unwieldy box. He stopped to catch his breath. Dave

wiped the sweat from his forehead, and said, "It's from you know who."

Guy tore into the box. Wow! A slick, titanium frame, professional grade, mountain bike!

Here was the card attached:

"My dearest son, I thought you might enjoy doing some other kind of exercise besides running. Something that I hope you can enjoy with people. I found out about a bike club that meets at the YMCA on Saturdays. All you have to do is to ride over to the bike shop and sign up. I had them attach a map for you so you can get down there today. Have fun, but be safe! Always wear a helmet! Love, Mom."

Cool! Guy had wanted to get into mountain biking for a while, but he just couldn't face haggling with manipulative bicycle salesmen.

He rolled his shiny new toy outside, said a quick goodbye to Dave, and pedaled over to the shop to find out about the club.

Guy was in luck. The Pushers & Peddlers, he was told, would be gathering this Saturday for their annual ride up to Bates Peak. It was a strenuous ride, the bike clerk warned him. But Guy figured he was in good enough shape from his running to make the trek.

And so, early that Saturday morning, he and a dozen other cyclists gathered in front of the Y. The club members warmly greeted their newest rider. Then they all took off.

As the group cycled out of town and started their climb in the foothills, Guy rode tandem with a cute, athletically built thirty-something woman, with blond, spiky hair. She said her name was Dee and that she'd joined the bike club a year ago when she moved to Seward. She told him that she lived up in Shady Hills, one of Seward's better neighborhoods, and that she was a hardcore rider. She rode hundreds of miles each week, year round, in ice, snow, hail, rain, and extreme heat. One time, like the wicked witch, during a cyclone.

Guy asked her what she did when she wasn't riding.

"I play games – *you* might call them video games. And I play all night, *if* you know what I mean." Dee winked at him.

No, Guy did NOT know what she meant. Was this some hip drug or sex lingo, some local patois from wherever she was originally from?

Suddenly the grade got steeper. As they began to reach their final ascent, Guy started huffing and puffing, but Dee took off, leaving everyone else in the dust.

By the time the rest of the group reached the summit, she had already patched her front tire and was leisurely kicking back and vaping an herbal e-cigarette.

Everyone, except for Guy, sat down and ate their lunches. He hadn't had the sense to pack something (where was Mom when you needed her?) and he was starving. Dee offered him half of her sandwich, but he politely declined, just as Joan had taught to do.

"Ah, don't be shy. I hope you like peanut butter and honey."

"Are you kidding? It's my favorite!"

"Mine too." She handed him half of the sandwich. He immediately wolfed it down.

"I guess we have a lot in common," said Guy with a laugh. "Do you like running, too?"

"Fuck yeah! I do marathons four times a year."

"Do you like the Discovery Channel?"

"Love it. Second only to NatGeo."

"That's awesome too!" He was starting to really like this woman. "How about model trains?"

She grimaced. "Hell, no. That shit is weird."

He laughed, though mainly out of embarrassment.

After a short silence, Dee asked, "What's the deal with your 'stache? Did you lose a bet or something?"

Guy was about to say that it was his mother's idea, but thought the better of it. "No. I'm not much of a betting man." That didn't really answer the question, but they left it at that.

"I'm just fuckin' with you," she said with a smile. He smiled with her, though he didn't know why, other than the fact that Dee was pretty.

When the cyclists had all eaten and had begun to feel the effects of their sugar and caffeine-laden nutritional sports drinks, Dee led them all down the steep and winding road back into town. When they finally reached the YMCA, everyone high-fived each other and said their goodbyes until the following Saturday.

Dee told Guy that if he ever wanted to share a P, B, & H sandwich and play some wicked video games, to give her a call. She gave him her business card and asked for his phone number. Then they said goodbye.

On his ride home, he couldn't help thinking about that sexy, spiky blond. All the same, he wished he hadn't given Dee his number. He knew he should have been straight with Dee from the start that he was seeing someone. He really liked Claire and knew it would hurt her if she found out that he was dating someone else. But Mom had told him to date other women before settling down. Besides, he reasoned, he and Claire never made *explicit* promises about being monogamous.

When he finally made it home, the sky was dark. It wasn't until he plopped down on the couch that he realized that he every muscle in his body was sore and he was utterly exhausted. Still, he had genuinely loved biking today. And he liked sharing lunch with Dee. Reaching into his pocket, he took out the card she'd given him. It read, "Denise 'Dee' McIntyre, C.P.A."

C.P.A.?! This sexy, athletic, and outgoing lady was an accountant? Even more surprising was her real name: Denise. That's the name his mother had told him to look for!

But how could Mom have possibly known about *this* Denise? After all, the young woman had told him that she'd just moved to Seward last year. And that was long after Mom's passing. Someone must be playing a sick and morbid joke on him, he thought. Perhaps all these emails were coming from some Dutch scammer. Or maybe from some hacker *slash* overbearing Jewish mother from Eastern Europe? But that didn't seem right, either. The missives sure looked like Mom's style of writing. Still…

His phone rang. Before he could even say hello, he heard, "Hey, it's Dee. You remember, right? Denise, from the bike club?"

"Yes, of course I remember. It's only been a few hours."

"Good, then there's nothing wrong with your short term memory." She added, with a slight laugh, "Not yet, anyway."

Guy felt like mentioning that he thought he might be going crazy on account of his dead mom's emails, but he certainly didn't want to get into that right now.

"Anyway," Denise asked, "Is it too soon to call?"

"No, not at all, it's good to hear from you."

"Now that we've got all that out of the way, you want to come over and play some games?"

Hell yeah! She gave him her address then grabbed his bike and pedaled up a series of steep hills to get to her place. Denise greeted him at the door in a sweat-drenched aerobics outfit. She told him to rest on the couch while she went into the kitchen to make him a sandwich.

After he ate she showed him her collection of some of the most violent video games he'd ever seen. Guy liked shoot 'em up video games just like the next bro-gamer, but *these* obscure role playing games - which she said were delivered in plain brown paper packaging – these were something else. To Guy, they seemed like nothing more than digitized snuff films. All this snuff-smut looked so vile that Guy couldn't decide among any of the games, so he let her pick one. Denise chose "Penitentiary" her favorite. In that game, she played a sadistic female guard who rapes the male inmates using various instruments of brutality: sticks, bottles, sifters, can openers, bowling pins, golf clubs, etc. Perhaps unsurprisingly, Guy's character was one of her prisoners.

Sitting side-by-side on her love seat while they fired up the X Box, he turned to get a closer look at

Denise. He'd never been attracted to a woman with short hair before, but Denise also had seductive lips and a smoking-hot body.

"You don't look like any C.P.A. I've ever seen," he told her.

"Is that good or bad?" she asked, pretending to not know the answer.

He stammered something about how, no offense, accountants are pretty staid. "I mean, look at you, you look sassy, and, if you don't mind me saying, sexy."

"Thanks, but I'm just squeezing your shoes," she said.

"You're what?"

"I'm just shitting you. I've been told that I don't look like an accountant about a million times," Denise rifled through a stack of papers on her coffee table but then gave up. "Actually, there's an interesting study around here somewhere that found that CPAs, on average, and adjusted for age, have twice as many sexual partners as those in other professions."

Guy frowned. "More sex partners than dentists? No way."

The two of them went back to another gory round of shootings, stabbings, electrocutions, and male genital mutilations.

By about the tenth game, Guy casually asked Denise whether she had known his mother, Joan Moulton.

"No, should I have?"

He shrugged and they went back to another game.

After she beat him 21 rounds to 2, he checked his watch. It was one in the morning. "I've had a great time, Denise, but I'd better be going."

"'Denise'? Only my lovers or clients call me that. Hold on a sec." She went into the bathroom. When she came out, Denise was naked except for a backwards baseball/bro-gaming cap on her head. With a lascivious smile, she said, "Since you don't look like of my clients, you'll have to be my lover for tonight."

She threw her arms around him and forcefully ground her pubis into his. Then she kicked aside some joysticks and other gaming devices and pushed him on her bed. They made love, or, rather, she ruggedly mounted him and rode him for two hours. When she was done – and she let him climax - his body was completely spent. Guy fell into a deep sleep at the foot of her bed.

Denise woke him up very early the next morning. She said she was teaching a kick boxing class in a few minutes and that he'd have to leave. So Guy splashed some water on his face and biked home.

As he walked up the steps to the front door, he thought about going upstairs and crawling back into bed. But there was too much on his mind. Instead, Guy just zoned out in the living room, trying not to look at his mom's closed bedroom door, which still made him sad to look at.

Guy thought of the emails again. Could Denise have had anything to do with them? That seemed doubtful. She sounded truthful when she said she didn't know his mother. Anyway, Denise hadn't met him until yesterday - unless she'd been stalking him this whole time…No, that was nuts. He was too tired to think straight, so he reheated an old pot of Folger's and parked himself in front of his new flat screen TV.

Sipping the barely palatable brew, Guy wondered whether it was Claire who was behind the emails. But why would she encourage him to date Denise? Was this Claire's way of getting rid of him - letting him down gently by finding him a replacement? That didn't make sense either. Claire obviously cared for him and wouldn't want to lose him.

Maybe Dave the U.P.S. guy was the one who was messing with him? True, he had a ponytail, which, Guy's mom always considered to be untrustworthy on a man. But Dave didn't seem bright enough to have concocted this email scheme, plus he seemed like too nice of a guy to do that. Could it be just some random hacker? But why would someone other than Mom go to the trouble and expense of buying all those expensive gifts that corresponded with the emails? Maybe it started out as Mom's emails but then the account got hacked?

Guy chugged down the rest of his coffee but the caffeine did no good. Within minutes he was fast asleep on the couch.

Over the next few weeks Guy continued his usual routine, though he now added Denise to the dating mix. He was still seeing Claire, who didn't act strangely or, in fact, any differently toward him than before. That made it even more probable, in Guy's view, that she had nothing to do with these crazy emails. On top of seeing Claire at work, he spent nights at her place on even days. On odd days, he'd hook up with Denise. It took a lot of energy keeping Claire and Denise from catching wind of each other. He knew Claire would be upset if she found out about his double-timing, though he wasn't so sure that Denise would've cared one way or another. Either way, Guy knew at some point that he'd probably have to choose between the two, but he put that out of his mind for now. Maybe Mom or whoever the joker who was sending those emails would help him with that decision.

Guidance did come, on his 29th birthday. Guy spent his day in the office and had dinner with Claire after work. Then, he kissed her goodnight and rode his bike up the hill for a late night of "games" with Denise. After some cyber ultra-violence and sexual activity, Guy finally made it home in the wee hours of the morning. He knew he'd only get a few hours of sleep before having to get up for work.

But just before hitting the sack, Guy checked his phone for messages one last time. There were birthday wishes from Claire, Denise, and Dave.

Then, there it was, the email he was looking for!

Mom wrote to wish him a Happy 29th Birthday. This time, she communicated in a passionate and very personal way of her love for beloved son. She recalled some of their memorable times together, like his tenth birthday when he lost his Fudgsicle in the back of their car, forever making their Corolla smell like a rancid ice cream truck driven by a serial killer. (At that time she was gripped in fear of the so-called "Iceman Killer.") Mom wrote tenderly of holding Guy's little hand on his first day of kindergarten, and of comforting him from his childhood fear of rats whenever he saw one in their basement.

Joan said she forgave him for making fun of the stories she'd told him, like those from her own youth; she reminded him of his sarcasm when she'd told she had fallen madly in love with, who disappeared a few days after she met Guy's father. (Joan blamed her own mother for that.) Joan also said she forgave Guy for mocking her beliefs in Jesus and Astrology, and for chastising her for spending money on psychic hotlines. She quoted scripture: "Forgive them, Father, for they know not what they do."

Who else but his own mother could have known about these things? Now there was no doubt in Guy's mind that Mom was truly the author of all these emails.

Next, Mom's tone turned dire:

"My successful and responsible son, PLEASE LISTEN TO ME! I have a gut feeling that you need to get a prostate exam right away. There's something very wrong. I know you're young still, but please, PROMISE ME YOU'LL GO TO THE DOCTOR!"

On a lighter note, she added that she hoped Guy was still enjoying dating Claire and Denise.

But she warned:

"Don't be like your father - God rest his wicked, philandering soul. You need to choose *one* girl and be faithful to her. I know with your limited experience that it might be hard for you to make the right choice. Maybe expand your pool. Have you considered Courtney? You remember Courtney, don't you? Hint: where did I used to buy your peanut butter?"

Guy thought about that, but his mind turned back to Mom's warnings about his prostate. He was so worried about his health now that there was no way he could sleep. He tossed and turned, alternating between fearing his impending death from cancer, and steaming about Mom's incessant meddling in his love life.

When his alarm went off that morning, he knew that there was no way he could go to work, so he called Mr. Dichard and told him he was sick. Guy didn't feel any guilt about blowing off work (well, maybe a little), since it was his first sick day in his four years with the department.

After making the call to his boss, he went back to bed. He was just on the verge of sleep when he was awoken by a pounding that shook the whole house. Guy literally jumped out of bed. But once he realized that there hadn't been an earthquake or that a drunk driver hadn't rammed into the house, he knew it must be Dave.

Sure enough, with bouncing quads and ponytail, Dave delivered Mom's latest birthday gift: an elegant men's wardrobe, complete with a dark, pin-striped suit, a fine cotton white shirt, silk tie, and dress shoes. The note read:

> "Happy Birthday! Wear this on any date and the ladies will swoon. But don't kill 'em! Ha! And just make sure you see about that prostate first. OK? Love, Mom."

Dave had another delivery for Guy: an unsolicited pair of running shoes from that annoying online company. Guy wrote "Return to sender. Did NOT order!" on the outside of the box and the two of them played a quick game of football catch with the package.

After a few minutes, Dave reluctantly said he had to get back to his appointed rounds. "Neither sleet, nor snow, that kind of thing," Dave solemnly told Guy . "Actually, that's for the Postal Service, but you get the idea."

As soon as Dave was gone, Guy called his doctor's office. He spoke to a nurse who tried to talk him out of scheduling a prostate exam, saying it wasn't a recommended procedure, absent symptoms, for men under the age of fifty. But Guy pleaded with her. Fortunately, there had just been a cancellation, so they were able to get him in that day.

Good thing, too, because Dr. Kamena quickly discovered something suspicious. She did a biopsy, and then performed emergency surgery to eradicate a rare and aggressive type of cancer. Luckily, the disease was still in its early stages. Had it not been for this early detection, the doctor said, Guy would most likely have died within a year.

Now he decided that it was time to heed the rest of Mom's advice and to go and find this Courtney girl. He went over to Big T, the supermarket where Mom used to shop. He went around the store furtively checking out every female clerk's nametag. There was a Tiffany, a Britney, a Gabbie, and a Hayden, but no Courtney.

Then Guy spotted a very pretty, fresh-faced young blond who was stacking turnips in the produce section. Though she wore Big T's silly gingham dress uniform, Guy could still see her sexy, hourglass figure. Guy walked close to her, pretending to check out the radishes, so he could get a good look at her name tag. Sure enough, it read "Hi, How Can I Help You Today, I'm Courtney."

He smiled at her. Then, desperately searching for something to say, asked her how to check for the perfect radish. Courtney earnestly showed him, explaining her dubious theories on how the shape of each radish affected its taste.

Guy thanked her, paused, and then asked, in as much of a matter-of-fact tone as he could muster, "Did you, by any chance know my mother, Joan Moulton?"

"I'm not sure. Does she shop here?"

"She used to shop her all the time."

He showed Courtney a few of the pics of Mom he had on his cellphone.

"Yes, I *do* remember your mother," said Courtney. "A real nice lady. She used to come in here a lot, finicky about avocados. But I don't think I've seen her in here for a long time."

"That's because she died two years ago."

A pained look came over Courtney's face. "Oh, I'm so, so sorry," she said. She daubed her eyes with her gingham apron. "Did you just ask me that to make me cry?"

"No, of course not," Guy said. But he didn't want to tell her that he was here on account of Mom's posthumous emails. Though Guy wasn't all that experienced in the dating world, even he knew that this wouldn't go over well. Perhaps Courtney would understand someday, but not now.

"No, I'd never try to make anybody sad," was all Guy could think to say.

"But you did!" She turned to leave. "And, here I thought you were a nice man."

"I am," said Guy, "At least I think so. I only asked because my mom had mentioned that a kind, young woman named Courtney at Big T was always so helpful whenever she came in looking for good avocados."

Courtney turned back toward him and smiled proudly. He had to hand it to Mom: this girl *was* beautiful. With her flawless skin and light blue eyes, Courtney was far prettier than Claire or Denise. They talked a little more and Courtney told Guy that she'd just turned twenty-one. While that was a little too young for him, she *was* sexy and sweet. Plus, he did the classic male rationalization: deciding that she seemed very mature for her age.

Courtney gave him her phone number and, within days they had their first date, at Il Travolta, Seward's popular date restaurant. Guy planned to wear something casual but at the last moment succumbed to Mom's advice by wearing the suit she'd bought him.

That turned out to be the right move. When the valet took his car and they were about to go inside, Courtney sized him up and said, "Don't let it get to your head, but you look very handsome and sophisticated tonight, all dressed up like that."

During dinner, Courtney laughed uproariously at nearly everything that came out of Guy's mouth. Like most men, he was flattered, but he was also unnerved too, for he was hardly known for his wit. Or his scintillating conversation.

"Guy, you are *so* hilarious," she said, in between bites of linguini. "You're a funny guy, Guy!" She took a big gulp of her wine, her third glass so far. She was undoubtedly an alcohol lightweight and was clearly catching a buzz. "Yes, I think you're excellent, puppy."

"Thanks, I guess. But what does that mean?"

"It means," Courtney stopped again to chug down the remains of her glass, "That maybe you should take me home and hump me."

He liked her direct approach, so unlike Denise's oblique sexual innuendoes about "games" and "doing time." And a change from Claire's prudishness and passivity in the bedroom. Upon hearing Courtney's remark, Guy sat up, straightened his tie and adjusted his penis. He decided that he liked this young lady. A lot. Not merely as a sex partner, but also as…well, he'd think of the reasons later. Right now his gonads were doing some serious thinking.

After dessert, Guy settled the tab and drove Courtney back to her place. There, she showed him volumes of photos of her family back in Oregon; she displayed her tattoos, telling him the story behind each and every one of them. Next, she told him of her dreams and ambitions, and then her hopes and fears. Finally, they got down to do it doggy style.

Over the next few months he dated Courtney, in addition to Claire and Denise. Guy hated deceiving his ladies, least of all, Claire. Not only was he uncomfortable with all these private trysts, he never pictured himself as the Don Juan type. Having to juggle three women was a quandary of his own making, he knew that. But he also thought that the ultimate cause of this problem was his controlling mother. His problem could and should *only* be solved by Mom. Guy longed for her next email so that she could give him a sign as to which gal to choose.

Luckily, he didn't have to wait for the next holiday. One September evening she wrote:

> "Dearest Son, Happy 9/11 Day! I trust you got that prostate handled – so to speak! And I hope you'll realize now that I gave you a lot of good advice while I was alive, but you didn't always listen to me, did you? Now that I'm dead, I'll bet you NOW listen to Mommy's little hints. But we'll say no more about it!

> "Guy, I need to tell you that I've been getting a strange feeling about Mr. Dichard. I'm sorry to tell you this honey, but I think your boss is going to die soon. Why don't you spend the next couple of weeks working real hard at the office so that when Old Man Dichard croaks you'll be in line for his job? I'm sure you don't want to be a second class worker all your life! Love for eternity, Mom."

Goddamit! How many times did he have to tell her that he was a Class II employee, not a second class worker?! Guy had long suspected that she called him second class on purpose in her misguided belief that it would motivate him to climb the Department ladder. "When you're at the top," she'd once told him, "You'll attract top-shelf ladies."

Mom's ribbing was annoying enough, but what really disturbed him was her premonition about his boss. Dichard had always been a decent man to work and Guy certainly didn't want to see anything bad happen to the man. Guy's fears were justified too: he'd long known that Joan's premonitions came true, more often than not.

Nevertheless, he followed her advice, and over the next few weeks, Guy put in extra hours at work. He volunteered for extra assignments, like alphabetizing all the microfiche in the office, and made sure that Dichard's boss, Ms. Gowan, also noticed all the work he was putting in.

Guy observed Dichard's health over the next few weeks. The man looked fine, despite Mom's warning. But then, on Halloween night, the small plane Dichard was flying crashed into a mountain en route to a city planner's convention. Dichard was killed along with everyone else on the plane. Just as Joan had predicted, Guy got his boss' job, having been promoted over co-workers like Claire, who had more education (a master's in mechanical engineering) and greater seniority.

Initially, Guy was thrilled with the increase in pay and prestige. But he also felt guilty about the promotion, especially when he learned that Claire was disappointed that she failed to get it. Even Guy thought that this was pure sexism, since it was obvious that

Claire was far more qualified than he was for the Supervisor, Class I position.

Claire's inability to get the promotion, plus the fact that Guy hadn't been making any effort to get closer in their relationship (how could he, when he was secretly seeing two other women?) caused Claire to become more distant toward him. They still went out twice a week, though, and she never complained about anything in particular. But Guy sensed that there was now a wall between him and Claire, which did not sit well with him.

Plus, Guy had this feeling, which he knew was irrational but still couldn't help dwelling on, that he and Mom had had something to do with Dichard's death. Guy was so upset by these feelings of guilt that he nearly cried when his former boss' widow and their three young children came to the office to retrieve the man's belongings the following week. Guy had to excuse himself to go to the men's room just so he wouldn't have to look them in the eye. Ms. Gowan looked equally upset and ran into the ladies' room until Dichard's widow and her kids left.

Guy wasn't sure he even liked the responsibilities and additional work the supervisor job entailed. Even *before* the promotion, he wasn't getting enough rest, what with dating three women, biking, running, and his model trains. Now, he was lucky to get by with three hours of sleep and with a few cat naps here and there. Worse, Ms. Gowan, apparently so distraught about missing her lover, Dichard, now began making untoward passes at Guy. In his increasingly addled and sleep-deprived state, whenever he thought about all the advice Mom had given him from the grave, he felt angry at her for giving it. And even angrier at himself for being too much of a wimp to stop taking it.

Now, Joan's emails were becoming more frequent. No longer were her communiques confined to major holidays; – now he got them on Halloween, Veteran's Day, even JFK Assassination Day. Then he got them on the birthdays of various Christian celebrities. It was only a matter of time, Guy knew, that her emails would come in every minute of the day.

He became so rattled that he seriously questioned whether he was losing his mind altogether. Maybe, according to one mental health website Guy visited, he was having a psychic breakdown due to unresolved feelings about his mother. Could all these communications merely be figments of his imagination? He hated to involve anyone else in all this, but Guy wondered whether he should share these emails with someone. Someone who could assess their veracity. And possibly assess his sanity.

As if anticipating what Guy was planning to do, the next morning Mom sent this stern message:

> "Son, remember that these letters are OUR special secret and they're private. Don't mention them to anyone else, my dearest. It's not nice."

Not nice?! Mom telling him what to do and driving him crazy - *that* wasn't nice!

Now he was dead-set on reaching out for help.

Guy decided he'd show the emails to Denise. Despite her penchant for unbridled violence and gory sex, she seemed to have the most logical mind of anyone he knew. He also felt certain that Denise had nothing to do with writing them, so she could be somewhat objective.

So, that evening he invited Denise over and showed her everything: the emails on his server and all the notes that had accompanied his gifts.

Denise took a quick look at them and let out a chortle. "Very funny, pulling my leg like that." She even belittled him, saying this was a lame ass way of trying to scare her off.

"Look, when I want to fuck," she said, "I fuck. And no one, I repeat NO ONE stops me. You got that?"

Denise added that she would expect immature hijinks like this from her fellow accountants or from some crazy lady ex-lover of hers, but not from Guy.

But she forgave him for his "adolescent humor," because, she said, she was turned on by younger men, "especially ones with a naughty side." To emphasize her point, she rubbed his crotch, unzipped his pants, and straddled him on the living room sofa.

Since Denise had been of little help - except for relieving his sexual tension – he invited Courtney over to show her the emails. Courtney's response was to erupt into tears. Then, after regaining her composure, she said how sweet it was that his mother would have taken time in her final days to write such loving notes.

"I wish," she said, stopping to blow her nose, "I had gotten to know that wonderful lady better back when we were picking out avocados." Courtney said she felt so sorry that Guy lost such a loving inspiration. Then she started to cry again, saying that this was just *her* luck, her CURSE, even: she would date older men but never get to know their parents because they were already dead.

"All of this talk," Courtney said, "Makes me want to bus on out to Oregon to give my mother the biggest hug in the whole entire world!"

Still teary, Courtney asked Guy to hold her and make everything alright. He put his arms around her, comforting her as best he could. Courtney then pulled him on top, kissed him, and lifted up her dress for a pity fuck. She was comforted. He was spent.

VI

Finally, and with extreme reluctance, he showed the emails to Claire. He knew she'd be upset to discover that Mom nagged him to date that "mousy girl." And he assumed Claire would be mad when she learned that he'd been seeing other women.

He was right on both counts: Claire became angrier and angrier when she read that Guy's mother had advised him to date Denise and Courtney. Then she became livid when he admitted that he'd taken Mom's dating advice. Courtney even kicked a small hole in his wall when she learned how Joan's interference – and Guy's complicity - had caused her to lose out on the job promotion. Guy was freaked. He'd never seen Claire so enraged before and he was afraid that she'd hurt him physically *and* ruin his career at the office.

After Claire voiced her profound feelings of disappointment, frustration, and betrayal, she put her head in her hands and broke down. Guy reached out to comfort her, but she pushed him away. Amid her sobs, he told her how very sorry he was about the other women. To prove it, he told her that he recently learned, in a prostate follow-up with his doctor, that Denise had given him chlamydia. (When Guy had confronted Denise and asked why she hadn't previously disclosed her STD to him, Denise callously told him, "Because that's how accountants roll. Deal with it, bitch.")

Guy spoke from the heart, telling Claire, for the first time, how much he loved her. He wanted Claire to understand that his mother's advice had always been hit and miss. If he hadn't listened to his mother, he said, he wouldn't even have worked up the nerve to talk to Claire. So, that was good. Mom saving his life by telling him to get a prostate exam? Also good. But Mom telling him to date the other gals, well, that was not so good. Claire glared back. He revised his assessment: dating other women was a *really, really bad idea*.

After she calmed down, Claire decided she was willing to help him. She told him that, while she had no idea who was behind these emails, one thing was certain: Guy had to stop letting them control his life. And he had to stop letting his *mother* control his life. Claire told him that she'd do everything possible to stop these missives from coming in, but made clear to him that from now on everything would have to be done *her* way. Guy wasn't sure he was all that crazy about this new, more controlling Claire – it reminded him way too much of Mom. But these ever-increasing messages were driving him to the point where he felt like he had no other option than to follow his girlfriend's instructions to the letter.

Claire's first step was to get rid of her rivals. She "borrowed" Guy's cellphone and separately texted Courtney and Denise, telling them to meet him in front of the library after work. When 5:30 arrived, Claire strolled hand-in-hand with Guy to the library, a short distance from their office. She asked him to kiss her and to tell her how much he loved her. Guy complied, completely oblivious to anyone else around. Courtney saw the whole thing and ran away in tears.

But Denise, who waited to see every last tongue action, was more intrigued than perturbed. She sidled up to both of them, dropping hints about doing a "twa. "It took Claire and Guy a few moments to realize that the hell she was talking about. But if Claire didn't like Val's pizza and porn parties, she certainly wasn't going do a three-way with anyone, least of all, one of her rivals. And one with an S.T.D. to boot.

The next day Claire finally got rid of Denise once and for all by sending a letter purporting to be from an investigator with the State Commissioner of Accountancy. It warned Denise that her CPA license would be revoked if she continued to have sexual relations with anyone without first disclosing in writing all her sexually transmitted diseases. The letter further warned Denise that "the licensee shall forever stay away from Guy Moulton, who, it is presumed, will soon be filing suit against her."

Claire felt pretty clever as she made the ninety minute drive to the state capitol to drop the letter off. After that, Denise was never heard from again – a week later, The Seward Sentinel reported that Denise had been stabbed to death in an unrelated incident.

Meanwhile, Joan sent a new threatening message of her own. She had a strange feeling, she wrote, that Guy had been sharing her emails with others – and with other *women*, no less! She reminded him of her admonition to NEVER do that, adding:

> "NEVER stop listening to my advice.
> Otherwise, things will get worse for you, Son.
> Much worse."

Guy was spooked by his mother's not-so-veiled threat. He knew, from many painful experiences, just how vindictive Mom could be. But he'd already promised Claire that he'd get rid of his laptop and change his email accounts.

So he continued to do everything Claire had instructed, and all was quiet…for a few days.

Then one early morning, at three a.m., he was awoken to a cacophony of beeps and dings from his cellphone. He checked it to find that Mom had just sent him hundreds of text messages.

The next day he got a new phone number and changed phone carriers. Still, every day he'd get another text message with the heading "MOTHER'S LITTLE WARNING."

On top of the texts, Joan's emails resumed, forwarded to every one of his new email addresses. He set his spam filter to catch the messages, to no avail: his inbox was still flooded with a multitude of warnings and threats, such as "exposing you Mr. Dichard's murderer."

Then Joan's poison-pen emails got through on his inter-office email too. He desperately tried deleting each nastygram before anyone near his cubicle saw what was going on. Guy asked the city's IT hotshots to solve the problem, telling them only that he was getting barraged with spam. Unfortunately, the best the city's tech nerds could say was that the messages were probably coming from some remote offshore server. In any case, there was no way they could permanently stop the messages from coming in.

Worse, Guy learned from the company his mother had contracted with, that, according to the terms of the Eternity Plus Plan, they were legally bound to track him down for up to ninety-nine years. And he learned that Mom had given the company all of his personal data, including a sample of his DNA, which apparently came from a hair sample she collected from a toilet. Thus, he and Claire realized that it was going to be much harder than they'd originally thought to rid themselves of this constant torment.

Still, Claire did what she could to try to get Joan out of their lives once and for all. She convinced Guy to put the house up for sale. To that end, they tossed whatever junk was still around after Guy's remodel and she helped him to get the house ready to show.

Unfortunately, in the midst of all this activity, Guy's electric train set sparked, causing a fire in the living room. Guy managed to douse the flames, but only after the fire burned his drapes, sofa, and video collection, including the DVD engineering series that Mom had sent him. His trainset still ran, but all of the model's buildings burned, making the pint-sized Seward replica look like the aftermath of the bombing of Dresden. Because of the fire, he and Claire had to spend an extra week just to clear out the charred remains.

The chore that Guy dreaded most was cleaning out Joan's room. Claire offered to go in by herself and clear things out with an iron broom, but he felt that he needed to go in there too, figuring that only he would know what to save and what to throw out. Still, he was nervous. Mom had specifically told him not to go into her room until she'd given the OK. But the thought of having to get permission from his dead mother made Guy furious. He was a grown man, for God's sake! This was now *his* home! He didn't have to take orders from anyone!

With Claire by his side, he slowly crept over to the dead woman's door and jiggled the knob. It was locked. He had no idea where the key could be so he broke the door down. He did it just like they do in the movies, only it took him a dozen tries and practically dislocated his shoulder.

Once the door came down they surveyed Joan's room. They found, much to their surprise… almost nothing.

Guy vaguely remembered that Muriel, from Mom's church group, had looked in on him around the time of the funeral. Muriel had said something about tidying up the house and clearing out some trash. But she must have done far more than that: all that was left was a gaudy faux gold night stand and three books, stacked on the floor, evidently meant to be cleared out later, but somehow forgotten. To Guy, thee books neatly summed up his mother's interests: a dog eared

Gideon's Bible, "Astrology: from A to Z", and "The Psychic's Connection."

Guy and Claire opened up Mom's bedroom closet and found that it too was barren, except for the laptop that Guy had given Mom.   They plugged it in and tried to boot it up, but the computer was completely dead. Guy took it to The Geek Squad, but the squad of geeks told him the hard drive was fried and unrecoverable. He took it to Devon, the teenage hacker next door, but he couldn't fix it either.

Meanwhile, Claire found a realtor to list the house. Guy's plan (actually, Claire's idea) was to buy a house across town; they'd find a place large enough for both of them, and for their children, if and when they were ready to start a family.   Claire had been right when she'd told him that it was a good time to sell because, sure enough, within a week, Guy got three offers. He even ended up selling at a higher price than what he'd originally asked for. A thirty day escrow was opened.

The next day, Guy checked his emails and saw a new one from Mom. He had the urge to delete it, but the subject line said "I'm Not Angry." He opened it up:

> "Dearest Guy, I hope you're not feeling bad
> about selling the house. By now, it's the right
> thing to do. You've lived here almost all your

life, and I guess it's time for a new chapter. By the way, I didn't tell you that I asked the church ladies to clear out all the junk in my room. There wasn't anything you'd need in there, so why trouble you with having to clean it? I do hope you can find a new place, a better place. Don't worry, though: wherever you go, I'll always be with you! Remember the time when you were little and I took you to that church outing at the lake and you fell out of the boat? You were so scared and everyone was screaming and I had to push that good-for-nothing Pastor Yarborough into the water to save you. Remember what I told you then?"

Guy felt a lump in his throat. Never had he felt happier to be alive then after the preacher pulled him back on board. Once he had coughed the water out of his lungs, his mother told him that she would ALWAYS look after him, no matter what. That day he felt so loved, so comforted - though, he did develop a lifelong fear of drowning.

Joan continued:

"I miss you so much and hope you can come and be with me soon. Don't worry, neither your father nor Mr. Dichard are up here, ha! Oh, before I forget, be on the lookout for a new gift

– nothing fancy, but I think you'll have a lot of fun with it! Love forever, Mom.

P.S. I hope Claire's father's OK."

Guy was happy now that Mom wasn't mad anymore. And happier still that for the rest of the week she didn't send any more messages.

Unfortunately, Claire's father was suddenly and tragically killed in a hit and run accident. She had to fly out to Indiana for the funeral. He wished he could've joined her, but Ms. Gowan told him, while putting her hand on his knee, that he was needed at the office.

For the past few months, Guy had been spending most nights at Claire's, since she refused to sleep at his house after she claimed to have heard moans coming from Joan's room. Now, though, he was happy to be sleeping at his place, where he'd have a little time alone before having to vacate at the close of escrow.

But he was surprised to find that he was lonesome without Claire, even though she'd only been gone for three days. It was a good thing she'd be flying in that afternoon.

Guy was just finishing up his Cream of Wheat when the U.P.S. truck rolled by. Dave was startled to see him: wasn't Guy supposed to biking with the club today? Guy said he quit the group at Claire's insistence, since, even though Denise was dead, his girlfriend didn't want him fraternizing with any other sex freaks he might have met there.

Dave handed Guy a package. The deliveryman flexed his quads in anticipation as Guy ripped it open. Yes! A sleek pair of rollerblades!

The attached card read:

"Happy Birthday, my dear, and be careful with your new gift. They're supposed to be the fastest pair money can buy!"

After Dave took off, Guy couldn't wait to take the blades out for a spin. Mom was right, these suckers *were* fast. So fast that, once he started rolling, it was nearly impossible to stop. He had to purposefully fall over a few times just to slow his ascent and avoid shooting into traffic. At one point he hit a rock at full speed, causing him to fly into the road, just barely avert an oncoming car. The death seat passenger, a woman, flipped him off and called him a motherfucking dick-suck. After an hour and a dozen more tumbles, he decided he'd had enough skating – and pain - for today.

Guy limped home. In the kitchen, he grabbed his first aid kit so he could salve and bandage his bloody and skinless knees. Then he threw the rollerblades on the steps, next to his running shoes, and hobbled upstairs to change his blood soaked pants. The laptop in his bedroom beeped, telling him he had a new email. He limped over to take a look:

"Did you like your rollerblades, Son?"

Without a second thought he typed back, "You bet!!!!! Thanks Mom, I love you!"

Mom instantly messaged back. "I love you too. And I just can't wait to see you!"

What did she mean by that? He typed "???", hit enter, but received no response.

Guy checked the clock. Uh oh, he was running late. He'd have to wash up and get ready ASAP if he was going to get out in time to pick Claire up at the airport. He went in the bathroom and peed, but it felt like he was pissing out razorblades. He inspected his member: it was encircled with runny, pus-filled sores. Denise, that number-crunching disease-ridden slut! He made a mental note to see Dr. Kamena next week about his genitals.

First, though, he'd have to shave and give his moustache a trim. He filled the sink and added a little mint soap, which Claire liked because it made his facial hair smell fresh, and not like the hormonal billy goat she said it usually smelled like. He leaned over the sink and splashed the water on his face. Then he plugged in the moustache trimmer and let the blades whirl to clean them out. Tiny hairs trapped in the blades flew out and landed in his eyes. He rubbed his eyes, trying to see.

Suddenly there came a series of rings at the doorbell, knocks on the door, and pounding on the front window. It sounded like the Gestapo. Maybe it was the cops. But why would they be here? Had he been rollerblading without some official permit or something? Did this have anything to do with the train-set fire?

"Jeez, I'm coming!" Guy bounded down the stairs. But his eyes were burning and his feet collided with those new super-duper roller blades, causing him to roll down the rest of the steps. He hit his coccyx bone on one stair and the base of his skull on another. It hurt like hell but somehow he managed to get up and get the door. Still dazed from the fall, it took him a moment to even recognize his friend.

Dave looked somber and penitent. "Dude, I'm very, very sorry," he said. "I should also have given you this box when I was here, but I forgot."

Dave handed it to Guy, who immediately saw that it was from that dumbass shoe company again. Guy was steaming. This is what he'd run down here and almost killed myself for?! He wrote "RETURN TO FRICKIN' SENDER!!!!" threw the box at Dave and practically slammed the door on him. Through the front window Guy saw the ponytailer mouthing the words, "I'm sorry, I won't forget again, I'm real sorry…"

Guy turned around and checked his clock again. Now he was running twenty minutes late! He'd have to haul ass now. He tried to run up the stairs to get back to what he was doing, but with his tail bone aching with every step, he could only muster a slow, palsied crawl. When he finally reached the top landing. his cellphone rang. It was Claire.

"Hi honey, I've missed you," he said, trying to catch his breath. "I can't wait to see you."

"Me too, sweetheart, but where ARE you?"

"I'm at home, just getting ready so I can get out of here to pick you up by the time you land."

"But Guy, I've already landed!" She made a deep, almost theatrical sigh. "Didn't you get my texts?"

He hadn't. Between the rollerblading and the interruptions he'd had no time to check his phone.

She spoke to him slowly and patiently, as if giving instructions to a child: "I told you to always check your phone because the airline might post updates on my arrival time. This time, the flight captain said something about us catching a tail wind, so we touched down early. Guy, don't you remember what I told you about checking your phone?"

He told her he was sorry and that he'd leave the house in a minute and hung up. He put the phone down, this time keeping it close by, next to his moustache trimmer on the glass shelf above the sink. He *was* sorry that he hadn't checked for flight changes. And, now that she mentioned it, he did have some memory of her telling him to keep his cellphone on hand.

But he did NOT appreciate being dressed down like that by Claire, or anybody, even his mother. Especially his mother. He wasn't some child who needed to be spoken to like that; he was almost thirty! And he was the most responsible person he knew. His phone rang again. It was Claire calling to nag him again, he was sure of that. This time he let it go to voice mail. *To hell with her*, he thought, *she can wait until I'm good and ready to get her!*

But the damn phone just kept ringing and ringing. He was about to pick up the trimmer to finish what he was doing, but just seeing that fucking thing, a reminder of his manipulative mother, infuriated him. MOM was the one who had almost caused him to die with those fucking rollerblades. And SHE was the one who made him date Denise - that sex freak who gave him who knows how many diseases. And Mom made him take Claire into his life, another controlling woman. *I'm always following everyone else's orders. And I'm tired of it! I. AM. A. GROWN. MAN!!* With each insistent and annoying ring Guy turned from furious to livid, and finally to violently enraged.

"Shit! Shit! Shit!" His mother had taught him not curse, but here he was screaming every obscenity he could think of, as if he had Tourette's.

"FUCK, FUCKING, FUCKAROONY!!!" Guy cried, pounding his fist with a SMASH! right down upon the glass shelf.

Shards of glass exploded everywhere, even in one of his eyes. His toothbrush, cellphone and electric moustache trimmer plopped into the sink filled with mint water. Guy's hand was bloodied and he had to use his other bloody hand to pull a jagged, L-shaped piece of glass out of his palm.

When Guy saw the mess he'd made, he immediately felt sorry. *What if Claire were in trouble right now and needed to reach me? Here I am behaving like a two year old!*

So Guy reached into the bloody sink to grab his cell phone and... ZAP! One hundred and twenty painful, deadly volts arced from the submerged moustache trimmer, sparking through the water and jolting every nerve ending, every muscle, every tissue, and every organ in his body. He shook violently, seized up, and then fell face forward into the sink with a SMACK!

At the age of twenty-nine, Guy Moulton was on his final journey to see his dear, dead mother.

COMMITMENT

I

WITNESS #1: Like I told you, I really didn't know the guy. My old roommate moved out and I was short on rent. Randy was the first sane and clean enough looking guy to answer my Craig's List ad, so he got the room. He moved in about two weeks ago, bringing only an old futon and a couple of boxes. That's his bedroom on the door to the right.

All I know about Randy was that he told me he'd come to New York to act. I don't even know what his day gig was, or if he even had one. Even after he moved in, he wasn't around here very much. As it happens, I woke up late yesterday afternoon (I'd been writing all night) and I hobbled over to the kitchenette over there to make some coffee. Randy was already at the table, sitting on one of the two stools. Something smelled like wet paint. He apologized for the mess and cleared away his paintbrushes and gift wrapping stuff - bows and ribbons, whatever - into a grocery bag so that I could sit down. I was too hung over to make small talk so I didn't ask him what he was doing, but I remember him saying something about painting a prop for a monologue. He said he was performing a scene he wrote at some space on Avenue D and would I like to come? I told him that I had other plans, which wasn't true, but I spent four years at Tisch School of the Arts

and I couldn't stomach any more avant-garde incense –
laden, half naked, men dancing in hula skirts, 9/11 and
AIDS- as –metaphors, performance art.

I didn't know really what Randy would be
doing, but I knew the theatre he was performing at, so I
knew I didn't want to go. Now that I know what
happened, I'm kicking myself about not being there!
It's not like I could've stopped it or something. Hey,
I'm not trying to be callous or anything, but I'm a
writer, I'm always looking for new material…maybe if
I'd known Randy a little better, I'd feel differently.

There's a guy down the hall, Nelson – he was at
the theatre last night. He told me all about what
happened just before you guys knocked.

II

WITNESS #2: Yeah, I was there last night.
Jesus, what a show! I don't know if you guys have seen
the layout of the theatre yet: you go down several
flights of stairs in a dark and musty stairwell to reach
the place. I think during the day it doubles as one of
those hot, stinky yoga joints. I went there to see my
girlfriend do an improv piece…What's her name?
Meghan, Meghan O'Farrell. She was doing something
with another actor, Cal, I think that's his name.
Anyway, I got there late, after my shift ended (I bus
tables at Veselka) since I knew she was going on last.
By the time I found a seat (for some reason the theatre

was packed last night) – some naked woman was onstage smearing feces and yams up her you know what, and saying shit like, "stop making eyes at me, you make me feel dirty" over and over AND over again until she'd run out of yams.

Then this tall skinny guy with black hair and a pencil thin mustache takes the stage. I do a double take – whoa, isn't that guy Ben's new roommate?

He starts by just staring at the audience for about a minute. I can't tell if it's some dramatic effect, or whether Randy's nervous, or forgot his lines, or what. But then, after introducing himself, he really starts cranking. The guy's so good I was spellbound; I hung on his every word; in fact I could probably give you his whole act word verbatim. Randy launches into a tale about what happened to him last Christmas. He says he hates the holidays because he has to go back home to see his wretched family. His mom and dad are hateful and never miss a chance to remind him that he's a failed actor. To them, Randy's just loser who doesn't get paid for his art. (Believe, me, I'm a struggling actor too, and I know the feeling – my grandmother's always giving me shit about the acting world how I'll never make it. But I don't have the balls to pull off what Randy did that night.)

So, onstage, Randy, I guess you could say, paints this scene: it's Christmas dinner at his folks' house – they live upstate, out in the 'burbs somewhere - and he's sitting down with his mom and dad, uncles, aunts, and cousins, to eat. As usual, Aunt Phoebe (I remember her name cause I have an Aunt Phoebe, too) insists on saying grace, and everybody is expected to hold hands and pray with her. They all say amen and start eating. Randy grabs a drum stick and digs in for the first good meal he's had in a long time.

Randy's great uncle, Dick, sitting directly across from him, asks him (for the umpteenth time) what he does for a living. "I'm an actor", Randy tells him. Uncle Dick, who is hard of hearing, looks at Randy blankly and asks again.

"I SAID I'M AN ACTOR!" Randy repeats, loud enough for everyone at the dinner table to hear. They all start to laugh. Out of the corner of his eye, Randy sees his dad's annoying smirk.

His Mom wipes her lips and says "No honey, Uncle Dick asked you what you did for a *living*."

"What have you been in? Anything I'd know?" Uncle Dick asks, leaning in toward Randy to hear him.

Dad chimes in, "Yes, son, what *have* you been in?"

"Yes, anything dear?" Mom asks then slugs down the rest of her wine. "What about Broadway?" The table grew quiet. "Uh, that would be a no. Off-Broadway? Nope. How about film? Again, the answer is no. Television? I guess that would also be a big, fat, NO."

Dad chimes in. "What about a performance that's played west of Avenue A? Anything that's not in a black box with 'actors' re-enacting Shakespeare on L.S.D.?"

"Or anything at all," Mom laughs, "Anything that would make us proud of our only child?"

Randy's cousins are cracking up; they join in the fun by pointing to Randy and making "L" for "Loser" signs with their fingers. And these cousins, Randy says, aren't kids, either, they're in their thirties

.

Then Randy tells us how he finally responded to his family's mockery. He tells Uncle Dick that he truly is a gifted actor *and* he can prove it. He just wrote a special scene for the Holidays, which he'd be pleased to perform at the dinner table.

"Would you like to hear it, Uncle Dick?" asks Randy asks loudly, as if playing to the back row.

Cupping his hand to his ear, Dick politely says yes. Randy rises from the dinner table and stands before the family to act out his scene.

The scene he has written for this yuletide occasion, Randy tells us, was intentionally written to be over the top, to be like a ham actor's parody of hammy acting. Randy recounts for the audience the monologue he gave on Christmas night. I don't remember the exact words of the piece he wrote, but it made William Shatner's *Hamlet* seem as nuanced as a haiku by comparison. The piece he wrote for his family was pretty funny in places, but also kind of sad and pathetic, especially in retrospect.

Randy's Christmas monologue ends with him pulling out a toy gun. "A little toy gun that looks just like this." He shows us the ridiculous replica, painted with candy stripes and topped off with frilly laces and bows. I heard some titters in the crowd.

He tells us that he put the toy up to his temple, right in front of his family, and threatened to kill himself. By now, Uncle Dick, who apparently still can't really hear what Randy is saying, is the only family member smiling.

In the theatre, the spotlights follow Randy's every move. I don't know if this guy studied

Stanislavsky or Meissner, or maybe he's just a natural. The main thing is that he's really getting into character.

He taps the pistol against his head. "I looked in Mom and Dad's eyes and I went 'bam' just like this – "

Onstage, right in front of us, Randy pulls the trigger and…. he blows his head off!

I don't mean part of his skull or something – I mean, his whole freakin' head! SUDDENLY BLOOD IS EVERYWHERE; PARTS OF HIS BRAIN AND BRAIN FLUID ARE SPLATTERING OUT TO PEOPLE, ALL THE WAY FROM THE FRONT ROW TO THE BACK. THE GORE, THE GOUP, THE BRAIN TISSUE, IT'S EVERYWHERE! MAN, IT WAS HORRIFYING! BUT, STILL IT WAS AWESOME!

At first, there was a delayed reaction. It's like all of us in the audience needed a few seconds to wrap our heads around what just happened. THE SCREAMING, THE PUSHING, AND STAMPEDE BEGINS. EVERYONE, EXCEPT THE MOST MORBID FREAKS LIKE ME, GET THE FUCK OUT OF THE PLACE A.S.A.P.

I looked at my girlfriend and she went nuts, the girl with the ass-yams went nuts. I went fucking nuts too!

Once I calmed down, I offered to help clean up the stage too, but by then the cops were there and they made us all leave.

I really can't tell you anything more about Randy. I'd only said hello to him maybe once or twice in the hall here before that. No one else I know knew him either. But I'll tell you this much: that was the best performance I've ever seen, hands down. That may have been some lame ass theatre, but that guy gave it everything he had. Great career move, too.

III

The investigators determined that Randy's monologue was made up in more ways than the obvious fact that his Christmas dinner did not end in his death.

Interviews with family members suggest that the actor, whose full name was Randall Thomas Crenshaw, actually had been raised in a close-knit family, not in upstate New York, but in another state, in a town called Seward. By all accounts, Randy's parents actually *encouraged* his acting aspirations, beginning as small child. It's highly unlikely that his parents would have told him to get a "real" job, since everybody in the family was involved in the arts in some way (Mom and Dad were sculptors), and though seemingly happy, no one seemed to care about having much money. Randy's two older sisters proudly sported

photos on the walls of the home they share together –
pictures of him in various onstage roles. There was no
aunt named Phoebe or any uncle named Dick. And,
with a bitter laugh, Randy's father added, he could not
remember a time when this family of agnostics had
ever said grace before a meal.

Investigators asked his friends and family
whether Randy had been depressed. No, to the contrary,
he had been excited by his recent move to New York.
Any history of mental illness? No. Substance abuse?
No. In fact, toxicology reports confirmed that he had no
drugs or alcohol in his system at the time of his death.

Could the gunshot have been an accident – did
Randy think the gun wasn't loaded or did he forget to
put the safety lock on? That's also unlikely, since,
according to Rachel Planck, a childhood friend, Randy
was a nut about gun safety and had always kept the
pistol under lock and key. Ms. Planck suggested they
go out to a shooting range sometime, Randy had testily
told her that you don't just shoot a gun without first
knowing how to handle it safely.

Randy's childhood friend said that she had been
surprised when Randy had first showed her the gun
since Randy didn't seem to her be the kind of person
who would own a firearm. Randy told him that it had
been his grandfather's gun. Randy' grandfather, he was
told, had been a policeman who was killed in the line of

duty. In truth, however, both sets of his grandparents were still alive.

Except for Ms. Planck, no one else was aware that Randy had even owned a pistol. In fact, the firearm wasn't even registered. At least, not to him.

The gun's last registered owner – a retired NYPD captain - reported it stolen, way back in 1978. Now, decades later, that former officer is still alive, and living in the Bahamas. He could not be reached for questioning.

In separate interviews, Randy's high school and college drama teachers remember him as a promising actor, a focused young man with a strong, life-and-death commitment to his craft.

THE PAMPERED PET

Dear Mom and Dad:

I'm sorry I haven't written for a while but I've been pretty busy fixing up the dollhouse, and getting used to my new owners. Can you believe it's been almost one year since I left the Hab? I'll bet you'd barely recognize me now. I've put on 15 earth-pounds, and 12 have come from my new family alone. You wouldn't believe the awesome morsels they feed me!

Please don't worry about happened with the first placement. The aliens liked me a lot, and I was starting to grow fond of them, too. But they were reassigned to another constellation and I wouldn't have survived the Earth years it would've taken to get there, like 250 years or something. So, two months ago the placement service found me a new home.

Where I'm at now, there's a pod of four. At least that's what I think. Something pops out of one of these guys sometimes, but I don't know if it's a separate alien or just an appendage. Oh, and besides the great food here, my new family spoils me with a swimming pool, gym, pool table, a running wheel, a maze, and all sorts of modern things like Experience Modules.

And, this is really cool for history buffs like us: books of every kind. Old time paper books, too. No screens or anything. And some look like first editions, like there's even an ancient and dusty King James Bible. God knows (ha ha) where they got that, but you know how the aliens who visit our Habitat are about human history and its relics, right? You guys would love this too: a first edition of "Pilgrim's Progress"! I've learned how to read on paper – it's not hard, once you get used to it – and have started to read it. (Yeah, I know I've never been much for reading, but there's a lot of down time around here. Time to – don't laugh – improve my mind.)

My new family, on top of giving me amazing food whenever I want it, is pretty chill. Especially compared with the last one. My last owners liked to dress me up all the time in period costumes (BTW, did you get the pics I sent earlier of me as a Russian Cossack, Dutch Boy, and Terra Cotta Warrior? What a hoot!), my new folks don't care what I wear. In fact, they pretty much let me do what I want most of the day. My only real job is in the evenings, when they want me to entertain them with acrobatic tricks I do in my mirrored play pen.

I'm sure Adoption Services already told you that I live with another human, a female who looks about the same age as me; though she can't say her age for sure. (She was adopted at birth, just before they changed the law.) My creatures call her a name that I don't quite get, but it sounds like "Vsht." She doesn't remember her Earth name, or if she even had one at all, so that's what she calls herself. She says I have to call her that too. Vsht's understanding of the alien language is good. Sometimes she translates when our owners say something to me. Sometimes she doesn't, though. She says I've got to learn things for myself.

And I am trying to learn. I know what an honor it is to be here, so I'm doing my best, I want to assure the both of you. And, yes, I do the best I can to pay attention to my owners. I do it out of respect, sure, but I also pay attention because you got to move around all the time to avoid them accidentally stepping on me. I can tell you it hurts like heck.

So you have to be on your toes all the time around these aliens. But at the same time, you kind of have to learn to tune them out most of the time, unless they're talking to you, of course. See, aliens, at least the one's I've lived with, make noises ALL the time. Even the best human-to-alien translators I've read about can only understand a fraction of what they're saying. And believe me, I'm nowhere near the best at knowing their language. But I'm starting to pick it up! I'll make you all proud, you'll see!

I know you read the pamphlet that the adoption folks gave both of us, and saw the video, so you know

how big these aliens are. That's one of the reasons it's
so hard to learn their language: their sounds are made
through blowholes and talking eyes twenty feet above
our heads. And, boy do they talk LOUD! Vsht says
their speech averages 100 decibels (about the sound of
ten town criers at home, all jabbering at once), which is
another reason you have to learn to tune them out.
Otherwise, I swear, you can't even hear yourself think.
You'll find this funny though: sometimes, when I'm
talking to Vsht, I have to shout over aliens. And one
time, when Vsht said my owners though I was making
too much noise, they squirted me with some unknown
but cold-as-a black hole liquid. I'll tell you, feeling that
will shut up anyone in a jiffy! Don't worry though - the
spray doesn't really hurt that much, it's just unpleasant.
I think it hurts more to know that I've displeased them.)

Though I enjoy hanging in the dollhouse or
amusing my owners with new tricks I've learned (and I
love it when they tickle me or give me one of their
famous massages!), the highlights of my day are my
daily walks. One of my favorite aliens here - the one
with the oblong shaped head - pays the most attention
to me and takes me out twice a day. (Of course the days
here are not quite the same as yours, but you get the
idea.) The best part of the walks is seeing other
humans. We get to play together, and sometimes when
we're out on the AstroTurf, away from everyone else,
we talk about things, like what Earth habitat are you

from, what are your owners like, you know, that kind of thing. Just chilling without the aliens.

There's a young lady down the street who belongs to a real nice bunch of aliens. Her people name is Madeleine, but they call her something like "Mdlsplchzorfn". She's very nice. And intelligent too. Madeleine's one year younger than me, and she says she got adopted three years ago from a Hab in Quebec. Did I mention she's pretty? Now you know!

How is everyone doing? How is good old Earth? Also, how is Ezra doing at Pilgrim Plantation? Did he end up taking that job apprenticing with the farrier? (Oh yeah, what happened after his fight with the broom maker? Did the guy press charges?) How are Tab and Abby? If I'm not mistaken, they should be starting middle school about now, right? Tell them I'll write them shortly. Oh, and before I forget, I'm enclosing a serving set my owners gave me to give to you. It says on the box that it's "archeologist-certified pre-Columbian." Maybe you can use it to entertain your pre-Columbian friends, ha ha! Well, that's all for now.

Love,
Silas

Our Dear Silas,

How wonderful hearing from you! To know that our big shot son of ours is doing well in his new placement is indeed great news. It sounds like you're having a great time. And reading too – well, that makes Mom especially proud ! Actually, we're ALL so proud of you. Nobody anywhere in Plymouth Hab can believe that a 19 year old kid could ever get adopted! We always knew you were destined for greatness. (Dad here: you're good, kid, but don't let it get to your head!) Here's some other good news: the lady at Interstellar Placement (you remember Ms. Skinner?) says that if you are able to develop a good bond with your new family, you'll be able to come home to visit us in four years. So get ready!

Your sisters are starting seventh grade tomorrow. How time flies here! It seems like just yesterday that you and Ezra were still in Blab School and the twins were in their prattlers! Tabitha has been a little apprehensive about going to a new school (though they have a couple of friends who are transferring with them from William Brewster) but Abigail can't wait until tomorrow - she's really excited to start her AP space science class. They're both taking five other advanced level classes so they'll be plenty busy this semester. Unless, of course, they make it in the adoption rush.

Ezra is doing alright. He's still disappointed that he wasn't picked by an alien family during the spring rush. But we keep telling him that we love him just the same and that, at least this way, he gets to finish high school. We're happy – surprised, really – that he's enjoying his work at the Plantation. And, yes, he ended up taking that apprenticeship to the knife maker. Your father suspects that Ezra likes his job because he likes being close to the knife maker's daughter, who hangs out there a lot. (You may remember her – her name is Prudence and she used to work at the Taco Bell that's near the thatcher's house.) We suspect (and fear) that your brother and this girl might be more than friends.

Speaking of love, it sounds like *you* are having a good time yourself with this girl Madeleine, no? Your father says you should be extremely careful. He says those French-Canadiennes are wild. (Your dear mother wants to know how and where your dad learned that!)

We made some inquiries and learned that your new aliens have a good reputation. That's all the more reason to remember to heed them, mind your manners, and behave yourself at all times. But we guess we don't need to tell you that. We know you'll do well! You should know that you're a great inspiration especially to your sisters. That's why they're scrambling around getting ready for fall rush.

In the meantime, keep us up to date on your adventures!

Love,

Mom and Dad

Dear Tab & Abby,

Greetings from Lyra Constellation! I've been thinking a lot about you two lately and miss you both. I miss playing in the indoor forests, and, man, I could really go for a Pious Burger right now! But I guess you wouldn't have much time for playing, much less hanging at Pious, now that you're starting sixth grade. I'm glad that you're both still concentrating on your studies (unlike a certain brother we know) and I'll bet you'll be learning a lot this year. I know I am.

For one thing, I'm learning that living with aliens is a lot harder than it looks. Just trying to decipher what they're saying to you can put your brain in knots. The floaters here all sound different too: one makes weird "e-e-e-e-e-e-" sound that don't even sound like speech at all. More like whale sounds being sped up. Another one talks all the time, that is, if you consider speech to sound like a child slurping a Coke through a straw. The other two aliens communicate only between themselves. And they do it in a dialect (or maybe it's another language entirely) which alternates between clip-clopping, rattling, sneezing, whistling, and laughing like a hyena.

I think both of you would get a kick out of this: with my first alien family, the "man of the house" (I say that because "he" was the largest) would sometimes lower one of his thousands of eyes on me, shine a laser beam-like light on my face, and would shout something like "FTFFFDGTEEEEESKAMO!" if I didn't listen up or doff my hat, bow, or curtsy, or do whatever it is that he wanted me to do. If I still didn't understand, he'd yell something even louder like "ZYXTGDTEEEESMATCHT!!!" and swat me on the head. It didn't really hurt though. Like most of the other aliens I've met around here, they were pretty gentle. They'd just box me on the ears when if they thought I was out of line. Even though they could easily hurt or kill you if they wanted to.

As both of you know, they are HIGHLY intelligent. Certainly, it's both exciting *and* challenging to learn from beings that far more advanced than we are. The other good thing about aliens, or at least the ones I've known, they really know how to make you feel good when you're sick or sad. Like, they'll hug you or bring you nice clothes or jewelry. That's probably why so few people ever dream of leaving their owners. It would be pointless to try to do that anyway, since, if they're within a few feet of you, they can read your thoughts, so they'd already be blocking the door if you even *thought* of getting away. Yesterday, I saw this disgusting news piece about some feral humans who attacked their owners. They said on that it takes a pack of five or six people to take down a single alien. And they have to manage to find one of them alone. I guess these human scoundrels attacked a well-known alien (and human rights proponent too!) and escaped from their pod. They were caught after two days on the run and eventually were put to sleep. Luckily, I've never run into criminals like that. The humans I've met here (especially the ones who were adopted from the baby mills) are generally happy where they are, and they identify with their owners. They're too busy jockeying for their place in the pod to think evil and murderous thoughts, anyway.

But just so you know what you might be getting into if you get picked for adoption, I have seen a few aliens mistreat their humans. Of course, the Humane Society is supposed to root this kind of stuff out. But, in reality, they're pretty toothless. And they're spread too thinly around this galaxy. So there's abuse, as close as next door, where a group of pint-sized people were bred by their owners to be tiny, like bonsai trees. I've warned the Society, but they've done about it. These poor bonsai people are forced to dress up in ridiculous costumes to make them look like famous people of the past: Leonardo da Vinci, Teddy Roosevelt, John Calvin, even a pock-marked Kevin Spacey (an actor from before your time). And these poor little guys are expected to do tricks - sometimes a hundred times in a row - like rolling over, playing dead, singing "It's a Small World" or reciting the Gettysburg Address.

Also, if you two REALLY want to get adopted, you ought to know what aliens are looking for in a person. Since most floaters seem to be almost as clueless about human speech and behavior as we are about theirs, they tend to choose, and, still sometimes, breed) solely on the basis of looks. But they don't share our ideas of beauty. Their tastes in humans are bizarre. Sometimes even funny. They especially go for exaggerated doll like features in people, which is the case with the female in my new home, Vsht. I suspect she was bred from a mill, but she claims she came from the Seward Settlement (I've never hear of it, have you?). Now, this is for your eyes only, but if her features were normal size, Vsht wouldn't look half bad. But her eyes are huge – it's like they take up a third of her face. She reminds me of that freaky cow-eyed actress before she died, Anne Hathaway. Or the goat-eyed one, the old time cinema star Michelle Pfeiffer. (I think spend too much time in the Experience Mod to know stuff like that!) Anyway, Vsht's breasts and hips are ridiculously large for the rest of her body. Her caked on makeup and bright red rouge and lipstick make her look like Raggedy Ann dressed up to look like a child prostitute. OK, to be fair, I guess she's not bad looking, but it's her personality that's ugly. She's prickly all the time, neurotic, and pathologically competitive. And geez, territorial too! She acts as if she owns the place! Why, if I even <u>try</u> to go near what is supposed to be OUR bed, she'll hiss, scratch, and bite. My friend Madeline says that's because Vsht was taken away from her mother way too young.

Since I hear you're both trying out for the fall rush, I want to wish you two the best of luck. But if you don't get adopted, or if you decide you don't want to try out, that's cool too. Don't get me wrong, I know what an honor it is for me to be picked, but you two are so much better at school than I was, and I think the two of you are brilliant enough to get a sponsor or even a patron for college. That's another great way to get out of the Hab. I guess what I'm saying is, do what really makes you happiest. If you want to find an alien, that's ok, just so long as you know what you're getting into, and you enjoy it. Don't just do it just to impress your friends. Or to make Mom and Dad richer. Obviously, they can always use more money, but not at the expense of your happiness.

AND - speaking of riches, enclosed are two Roman brooches and a hundred bars of plutonium to spend on whatever you like. Great big hugs from me!

Silas

Dear Si:

Thanks *sooo* much for the brooches! And for
the money! You must have known we'd need the cash
for the adoption rush that's coming up – everything,
from wigs to makeup costs major Plutes!

Things here in the 'Tat are pretty much the
same. And Ezzy's still Ezzy: he got into three fights
last week. Yesterday we overhead Dad tell Mom that
Ez even got his pay docked at Pilgrim for slapping the
farrier! Before you get all mad at Ez, that horseshoeing
jerk deserved it 'cause he told Ezzy that if *his* son had
lived *he* would've fetched twice the price you had got
from the aliens!

Mom and Dad are still the same, but I guess you
already know that!

Keep your fingers crossed for us for the fall
rush!

xoxo,
Tab & Abby

P.S. We did some research on the Seward
Settlement. It seems that they've been running a
human mill for hundreds of years. So be careful of that
Vsht woman!

Hey Ez,

It's Si. What's up? I heard you found a good situation over at Pilgrim. Knife-making, huh? I guess we've both come a long way from stuffing straw dolls at Ye Olde Square! Still, I'm sure it's pretty hard work, especially wearing those heavy cloaks and itchy underwear – and then riding that lazy assed mule.

Mom and Dad said that you're still pissed about not getting adopted. I know it should've been YOU that was picked and I wish I could tell you what was up with that. No way is it fair. I remember, even when we were both little, I was the one putting New World maps on my side of our room, while you were putting up alien posters up. And playing with alien dolls – sorry, bro, action figures. But to tell you the truth (and this is NOT to ever to get to Mom and Dad!) I think you're better off where you are. I don't want to sound spoiled, but NOT EVERYTHING IS ALL FUN AND GAMES WITH THE ALIENS. Things can often be pretty difficult here. You have to be on your toes all the time. And you sure as hell better learn what they're saying to you quick or they'll give you a swat – or worse. (If you ever get hit by one of their protruding eyeballs, you'll know what I mean!)

But my aliens are peaches and cream compared with Vsht. She's the other human here. She's young, about our age, but she pretends like she's older. And, if you don't mind her territorial biting, scratching, and peeing, and her general bitchiness, she's a lovely gal. My placement advisor told me that my new family used to have another human, an older male, but he died or had to be put down or something. So, I'm his replacement. And, from the way our bedroom is arranged – mirrors on the ceiling, vibrating bed, and the slutty outfits my family dresses Vsht in, it doesn't take an alien genius to know that my new family picked me to breed with her. But, I'd sooner be neutered than hump this vile creature.

And, speaking of breeding, ha ha, I heard you've got your eye on the knife maker's daughter. Nice! But, bro, you better be more discreet about your love life this time, unless you want a repeat of what went down with the cobbler. (Dude, what were you thinking, schtupping his wife?)

And, still on the subject of schtupping, could you do me a favor? There's this young lady who lives down the street, Madeleine's her name. I'd really like "get to know her better" (you know what I'm talking about), and I'm pretty sure she does too. But we're not supposed to hump and we'll both get in a lot of trouble if I put a bun in her oven. So would you mind sending me a couple cartons of Trojans? I can't seem to find them anywhere in this zone. Enclosed is 50 Plutes for your trouble. So, please send the rubbers as soon as you can.

Thanks, man, I owe you one.

Later,
Silas

Yo Silo,

Here you go, you lucky fucker! I rustled up the last ten cartons of rubbers at Ye Olde Apothecary. (These are Pilgrim Pride. They were out of Trojan's, BTW.) Also, I dropped a shitload of coins into a condom-matic machine in the Taco Bell john, so there's another thirty packets. Thanks for the Plutes - I was pretty low on cash, especially after getting my pay docked. (It's a long story.)

When the new shipment of cock hats comes in at the Apothecary, I'll send some more. And I'll grab a couple cartons myself, since I'm running low with me and – well, never mind. I still have some change left over from the Plutes, so any time you need rubbers (or love dolls, ben wa balls, or dildos – ha!) you just let me know and I'll send 'em your way.

I hope these "Puritan strength prophylactics" will be enough to tide you over for a while with you and your Madeleine! So have fun with your "dates." You've got enough now for 400 fucks!

Your prophylactic pimp,
Ez

P.S This is Dad: Hi son, I see what your dear brother has enclosed, so here's a few fatherly words of advice: first, you're doing the right thing - always use rubbers. Especially with gals of the Canuck persuasion! Just be cautious, and don't forget what Rev. Barnett used to say: long skirts carry dust, but short skirts carry away souls. But then again, he was an imbecile. All kidding aside, have fun with your little Madeleine (wink, wink), but remember to be careful – and I also mean with your new family. Respect and obey them. If they want you mate with that girl with the weird name then you better just bite the bullet and do it. You know how lucky you are? The odds of a high school senior getting placed by not just one, but now TWO pods of floaters has got be a about 100 million to one. It would've been easier me to get a cushy job at Bunyanville or Johnny Appleseed's than for you to have gotten adopted like you did. So, whatever you do, don't be seem ungrateful – you know what would've happened to us had the aliens not come here to save us in the first place. So don't piss them off! Love, Dad

To: Madeleine
c/o The Xwoekdcs

My dear Madeleine,

I haven't seen you all week and I'm hoping
you're ok. Are you sick? Is everything going alright
with you and your owners? I miss you a lot! Hanging
with Vsht is hardly the same as being with you,
laughing with you – and kissing you! Please drop me a
line and let me know how you are. I can't wait to see
you again…

Silas

To: Madeleine
c/o The Xwoekdcs
Dearest Madeleine,

Did you get my last letter? Have you been
getting *any* of my letters? It's now been over two
weeks since I last saw you. Two weeks since I held you
in my arms. Vsht says you probably found somebody
else, but I don't believe her. She lies. But if it's true, as
sad as that would make me, I really hope that you are
happy.

Vsht now claims that she overheard
Qmbsplaaaaatz (remember him, the tall, geeky looking

floater who picked me up at the park last time we saw each other?) say that your family moved to another galaxy and took you with them. If that's true I am TRULY heartbroken! If you really have moved, I hope to God that someone forwards this letter to you, so you'll always know exactly how I feel about you. I know we haven't known each other that long, but being with you these past two months is enough for me to say that you're the greatest girl I've ever met. And, ok, I've never said this to any else before, honest, but I've fallen madly in love with you. My heart will remain broken until I hear from you.

      Yours forever,
      Silas

To: Madeleine
c/o The Xwoekdcs

Madeleine, My Love,

Please write me. I miss you so much!!

Love,
Silas

Dear Family,

I'm sorry about the long delay in writing, even though I think about you all every day. To tell you the truth, I just haven't felt like writing, or doing much else, for that matter. Don't get me wrong, I'm not depressed or anything like that, so Mom, please don't worry. It's because of, well, you remember Madeleine, the beautiful girl I told you about? It turns out it's true that she and her owners moved away. Out to some solar system I've never heard of.

And to top it all off, my adoption counselor confirmed that soon I'm supposed to mate with Vsht (ugh!). Now I know you don't want me to anger the aliens (or Dad, God forbid!) but hell would have to freeze over before I did you-know-what with this repulsive female. This whole mating business makes me want to puke. I don't know what kind of creatures they've been breeding in Seward (if that's really where she's from) but remind me never to visit that ungodly habitat It's almost making me want to change my sexual orientation! (As if it really *was* a choice.)

Vsht has been getting dolled up for me lately but I'd have to down every last bottle of her schnapps and go into a psychogenic fugue before I'd touch that feral beast.

Desperately missing you all (and for the first time ever, hoping to stay celibate),

Silas

Dear Family,

You will be happy to know that hell did indeed freeze over last night. (You know what I'm talking about.) I won't go into the dirty details – especially with the twins reading this (and the details are indeed dirty) but it certainly wasn't a romantic night. And it did involve a massive dose of schnapps, "performance" drugs, and oysters.

Now I'm sore all over from all the bite marks, scratches, and gashes Vsht laid into me. Luckily, my owners brought in a people vet. The guy gave me some skin ointment, antibiotics and painkillers, so I'm doing ok now. Plus the doc said my penis should heal up ("good as new") in two to three weeks. One good thing that came out of all this, I suppose, is that Vsht now lets me sleep in our bed together instead of me sleeping on the floor. Actually she said she'll let me you it until I recuperate. But since Vsht is kind of digging me now (in her own obnoxious and repulsive way!) I have the feeling that I'll be sharing that comfy bed with her for a long time.

All in all, I guess you could say that things are starting to look up for me here. After last night, my owners are so pleased with what I did with Vsht that they're giving me special treats, like my favorite fish popsicles and bags and bags of Salty Asteroids. And they got me some cool presents too: an exercise wheel, silver-plated space boots, and an 18th century powdered wig. I feel like a male hooker, but what the heck, I guess there are worse jobs. (Like getting up every morning at the crack of dawn to trudge to work mining at the Earth's core – I know, Dad, I remember all your stories.)

Enclosed please find some extra cash: 200 Plutes for now, but more will be coming soon. That's what my owners gave me to send to you after my "experience" with Vsht. I hope it helps, since I know money's tight. But don't feel bad, it's not just you. I hear it's been tough for everyone on Earth, what with tourism down 'cause of all those travel restrictions.

That's it for now. I can't wait to see you all in four years! My love to everyone,

Silas